The Ghost
Who Stayed Home

HAUNTING DANIELLE

The Ghost of Marlow House

The Ghost Who Loved Diamonds

The Ghost Who Wasn't

The Ghost Who Wanted Revenge

The Ghost of Halloween Past

The Ghost Who Came for Christmas

The Ghost of Valentine Past

The Ghost from the Sea

The Ghost and the Mystery Writer

The Ghost and the Muse

The Ghost Who Stayed Home

The Ghost and the Leprechaun

The Ghost Who Lied

The Ghost and the Bride

The Ghost and Little Marie

The Ghost and the Doppelganger

The Ghost of Second Chances

The Ghost Who Dream Hopped

The Ghost of Christmas Secrets

HAUNTING DANIELLE - BOOK 11

THE GHOST
WHO STAYED HOME

BOBBI HOLMES

The Ghost Who Stayed Home
(Haunting Danielle, Book 11)
A Novel
By Bobbi Holmes
Cover Design: Elizabeth Mackey

robeth.net

ROBETH PUBLISHING, LLC

ISBN-13: 978-1544682044
ISBN-10: 1544682042

To my precious grandchildren, Addison and Evan.
To Evan for borrowing his name,
and to Addison for borrowing her age.

ONE

Gray storm clouds blanketed the sky, obscuring the sun and making the day feel more winter than spring. It provided a dismal backdrop for Marlow House, which seemed somehow taller on this day to Joanne Johnson as she pulled up in front of the house and parked her car.

With the engine still running and her hands clutching the steering wheel, Joanne peered out the car window, studying her place of employment. The towering structure, shielded from the impending storm by the mansard roofline, appeared lifeless and deplete of hope. Joanne knew if she sat there much longer, she was going to cry. Steeling her courage, the middle-aged housekeeper took a deep breath and turned off the engine. Removing the keys from the ignition and snatching her purse off the passenger seat, she opened the car door and got out of the vehicle.

Hurrying up to the front walk of Marlow House, hoping to get inside before the rain started falling, she heard someone call out her name just as she reached the gate. Pausing a moment, she turned to the street and saw Adam Nichols rushing toward her. She guessed he was coming from Ian's house.

Adam, in his mid-thirties, was a few years older than her employer, Danielle Boatman. Joanne had known Adam for as long as she could remember. He had been a handsome teenage boy and had grown up to be a good-looking man, with dark brown—almost black—eyes and shortly cropped brown hair. Real estate broker and owner of Frederickport Vacation Properties, he always dressed sharply, and if Joanne wasn't imagining things—he had recently improved his wardrobe. The slacks and dress shirts he wore these days seemed to be higher quality compared to his wardrobe six months ago. She liked Adam, even if he was something of a scamp with the ladies.

Slightly out of breath when he reached her, he asked, "Have you heard anything?"

"No." Joanne glanced up to the sky and pushed open the gate. "It's going to start raining. Come inside. We can talk there."

With a nod, Adam silently followed Joanne. A brisk gust of air moved rudely across the walkway. By reflex Adam tugged his light jacket tighter around his body and shivered. He picked up his step and caught up with Joanne, who was now at the front door, inserting her house key into the lock. Seeking warmth, Adam buried his hands deep in his pockets. He shivered and glanced around, waiting for Joanne to let them inside.

Rain started to fall just as the door swung open. Both Joanne and Adam rushed into the front entry hall of Marlow House. There were no overhead lights on inside, just a dim glow of randomly placed night-lights to break up the darkness. All the shades were drawn, but considering the cloudy day, even if they had been open, the sunlight would be minimal.

Inside, Sadie sat in the center of the entry hall, her tail wagging. Adam didn't notice her immediately—not until the dog let out a bark in greeting just as Joanne flipped on an overhead light. At one time the golden retriever had made Adam nervous, but he and the dog had since come to terms with each other.

"Ahh, girl," Joanne said as she turned to Sadie and put out her hand. The dog rushed to her, tail still wagging. Kneeling down, Joanne accepted the wet kisses and showed her affection by several energetic pats to the dog's furry shoulders. Joanne didn't have to tell Sadie to calm down—for in the next moment the dog let out a short bark and then sat down, no longer jumping on the housekeeper.

Adam frowned at Sadie and thought, *If I didn't know better, I'd say Ian—or someone—had just given Sadie the command to sit.*

"Come in the kitchen with me. I need to feed Sadie and Max." Joanne dropped her purse on the entry table and pulled off her jacket. She hung the jacket on the coat rack and then headed to the kitchen.

"I keep wondering what I'm going to do with them," Adam said as he followed Joanne.

"I'm trying not to think about that."

"I hope they're okay here." Adam watched Sadie, who trotted along beside Joanne.

"They are for now." Once in the kitchen, Joanne headed to the pantry for bags of dog and cat food.

Adam took a seat at the kitchen table and watched as Joanne filled two bowls with food—one with cat food and one with dog food—and set them both on the floor. Sadie went immediately for her bowl and started eating.

"Aren't you afraid Sadie is going to eat the cat's food?" Adam glanced around, looking for Max. The cat was nowhere in sight.

Joanne laughed and shook her head. "It's the strangest thing. Sadie never touches Max's food."

"Ian must have really trained her well."

"You want a cup of coffee?" Joanne asked as she reached for the canister with coffee and started making a pot.

"Sure, if you're making some." Adam stood up for a moment and removed his jacket. Before sitting back down, he hung it on the back of his chair.

"Cream, sugar?" Joanne filled the pot with water from the sink.

Adam shook his head. "Black is fine."

Joanne poured water into the coffee pot. "You can tell your grandmother I've been coming over here at least twice a day."

"I really appreciate it. But I'll admit, I was a little surprised they decided to leave Sadie here. I understand Max."

Joanne leaned back against the counter, waiting for the coffee to brew, her arms now folded across her chest. "Sadie is comfortable here, and her and Max get along. They can both get to the side yard by the doggy door. I guess Ian felt she'd be happier here than a kennel. And like I said, I try to get over here at least twice a day."

"I appreciate it. But this can't go on indefinitely."

Joanne closed her eyes a moment and let out a sigh. "I know." She opened her eyes again and looked at Adam. "I assume you were over at Ian's when I drove up?"

Adam nodded. "I came over to check on it. I stopped by Chris's too, I have the key. Making sure everything is okay."

Joanne laughed bitterly. "Nothing's okay." She turned back to the counter and pulled two coffee cups from the overhead cabinet. A moment later she brought two filled cups to the table and sat down. She handed one to Adam.

After taking a sip, she asked, "So what are you going to do with Ian's house?"

"He has a lease." Staring at the coffee cup sitting on the table before him, Adam absently fiddled with its porcelain handle.

"Come on, Adam, you know what I mean."

"The house belongs to my grandmother. Normally, I would be the one to make the call—even with the properties she owns—but we're talking Danielle here."

"How is your grandmother handling all this?" Joanne took another sip of her coffee.

"Not terrific. She stubbornly refuses to believe…" Adam let out a sigh and picked up his cup.

"She's pretty fond of Danielle, isn't she?"

"Oh yeah." Slouching down in the chair, Adam took a drink of the coffee and then set the cup back on the table. "She thinks of her as a granddaughter. She's pretty fond of Lily too. But it's different with Danielle."

"WHAT ABOUT DANIELLE AND LILY? Where are they?" Walt Marlow shouted to deaf ears. He sat on one of the *empty* chairs at the kitchen table. Frustrated, the ghost of Marlow House glanced from Joanne to Adam and back to Joanne. He was sorely tempted to command a pen to start writing his question onto a blank sheet of paper and drop it on the kitchen table, but he knew that would simply send Joanne and Adam running from the house—like Adam had run from the house some ten months earlier when Walt had hurled a croquet set at Adam and his companion Bill Jones after the pair had broken into the house, searching for the Missing Thorndike.

Had it really been ten months ago? Walt wondered. A spirit trapped in a house for almost a century didn't always have the best sense of time. Those past decades—from the time of his death to when Danielle arrived ten months earlier and helped him come to terms with his new reality—were primarily a foggy, unfocused haze. There were moments he could recall, such as when Joanne (when she still worked for Danielle's great-aunt) would show up to clean the house on a regular basis. Yet Walt couldn't recall the housekeeper before Joanne, and he was sure there had been one—or more.

When Danielle had appeared on his doorstep with Lily to claim her inheritance, Walt was fully prepared to call the police and have the young women escorted off his property. Of course, that was not really possible—something Walt hadn't quite grasped at the time. How could a ghost who was trapped inside Marlow House call the police? No one could see or hear him—except for Danielle—and Max and Sadie. There was also Chris and Evan—and perhaps Heather. However, Walt would rather avoid Danielle's quirky neighbor Heather, whose sensitivity to spirits seemed to be heightening in recent weeks.

The truth was, Walt was no longer trapped in Marlow House—not in the same way as he had been when Danielle had first walked into his life—or more aptly, his death. He could leave now, but once he did, he would never be able to return and would instead be forced to continue to the next level—whatever that might be.

Motion from the corner of his eye caught his attention. It was Sadie. She had finished her bowl of food and was now sniffing at Max's dish.

"Sadie!" Walt snapped.

The golden retriever looked up guiltily.

"Why don't you go tell Max he has food in his bowl," Walt suggested.

Letting out a grunt, Sadie reluctantly turned from Max's bowl and headed for the doorway.

"He's in the attic!" Walt called after Sadie.

"I can't believe that," Adam said. He had just noticed Sadie sniffing at the cat food. "She didn't touch it."

"I told you." Joanne set her now empty coffee cup on the table. "She never does."

"Forget about Max and Sadie," Walt said impatiently. "Keep talking. Tell me what happened to Danielle and Lily!"

"Are you going to the city council meeting?" Adam asked Joanne.

"I was thinking about it."

"Why are you talking about a city council meeting? What's going on with Danielle and Lily?" Walt asked.

"Are you going?" Joanne asked.

"I think I should." Adam glanced at his watch. "Why don't you let me treat you to lunch. I haven't eaten yet, and I'm starving. We can talk there."

Walt stood up abruptly. "No!"

"I am kind of hungry." Joanne got up from the table and picked up her empty coffee cup and Adam's, carrying them to the kitchen sink, where she quickly washed and dried them before returning the cups to the overhead cabinet.

"Is Pier Café alright?" Adam asked.

"Sure." Joanne walked to the coffee pot and turned it off.

"You can't leave yet!"

Walt's pleas went unheeded. Several minutes later he stood at the attic window, looking out, and watched as Joanne got into her car. Just before she pulled her vehicle from the curb, Adam ran back across the street to Ian's house, where he had parked his car.

Walt stood there a few minutes and stared outside. It was raining now, and the wind was starting to kick up, coming in from the west, sending the raindrops pounding against the windowpane.

A meow at Walt's feet broke his concentration. He looked down. Max stared up at him through golden eyes, his black tail swishing back and forth.

"Didn't Sadie tell you dinner was here?"

A bark came from the doorway. Walt glanced in that direction. He hadn't noticed Sadie when he had come into the attic a few minutes earlier. Max let out another meow.

"No, Max," Walt said. "We still don't know where she is."

TWO

Huddled under the blanket dome, lit flashlight in hand, Evan MacDonald studied the invitation to Trevor's birthday party. His father had promised to be home in time to take him to the party. It was tomorrow. He wasn't home yet.

Turning off the flashlight, Evan pulled down the blanket and glanced around the dark room. His older brother, Eddy, was sleeping in the next bed. They weren't at home. They were at their Aunt Sissy's house, but they were supposed to be home by now. Home in time for his dad to take him to the birthday party. His Aunt Sissy had said she would take him, but still—something didn't feel right.

The bedroom door was ajar, and the hallway light had been left on. Sitting up in the bed, Evan looked at the partially opened doorway. The house was quiet. Evan was pretty sure his aunt was still awake. His uncle had gone out right before he and Eddy had gone to bed, and he hadn't heard him come home yet.

Tossing the flashlight to the foot of his bed along with the birthday invitation, Evan thought about his Aunt Sissy. He and Eddy usually stayed with her if his father went out of town, like when his dad went to Hawaii before Christmas. However, Aunt Sissy was acting strange—strange for Aunt Sissy.

When he visited his grandparents—his mother's parents—he was used to his grandma always hugging on him and smacking kisses all over his face before he could wiggle away. He loved his grandmother, so he didn't really mind it. Plus, his dad said she acted that way because she missed his mother so much.

But Aunt Sissy wasn't like that—at least she hadn't been until this week. The day after he and Eddy had arrived, Aunt Sissy started getting all mushy and touchy, and if he wasn't mistaken, he could swear he saw tears in her eyes a few times after she captured him in a suffocating bear hug. He wasn't sure what was up with her, but it was starting to creep him out.

Lights from a car's headlights lit up the room for a moment and then it went dark again. His uncle was home. Very quietly, Evan slipped out of bed and made his way to the open doorway. He stood there and listened. A few moments later he heard the front door open and close, and then he heard the hushed voices of his aunt and uncle downstairs.

Instead of going back to bed, Evan decided to fill up his cup with water. Aunt Sissy called it a sippy cup—which Eddy found insulting. "Sippy cups are for babies," his brother, Eddy, insisted whenever she called them that. Their cups just had spill-proof lids and built-in straws. Aunt Sissy only laughed when he corrected her and then rolled her eyes and said, "Whatever." Evan didn't care what they were called, he just wanted to make sure his was filled before he went to sleep, in case he woke up in the middle of the night thirsty. His dad normally made sure they were full, but his dad wasn't here.

After making his way downstairs, Evan was just going into the kitchen when he heard his aunt and uncle talking in the den. They assumed he was still upstairs in bed. He intended to go straight to the refrigerator and use the water dispenser to fill his cup when he heard his uncle mention his father's name. Curious, Evan set the cup on the counter and made his way to the doorway leading to the den.

"I don't believe my brother's dead," Evan heard his Aunt Sissy say. He froze a moment, hiding in the shadows of the hallway, just outside the open door leading to the den, listening.

"I pray he isn't, but the city council needs to find someone to replace him until they know more. With both him and Morelli missing, what else can they do? Brian's in charge down there, but that's only a temporary situation. They feel it's necessary to find someone to replace Ed."

"And when he comes back, does that mean he's out of a job?"

"They didn't say that. But, Sissy, what if he doesn't come back? What if he's dead? We need to think about what we're going to tell those boys."

"No! I can't tell those boys they've lost their father too!" Sissy began to cry.

Evan listened for a few more minutes before he had heard enough. He ran back to the bedroom, leaving his cup sitting on the kitchen counter. Diving under the blankets, he pulled them over him and huddled in the darkness.

"No. Dad is not dead," Evan stubbornly whispered. "I would know. He would have come back here to say goodbye, like Mom did." Evan couldn't tell his aunt and uncle that. His father had warned him: *never discuss your gift with others, even Aunt Sissy. People wouldn't understand.*

One day his father had taken him to lunch with Danielle Boatman. His brother, Eddy, hadn't come along—it was just Evan, Danielle, and his father. Danielle was like him. That day, she told him if he ever needed to talk about his gift, she would be there for him. He had also met Walt Marlow. But that wasn't at lunch. That was when he had stayed at Marlow House.

Evan suspected Danielle wasn't there to help him—not if what he had heard his aunt and uncle talking about just minutes before was true. But there was always Walt Marlow. Considering his options, Evan came up with a plan—sort of. He decided to wait until his aunt and uncle went to bed and were asleep before he made his move.

Time passed. Wide awake, Evan waited. Finally, his aunt came into the bedroom. Closing his eyes, pretending to be asleep, Evan could hear his aunt walking to his brother's bed and then his. He felt her hand gently pat him before placing a light kiss on his forehead and then whispering, "You poor dear boy. Your Aunt Sissy will be here for you."

When he heard her walk out of the room, he opened one eye and peeked. The hallway light went out, and then he heard the door to his aunt and uncle's bedroom close. Evan waited for another thirty minutes or so before he finally climbed out of bed, careful not to wake his brother up.

His aunt had laid his clothes out for the next day—Aunt Sissy was like that, very organized. Unlike his father, who let Evan pick out his own clothes every morning. But tonight, he was grateful for his aunt's habit.

After dressing and putting on his shoes, he grabbed the flashlight off the end of his bed and stealthily made his way down the hallway and stairs, careful not to make a sound. Using his flashlight to help him see, he found his jacket on the coat rack by the front door and put it on. It was then he remembered the cup he had left downstairs. Going to the kitchen, he found the cup where he had left it, and filled it with water. After fitting its lid securely on, he placed the cup in his coat pocket.

He was just about to pick up his flashlight when he noticed its beam had landed on the covered cake plate sitting on the counter. His aunt had made homemade cookies that morning, and that was where she kept them. Easing the cover from the cake pan, he snatched several cookies, shoved them in his empty pocket—the one not holding the water bottle—and then carefully re-covered the cake plate.

Picking up his flashlight, he made his way to the kitchen door leading to the side yard. He opened the door, pulled the hood of his jacket over his head, and rushed out into the night—and into the rain.

Six-year-old Evan MacDonald didn't mind the rain. After all, he was a native Oregonian, and like his dad always said, "Rain is just a little water." The dark was another matter. Even with his flashlight, Evan wasn't thrilled about walking the streets of Frederickport in the middle of the night, but sometimes a person had to put his fears behind him because there were worse things than being out in the dark—like losing another parent.

Fortunately, his aunt and uncle's house was only a block away from his house, so he was familiar with the neighborhood. He was pretty sure he could find his way to Marlow House, even in the middle of the night. First, he would head to the pier. That was easy. He, his brother, and father had walked down to the pier together countless times. The street that ran along the ocean—and the entrance to the pier—was where Marlow House was located. The only thing that made him nervous was imagining what he might encounter on his way to his ultimate destination.

No cars or trucks were on the street, and the windows in the houses he passed were all dark. Rain continued to fall, pelting the shoulders and the hood of his jacket. He had walked about two blocks when lightning streaked overhead, briefly illuminating the sky. Startled by the lightning, Evan started to run, but when his right toe touched down in a water puddle, his foot flew out from under him, sending him butt first into a larger water puddle, soaking his jeans. In the midst of the fall, the flashlight flew from his hand. When it landed on the sidewalk, its batteries fell out, rolling off the curb and into the river of water running down the street.

Getting back to his feet, he located the flashlight, but soon discovered it wouldn't turn on; the batteries were missing. Another streak of lightning flashed across the sky. Tossing the flashlight to the ground, Evan began to run, heading for the pier, ignoring the possibility he might slip in another puddle if not careful.

Evan managed to stay on his feet for the rest of his journey. He passed several cars along the way, but without the lit flashlight in his hand, the drivers of the vehicles didn't notice the little boy—all alone—tearing down the sidewalk in the dark night.

He was out of breath by the time he reached Marlow House. His plan was to enter through the doggy door, yet first he needed to get in the side yard, but the gate appeared to be locked. He could see two cars parked in the drive along the side yard, but he knew their owners were not home.

Instead of climbing over the fence, Evan decided to take advantage of a nearby tree, whose branches hung over the top of the fence and into the side yard. Determined, the little boy made his way up the stout trunk, using knotholes as ladder rungs while grabbing onto dangling greenery. When he was about six feet from the ground, he wrapped his legs around one of the branches—it arched over the top of the fence and into the side yard of Marlow House. Evan crawled toward the far end of the branch. It was quite a drop to the ground, but that did not scare Evan. He had come this far in the dark and rain.

Taking hold of one of the narrow branches, he dropped from the tree, swinging Tarzan-like. He heard the limb crack, yet the injured branch remained attached to the tree. His feet dangled as if he were on the monkey bars at school. Once his shoes were as close to the ground as they could get—about two feet—he let go of the branch and tumbled onto the ground into a muddy patch of grass.

Scrambling back onto his feet, ignoring the mud now covering his jeans, he ran to the door leading to Marlow House's kitchen—and its pet door. It was pitch dark in the kitchen, but that did not deter Evan. Getting on his hands and knees, he crawled through the tight-fitting pet door, the top of his head pushing its flap inward. Once he was in the kitchen, he stood up and looked around.

In the next moment the overhead lighting turned on and Evan found himself standing face-to-face with Walt Marlow, a golden retriever sitting by his side, and next to the dog sat a black cat. The three stared at him.

THREE

"Evan?" Walt said in surprise.

The slender boy stood shivering, covered in mud. "You have to help me find my dad!"

Fifteen minutes later, Evan sat in a hot tub of water while Walt stood in the bathroom doorway, leaning against the door jamb and listening to the boy's story. Sadie curled up on the bath mat in front of the tub, keeping an eye on the child, prepared to leap into rescue mode should the boy slip under the water. Max napped in the hallway outside the door, content to be filled in on the situation later, after he got a little sleep.

After telling Walt all he knew, Evan stood up in the tub, droplets of bathwater clinging to his nude body.

"I knew something was wrong." Walt handed Evan a towel.

Drying off, Evan's eyes widened as a pink terrycloth robe floated into the room.

"You can wear this until we get your clothes washed." *I think I can figure out that newfangled washer and dryer contraption downstairs.*

"But it's pink," Evan grumbled.

Walt arched his brow. "I don't think we can have you running around here buck naked while we wait for your clothes to get washed and dried."

Begrudgingly, Evan dropped the towel to the floor and took the robe, slipping it on. It belonged to Lily, and considering her small stature, it didn't overwhelm the child.

Evan followed Walt from the bathroom and into Danielle's bedroom. The spirit of Marlow House pulled down the bedcovers.

Instead of getting between the sheets, Evan frowned at Walt. "Aren't you going to help me find my dad?"

"If I was a responsible adult, I would make you call your aunt and uncle and have them come get you. They're going to be worried sick in the morning when they realize you're gone. But I need you right now as much as you need me. So why don't you climb into this warm bed, get comfortable, and we'll try to figure this thing out."

Evan looked at the bed—it did look comfortable and warm. He gave Walt a nod and then scrambled up into the bed, still wearing the oversized pink bathrobe. Once he was situated under the sheets and covers, Walt pulled up the bedding, tucking Evan snugly into Danielle's bed. Instead of sitting on the mattress with Evan, as he normally did with Danielle, Walt pulled a chair to the side of the bed and sat down.

"I have to agree with you. I don't believe they're dead. I can't imagine Danielle or Lily would just move on without first coming to tell me what had happened," Walt said.

"That's what I think too. But my uncle thinks they're dead—everyone does." Resting against the pile of pillows, Evan folded his arms across his chest and looked up at Walt.

Walt leaned back in the chair and studied the boy. "You said your mother visited you after she died?"

Evan nodded. "Sort of. It was at the funeral. I think she was surprised I could see her. She told me not to be afraid, that she loved me, but that she had to leave. She said she would be watching over me and Eddy and Dad, but that she had to go."

Walt let out a sigh, and shifted in the chair, uncrossing and recrossing his legs.

With a serious expression Evan asked, "Why didn't she just stick around?"

Walt shrugged. "I assume it was her time to move on."

"But you're still here. Mom knew I could see her, so why didn't she just stick around so she could be with me? She didn't have to leave. You didn't. She said she was going to be watching over me anyway. I don't understand. Why did she go?"

Walt considered the question a moment and then smiled. "Danielle's always saying we aren't meant to hang around indefinitely—she's probably right. I imagine your mother was afraid if she did stick around, it would only confuse you. Especially if you started telling people you could see her."

"They might think I'm crazy?" Evan asked.

Walt smiled. "Yes, something like that."

"But now, now that Dad understands, why doesn't she just come back so I can see her again—talk to her."

"When we finally move on, we can't really come back. Oh, there are ways to communicate from beyond, but to be here like I am right now…" Walt shook his head.

"If you decide to move on…like Danielle says, to the next level…then you won't be able to come back?"

Walt shook his head. "No. Once I make that decision to go, well…you and I won't be able to talk like this."

"I hope you never go. I wish my mom hadn't gone."

Walt smiled sadly at Evan. "For now, we need to concentrate on getting your father, Danielle, and the rest of them back. And I tend to agree with you. I don't believe he would move on without first communicating with you."

"So what are we going to do?"

"I suppose the first thing we need to do is find out where they are."

Evan frowned. "You don't know?"

"Why would I know?"

"I just figured a ghost would know stuff like that."

"Unfortunately, it doesn't work that way."

Dejected, Evan slumped back in the bed. He looked like he was about to cry. "Then I came all the way over here for nothing."

"Hey, buddy, I didn't say I wasn't going to help you."

A tear escaped from the corner of Evan's eye and slid down his face. He sniffed. "How can you help me? You told me yourself you're stuck here, and if you don't know where they are…"

"Just because I'm confined to this house doesn't mean there aren't ways for me to figure out where they are."

"Like what?"

Walt smiled. "For one thing, I could try a dream hop."

"Dream hop?"

"That's what Danielle calls it. It's when a spirit goes into a person's dream, and they can talk to each other. It's also a way for a spirit—one that has moved on—to communicate with someone who is still living."

Evan gasped. "You mean she was really here?"

"Who was really here?"

"My mother. She visits me in my dreams…" Evan paused and shook his head. "No…it was probably just a dream, because Eddy has them sometimes too, and Eddy can't see ghosts like I can."

"Your older brother?"

Evan nodded.

"Technically speaking, your mother is not a ghost—she has moved on. She's strictly a spirit now. And she probably did visit your brother. A person doesn't have to be like you and Danielle to experience a dream hop. Did those dreams with your mother seem different from regular dreams?"

Evan considered the question a moment. "I can remember them. I always seem to forget my other dreams, but whenever I have one of those dreams with my mom—gee, I can remember everything about them."

Walt smiled. "That, my boy, is a dream hop."

"How will a dream hop help us find my dad?"

"If they are still alive—which I believe they must be—then they have to sleep sometime. I'll try to hop into one of their dreams. Lucky for me, I have four people who can help us: your father, Danielle, Lily, and Chris."

"I don't understand?"

"Lily and Danielle are quite used to my dream hops. The moment I enter one of their dreams, they'll understand I'm really there. As for your father and Chris, they both know about dream hops."

"And Chris is like me and Danielle," Evan said with a smile.

"Yes…yes, he is." Walt stood up. "Why don't you try to get some sleep. I need you to help me communicate with the living world. If I find out where they are, you and I have to figure out how to get that information to the right person, and I can't do it alone. I need you, Evan MacDonald."

BEFORE LEAVING Evan to his dreams, Walt rinsed and refilled the cup he found in the boy's jacket. He set it on the nightstand next to the bed. Unfortunately, there was no saving the cookies he found shoved into the other pocket—at least he assumed they had once been cookies. Now they were soggy mush.

Uncertain when Joanne would show up in the morning, Walt figured his first order of business was to straighten up the bathroom and wash Evan's clothes. He had watched Joanne use the modern washer and dryer enough times; he was fairly certain he could figure it out. When Joanne returned in the morning, Walt didn't intend for her to discover Evan—or any evidence of his presence.

After shoving Evan's dirty clothes and towels from his bath into the washer, Walt added the detergent, turned on the machine, and went into the kitchen. Sitting down at the table, he closed his eyes and thought of Danielle, hoping that wherever she might be—she would be sleeping.

In the dark kitchen, Walt sat at the table for about ten minutes, eyes closed—nothing. Opening his eyes, he let out a sigh and then closed his eyes again. This time he thought of Lily.

LILY, her red curls messily tied in a knot and pinned atop her head, sat on the desolate beach, her bare toes buried in the sand. The sleeveless sundress she wore covered her knees, while its pale green fabric complemented her fair coloring. She sat there for a few moments, staring out to sea, when she suddenly realized she wasn't alone.

Turning abruptly to the right, she spied Walt, who stood over her, smiling.

"Walt!" Lily gasped, jumping to her feet. "Oh my god, you're here, you're really here!" Throwing her arms around him, she began to sob.

"It's okay, Lily." Walt didn't believe that was true, but he found himself saying it anyway as he gave her shoulder a comforting pat. "But you must stop crying, or you're going to wake yourself up."

Pulling back, Lily wiped the tears from her face and looked up at him. "You're right. I can't wake up yet. What took you so long? We thought for certain you would have come by now."

His hands now clutching Lily's shoulders, he looked seriously into her green eyes. "Is Danielle alright?"

Lily nodded solemnly. "Yes, she is for now."

"What about the rest of them?"

Anxious, Lily licked her lips. "All but…Chris."

Walt frowned. "Chris?"

"Is that why you finally came? Did Chris come to you?"

"How would Chris come to me, Lily?"

"You know…"

"What are you saying, Lily? And where are you?"

Her eyes wide and frightened, Lily shook her head. "I have no idea."

In the next moment, she vanished.

Walt glanced around the beach; she was no longer in sight.

Wherever Lily was, she was no longer sleeping.

FOUR

Officer Brian Henderson sat at the chief's desk, sorting through papers. He hadn't had a day off since the chief and Joe Morelli had taken off—that had been over a week ago. Absently combing one hand through his hair while trying to find some order to the papers on his desk, he told himself he was too old for this crap. Just as he gathered up several papers and tossed them into a pile, a soft knock at the open doorway caught his attention. He looked up. It was the chief's sister, Sissy Conway, and by her red-edged eyes, it was obvious she had been crying.

Just as Brian stood up, Sissy rushed into the office and said, "Evan's missing!"

"Evan? What do you mean missing?" Walking around the desk to greet her, Brian gently took Sissy by the arm and led her to a chair. She sat down, her purse on her lap.

"When I got up this morning, he wasn't in his bed. We've looked all over. I think he's run away." Sissy started crying again.

Awkwardly patting her shoulder, Brian said, "Calm down, Sissy. I'm sure we'll find him with a friend, or maybe he went over to his house." Sitting on the edge of the desk, he looked down at Sissy, who fished a tissue from her purse and dabbed tears from the corners of her eyes. She stopped crying.

Shaking her head, she said, "No. Bruce went over there already. There was no sign of Evan. Bruce even went inside. We thought maybe Evan had a key we didn't know about. But the place was still all locked up. It didn't look like anyone had been there. Bruce checked all the rooms—even the closets. Evan wasn't there."

"Considering what's happened with his father—"

"He doesn't know," Sissy said before Brian could finish his sentence.

Brian frowned. "What do you mean he doesn't know?"

Sissy shrugged sheepishly. "We just told the boys the trip was extended for a few more days. We hoped…" She glanced down at the tissue in her hand, absently twisting it.

"Sissy, you do realize the entire town is talking about this. Hell, there was a city council meeting last night. You know that, I saw Bruce there."

Again, Sissy shrugged. "We just didn't want to worry the boys. It seemed premature."

"What about their friends at school? You don't think one of them heard something at home and then said something to either Evan or Eddy?"

"I know he was upset his father wasn't going to make the birthday party."

"Birthday party? It's Evan's birthday?"

Sissy shook her head. "No. One of his little friends. It was his birthday. Ed was supposed to be back in time to take him." She smiled up sadly at Brian. "Ed was scheduled to work this afternoon, so he promised he'd drop Evan off at the party first. Evan likes to show his dad off—you know—in his uniform. He's pretty proud of his daddy."

"When was the last time you saw him?" Brian studied Sissy. She was a handsome woman, a few years older than her brother, Police Chief Edward MacDonald. Tall and slender, she had the same blue-gray eyes as her brother, and Brian suspected her brown hair would have streaks of gray like her sibling's if she didn't have it colored. Sissy and her husband, Bruce, had never had children. Since the chief had lost his wife, Sissy had tried to step into the role of surrogate mom, but Brian wondered if she had the temperament to raise little boys—she seemed a little high-strung to him.

"Right before I went to bed last night. I never really checked the time. After Bruce got home from the city council meeting, we stayed downstairs and talked for about thirty minutes before going upstairs to bed. Right before I went to our room, I checked on the boys. They were both sleeping."

"What time did you get up this morning?"

"We always sleep in on Saturdays. It was around nine when I looked into the boys' room. Eddy was still sleeping, but Evan's bed was empty. I assumed he was downstairs, watching cartoons. But when I got downstairs, I couldn't find him." Sissy paused a moment and opened her purse. She removed a flashlight and stood up briefly, handing it to Brian.

"What's this?" Brian took the flashlight and studied it for a moment. Its end was missing, as were its batteries.

"That's Evan's flashlight. He always sleeps with it. After Bruce got back from Ed's house, we walked around the neighborhood, checking to see if anyone had seen Evan. We found this a couple blocks from our house, lying on the sidewalk."

"I assume you've called his friends?"

"Just the ones I know. But I did call Trevor's mother—he's the boy who's having a birthday party today. All of Evan's little friends will be there, so Bruce is going to go over there and talk to the parents and kids when they arrive, see if anyone knows anything."

"Where is Bruce now?"

"He's home with Eddy. We didn't want to leave him alone. Especially now."

Picking up a pencil from the desk, Brian absently tapped it against one knee. "What does Eddy say about his brother?"

"He doesn't know where he is." Tears filled Sissy's eyes again. "What are we going to do?"

"For now, we need to find your nephew." Standing up, Brian walked around his desk and sat down. Picking up the phone, he made a call.

Sissy sat quietly, listening. When Brian finally hung up, she said, "Thank you, Brian."

"We're going to find him. I promise you."

Shoving her crumpled tissue into her open purse, she pulled out a fresh one and blew her nose. "This has been absolutely the worse week in my life. Have you talked to the other families?"

"Joe's the only one—aside from your brother—who has family locally. Craig's been stopping in about every afternoon, checking for updates. As for the rest of them, I've been talking to Lily's parents every day. I can't help but feel especially horrible for them—they thought they lost their daughter once already. Of course, Danielle has no one for me to call, same for Chris. I've also been talking to Ian and Kelly's parents. And Carol Ann's brother. Thanks for giving me that number, by the way."

"I wasn't sure it was still good. Ed gave it to me when he and Carol Ann went to Hawaii last year."

"It's surprising how many of them have lost both parents—kind of makes me feel old. After all, they're all younger than me."

"From what I understand, Carol Ann was raised by her older brother. I believe he recently got out of the military."

"Maybe that explains his stoic attitude."

Sissy frowned. "What do you mean?"

"Lily's parents have been basket cases—can't say I blame them. Ian and Kelly's parents, not much better. But Carol Ann's brother, well, he didn't say much. Just thanked me for the information and asked me to contact him as soon as we found out something."

"I've never met the brother before. But I remember Carol Ann saying he wasn't an especially warm and fuzzy guy, but they were close." Sissy stood up. "I better get going. Bruce is waiting at home for me."

Brian stood. "If Evan shows up—and I have a feeling he's going to be wandering in on his own—call me immediately."

"I will. I promise."

EVAN HAD JUST CHANGED into the clean clothes Walt had brought him that morning. They were the same clothes he had been wearing when he had first arrived at Marlow House the night before. Standing by the dresser in Danielle's bedroom, Evan watched in fascination as the sheets, pillows, blankets, and bedspread from the bed he had slept in floated effortlessly in the air and then miraculously settled neatly over the mattress.

"Wow, that's awesome! I wish I had you at my house."

Walt chuckled. "If I lived at your house, you would make your own bed. But for now, we can't chance Joanne noticing anything out of place. As it is, this morning I had to wipe up the muddy footprints you left on the kitchen floor last night."

"Who's Joanne?" Evan followed Walt out of the bedroom.

"She's the housekeeper. She comes over at least twice a day to check on the house and feed Max and Sadie. We need to find someplace for you to hide when she gets here."

"When is she going to come?" Still following Walt, Evan took hold of the railing and made his way down the stairs.

"I'm not sure. But I have Sadie standing guard. When she barks, you need to hightail it to your hiding place."

"Where's that?"

Walt paused mid staircase and looked at Evan. "If we're downstairs, the closet in the downstairs bedroom. I can't see any reason Joanne would go in there." Walt continued down the stairs.

"Did you figure out where my dad is?"

"No. But I did find out he's alive."

"I knew it! How did you find out?"

"I managed to hop into Lily's dream last night. She told me right before she woke up."

"Did you try again?"

Stepping onto the first-floor landing, Walt looked up to Evan, waiting for the boy to reach him. "I tried. But I have a feeling, wherever they are, I don't imagine they're sleeping well. Dream hops don't seem to work as well on someone who's catnapping."

"Catnapping?" Evan frowned. He stepped onto the first-floor landing and then followed Walt to the kitchen.

"Someone who is restless, can't get into a deep sleep. Maybe dozes off, and then wakes up a few minutes later. I suspect wherever they are, the sleeping accommodations aren't the best. But I'm not giving up."

"Good."

Walt opened the kitchen door for Evan.

"I'm hungry," Evan announced as he walked into the kitchen.

"I'm afraid there isn't much in the refrigerator."

"I had some cookies in my coat pocket! Where's my coat?"

"I'm afraid those didn't survive your little adventure last night."

"Oh…" Evan's lower lip stuck out in a pout.

"Look in the pantry. I'm sure you'll find something there. Just don't mess it up. Joanne might look in there."

Before Evan had a chance to open the pantry door, they heard Sadie barking.

"Quick. To the bedroom you stayed in when you were here the first time. Hurry. In the closet," Walt ordered.

JOANNE HAD JUST PARKED her car along the sidewalk in front of Marlow House when something in the side yard caught her attention. Stepping from her car, she looked over and noticed one of the branches hanging over the fence appeared to be broken. Instead of arching over the fence, the limb hung limply from a larger branch.

Frowning, Joanne slammed her car door shut and headed for the side gate to have a closer look. After unlocking the side gate, she entered and made her way to the injured branch.

"I'll need to ask Marie if I can call the gardener," she muttered.

Turning from the tree, she headed for the side door leading to the kitchen. Just as she was about to step onto the side porch, she froze. Spatters of dry mud covered the patio and doggy door.

Joanne groaned. "Oh please, don't tell me Sadie came out here and rolled in the mud." Hurriedly, Joanne unlocked the kitchen door. The moment she did, she called, "Sadie!"

Tossing her purse on the kitchen counter, she glanced around the room and was relieved to see the floors were still clean. There was no evidence of mud. She still expected to find mud caked on the golden retriever. However, when a clean dog charged into the room a moment later, she began thinking cat. *Did Max make that mess outside?*

Kneeling down to greet Sadie, Joanne heard a meow. Glancing up from the dog, she spied Max standing in the doorway—his black fur shiny and clean, and the tips of his ears snowy white.

FIVE

Perched cockeyed on the gray head of hair was a lavender straw hat, its front brim folded back, which defeated its initial purpose: keeping the sun from Marie Nichols's eyes. She stood in the middle of the front yard, surveying the damage from the previous night's storm. It hadn't been a gentle sprinkle.

Early spring flowers, their heads weighed down from the recent dousing, dotted the fenced yard, while the lawn glistened. Behind Marie was her bright yellow beach cottage, its white trim clean and fresh from a recent painting. Hands on hips, she wore a pink floral, cotton housedress and lime-green rubber rain boots. Overhead the sun lit up the blue sky. Whatever rainclouds had been there the night before had vanished by noon.

Her grandson, Adam, found her still standing there when he pulled up in front of her house ten minutes later.

"I like your outfit," Adam teased when he met his grandmother at the front gate. In his hand he carried a sack of take-out food. He'd brought his grandmother lunch.

Removing her hat, she used it to swat Adam. "Oh hush." Turning to the house, the elderly woman led the way to her front door.

Glancing over her shoulder, she asked, "Any news on the plane?"

"Nothing."

At the front porch, Marie removed her boots. Once inside, she hung her hat on the coat rack in the entry hall. Minutes later she sat with Adam in the kitchen, unwrapping the sandwich he had brought her.

"I don't understand. They should have found the plane by now. They know where it went down," Marie said before taking a bite.

"The witness didn't give an exact location. That's an immense area. Nothing but forest."

Marie set her sandwich down on a napkin and looked at Adam. "Isn't there some way they can track its location? Don't planes send out some sort of radar when they crash?"

"I guess not." Adam picked up a small sack of potato chips and tore it open.

"I don't like this. It's been a week—how long can they survive alone in the forest?"

Assuming they survived the crash, Adam thought before saying, "I guess it's a good thing I don't have a girlfriend." He popped a potato chip in his mouth.

Marie frowned. "What do you mean?"

"Chris invited me to go along. But I felt like a fifth wheel. There wasn't really anyone I wanted to ask."

"Oh my! You never told me that!"

Adam shrugged and picked up another potato chip.

"I suppose in this instance, I'm glad you aren't in a serious relationship. If you were, you would have probably been on that plane, and then instead of worrying about Danielle, Lily, and the rest of them, I'd be worried about you too!"

"I just hope it's not too late. There're a hell of a lot of people on that plane that I'll miss if they never come home."

Picking up her sandwich, Marie started to take a bite but instead asked, "Do you know anything about the pilot?"

"Just that he owns the plane—runs a charter service. From everything I've heard, he's a damn good pilot—which gives me hope."

"You mentioned you were going to check on their houses. Did you?"

"I went over to your house yesterday and Chris's. Not the Gusarov Estate, but his house on Beach Drive. Everything was fine. But after last night's storm, I'm having Bill go around and check on all the vacant properties. I also stopped at Marlow House yesterday. Joanne was there."

"How are Max and Sadie?" Marie asked.

"Okay for now. Joanne goes over there every day and feeds them. I just hope we don't have to find homes for those two."

"I would take them in a heartbeat—but those kids are coming home!"

"Grandma, you hate cats. And you always said you'd never have a dog because they'd dig up your garden."

"I don't *hate* cats. I just don't like them using my yard as a litter box. As for the dog digging, from what I recall, Ian's dog is well trained. I expect Danielle and the rest to return safely. But if they don't—god forbid—I certainly would not turn my back on two helpless animals that meant so much to her. Absolutely not." Stubbornly, Marie shook her head.

Adam smiled weakly at his grandmother, picked up his soda, and took a drink while thinking, *Another reason to keep praying for their safe return. If they don't come back, I'm going to be coming over here every day to pick up Sadie's dog poop and clean Max's litter box.*

DANGLING from his lips was a lit cigarette, its prominent ash threatening to fall off at any moment. Bill Jones pulled his truck in front of the Gusarov Estate and turned off the engine. He removed his cigarette and flicked its ash carelessly out the open window before returning it to his mouth and grabbing the clipboard off his passenger seat.

Pulling a pen from the pocket of his blue work shirt, he scribbled a note on the clipboard's top paper and then tossed the clipboard back onto the seat before opening the truck's door. On his last stop he had fished out the key to the Gusarov Estate from his glove compartment and had shoved it into one pocket of his work pants.

Making his way up the walk to the front door, he wondered what was going to happen to the Gusarov Estate if the plane and passengers weren't found. *Would Adam be able to sell the property?* he wondered. *And what about the house on Beach Drive?*

Adam never came out and directly told Bill that Chris Johnson was in truth the wealthy and reclusive philanthropist Chris Glandon. But it didn't take him long to figure it out. He knew Johnson—or Glandon—whatever he wanted to be called—had purchased both properties. It wasn't exactly something Adam could keep a secret from Bill since he regularly sent him over to work on both properties.

At first, Bill didn't understand the significance. Around town, the word was that the Gusarov Estate had new owners and would be the new headquarters for the Glandon Foundation. Bill had no clue what the Glandon Foundation was, but he was mildly curious, and he knew his way around Google, so he gave it a quick search.

What he found out, the Glandon Foundation was actually the newly organized nonprofit entity formed by Chris Glandon, a young man who had inherited billions from his wealthy parents and who was known for his philanthropic work. Bill was shocked to learn the guy with the surfer-bum persona was worth a freaking fortune. No wonder Adam never hesitated to jump through hoops for the guy.

Bill just hoped the plane was found and its passengers were alive and well. Not that he personally cared about anyone on board. But he and Adam had been friends for years, and he seriously worried Adam might go suicidal if he lost his golden-goose client.

When Bill stepped into the front entry of what was now the Glandon Foundation Headquarters, he didn't bother turning on the overhead lights. The high-placed windows brought ample sunshine into the building. What had once been a living room was now the waiting area. Bill almost expected something more opulent—*didn't superrich people like real gold accents and lots of dangling crystal?* Instead, Chris had gone for classy yet understated. Whoever owned this place obviously had money, but they weren't trying to shove that fact down anyone's throat.

Begrudgingly, Bill approved of the décor. He hadn't been in the house since the final touches had been added. Making his way from the newly appointed waiting area, he went to inspect the rest of the house, beginning with the first floor.

Just as he was about to go up the staircase, he heard a strange clanging sound coming from the door leading to the basement. Bill stopped and listened. He heard it again. It sounded like someone was pounding on metal.

The house had been broken into once before—when some vagrant decided to camp out in the house after Chris's purchase. Bill considered briefly going back to his truck and getting something he could use as a weapon should he encounter a violent vagrant, but then decided he was being ridiculous. It was probably an issue with the furnace.

The moment he opened the door to the basement, he heard someone cry out, "Who's up there?"

Bill lurched back, almost tripping. He hadn't expected someone to actually be in the basement—having just convinced himself it was some explainable building sound. Instead of answering, he slammed the door shut and ran out of the house. Back at his truck and out of breath, he pulled his cellphone out of his pocket and called the police.

"AND HE HASN'T COME OUT?" Brian Henderson asked after he and another officer showed up ten minutes later. They stood with Bill by the sidewalk, looking up at the house.

"No." Bill shook his head. "I sure as hell wasn't going to just walk down there. No one's supposed to be in there. Of course, I guess it's possible whoever it was took off out the back door."

A few minutes later, Brian Henderson stood at the door leading to the basement, gun in hand. Just as he opened it, a voice called out, "I know someone's up there! Please! Help me!"

"Who's down there?" Brian called out.

"Oh my god! There is someone! Please, please help me!"

Whatever Officer Henderson imagined to find in the basement was nothing like what he encountered a few moments later.

The man handcuffed to the pipe looked like he had been there a while, if one took into account his unshaven face and his rumpled clothing. Next to him was a row of gallon water jugs, some full, some empty. Wrappers from granola bars littered the concrete floor. Brian was pretty sure he knew the contents of the nearby bucket.

The moment the man saw Brian's and the other officer's uniforms, he began to cry. "Thank god. I thought I was going to die here."

Brian winced at the sight of the man's wrist—raw and bloody from trying to pull the handcuff from the pipe. The other officer immediately called for help; this man would need to be checked out. It didn't look as if he was starving, and he had plenty of water, but he had been locked in the basement for a number of days. They were also going to need assistance getting the man out of the handcuffs.

"Who did this to you?" Brian asked.

"I don't know who they were. I came here to meet Chris Johnson. When Chris didn't answer the door, I walked in the house, and the next thing I know, someone hits me over the head, and when I wake up, I'm down here, handcuffed to that damn pipe."

"What day was that?" Brian asked.

After the man told him, Brian frowned. It was the day before the plane went missing.

"Who are you? Why did Chris call you over here?" Brian asked.

"My name is Mason Murdock. Chris hired me to fly him and some friends to Texas."

"Mason Murdock?" Brian blurted out. "You and your plane and passengers are missing."

"What are you talking about?"

"The day after you came here, your plane took off with eight passengers, and it went missing. You were listed as the pilot."

"That's impossible. I've been here all that time."

SIX

If it wasn't for the sunshine slipping through the occasional gaps in the metal paneling, Danielle would have no idea what time it was. She guessed it was late afternoon, considering the location of the brightest point inside the unlit building.

Sitting up, her chains rattled. She couldn't help but groan. She ached all over. Sleeping on concrete was not a recipe for a good night's rest.

"Dani, you're finally awake!" she heard Lily whisper.

In spite of the lack of light, Danielle's eyes had grown used to the darkness. She turned to Lily, who sat next to her. Like Danielle, Lily's ankle was manacled and chained to the floor.

"Did you talk to Walt?" Lily asked.

"I assume you're talking dream hop. But no. He still hasn't come yet. I knew he wouldn't while he thought I was still on vacation, he said he wouldn't be jumping into my dreams—not when I'm off on vacation with Chris. But since we should have been back by now, I sort of thought he would."

"I saw him last night," Lily said, her voice low.

"He came to you in a dream hop?"

Lily nodded. "He did for a minute. He knows something's wrong. He asked me where we were—of course I had no answer for him."

"Did you tell him what happened?" Danielle glanced toward the doorway on the far side of the building and then back to Lily.

"I started to, but then something woke me up."

"Getting any real sleep in here is virtually impossible. I was pretty restless all night. I didn't fall asleep until early this morning." Danielle brushed her hand through her long tangled hair. The elastic hair tie securing her braid had snapped off days earlier. "If Walt hopped into your dream—that must mean we should have been back by now. He's probably trying to figure out why we haven't returned."

"Why didn't he jump into your dream?" Lily asked. "I'd expect him to do that first."

Danielle shrugged. "If he tried sometime last night, probably because I wasn't asleep. Why didn't you tell me about the dream hop last night, when you woke up?"

"Because I tried to fall asleep again—just in case—in case he was still there waiting."

"Danielle," a voice called out from the other side of the building. It was Chief MacDonald.

"Chief?" Danielle shouted back.

"Roll call," the chief said.

"Damn, you're bossy," Danielle hollered.

"I see you haven't lost your sense of humor," the chief called back.

"Got to hold onto something!" she said in a loud voice before shouting, "Danielle. I'm okay, just sore. I managed to get some sleep in this morning. To Lily."

"Lily here. Same as Dani. To Kelly," Lily shouted.

"Kelly here. I want to go home. But I'm about the same. Still alive. To Carol Ann…"

Silence.

After a moment MacDonald's loud voice boomed from his shadowy side of the building, "They still have her. I'll take that to mean Chris is still alive. Early this morning, they let her come in here for a moment. She told me they're still treating her okay and not to worry. She didn't seem afraid—I think her focus is on pulling Chris through this. To Joe."

"Joe here," Joe Morelli called out from another corner of the building. "No change. To Ian."

"Ian here. The same."

"You think they still have someone listening to us?" Lily asked in a loud clear voice.

"I'd be surprised if they didn't," Joe called back.

After roll call, Lily, still sitting, reached to her ankle and repositioned the manacle. She couldn't decide what she wanted more—a backrest or some ointment for her ankle's raw skin.

"God, I hope the chief is right and this means Chris is still alive," Lily whispered.

"He must be."

Lily turned to Danielle. "Why do you say that?"

"I haven't seen him, have I?"

Lily shrugged. "You have a point. If he was dead, I'm sure his spirit would come looking for you. Has Percival been back?"

"No. But I wish he would. Maybe he can't help us get out of here, but he should be able to tell us where we are." Danielle stood up; her chain rattled. Awkwardly stretching, she rubbed her hip. Every inch of her body ached. "We have one thing to be grateful for."

"Please tell me what?" Lily scoffed.

"If we had to be in this situation, I'm just grateful we had a nurse with us. I'd feel better if Carol Ann was a doctor instead of a nurse…but I'll take a nurse," Danielle said.

"I'd feel better if this hadn't happened at all!"

"That too," Danielle said with a sigh.

"I swear, when we get out of here, I'm never going to look at another granola bar ever again."

"I guess we should be grateful they're giving us something to eat and plenty of water. When I was trapped in Presley House, I would have killed for water."

"Oh please," Lily snapped. "Don't go Pollyanna on me."

Ignoring Lily's comment, Danielle added, "And they chained us to the same spot. At least we can talk without shouting. Poor Kelly is stuck over there by herself, like the guys."

Lily frowned. "Yeah, why do you think they let us be together?"

"I suspect it had nothing to do with trying to make us more comfortable. My guess—they ran out of places to secure the chains."

Lily groaned. "I feel so damn guilty for how we used to chain our dog up in the backyard when I was a kid. What were we thinking?"

"I'm just relieved we haven't seen their faces. It gives me hope we'll get out of here."

"What do you mean? We saw the damn pilot's face."

"Yeah, but he was wearing a beard and those humongous sunglasses. And didn't you notice his hair color looked a little fake? I don't think he's a natural redhead. And I bet when he shaves off the beard and lets his hair go back to its natural color, we won't recognize him. For that I'm thankful, and it gives me hope in getting out of here alive. I mean, what would be the purpose of killing us all now? Hell, there are eight of us. If that wouldn't get them the needle, what would?"

"Dani, I hate to be the one to point this out—but if Chris dies, they might feel they have no option but to kill us."

Danielle shook her head. "I refuse to believe that. It would just make their situation worse, and we can't identify them."

"You're talking common sense," Lily scoffed. "Those guys are freaking maniacs."

BEFORE ENTERING THE HOSPITAL ROOM, Brian Henderson downed three aspirin. He had purchased them minutes earlier in the hospital gift store, along with a bottle of water. It had not been a good day. The chief's youngest son was still missing—he had literally vanished into thin air—and the pilot who was supposed to be on the missing plane had been found chained up in a basement. No, not a stellar day.

"Mr. Murdock," Brian greeted him when he entered the hospital room. "How are you feeling?"

Mason Murdock, now wearing a hospital gown, lay in the bed, an IV hooked up to his arm. With the backrest portion of the bed elevated, Mason remained leaning back, his head on a pillow. "Better. Thankful to be out of that damn basement."

"I understand they're going to keep you here for observation?" Brian took a seat next to the hospital bed.

"At least one night."

"I was hoping you could tell me a little more about what happened."

"I wish I knew more. I would love to help you get those creeps."

"Why don't you tell me again how you happened to be there?"

"Chris hired me and my plane. We were supposed to leave the next morning, when I got a call from someone who said they were from Chris's office. Officer Henderson, I know who Chris really is."

"Chris Glandon?" Brian asked.

Mason nodded. "When he first told me his real name, I didn't really know who *Chris Glandon* was—I mean, I had heard the name before, but I couldn't recall if he was an actor, politician—I really couldn't place the name. But then he explained that Johnson was actually his mother's maiden name—and he told me I could check with Police Chief MacDonald, that he and the other officers at your station could vouch for his identity. Of course, I didn't understand exactly how rich he was until I went home and looked him up online."

"Why was it necessary for him to tell you who he really was?"

"I imagine because he was considering hiring me for more than just one flight. He told me about his foundation, how he intended to get more involved in the charity work and that it would require more traveling—something he really didn't want to do on a commercial airline."

"So he was going to hire you as his pilot—his plane?"

Mason nodded. "I asked him why he didn't just buy his own jet—I mean, really, the guy could afford it. He told me he wasn't interested in owning a jet."

"This person who called you, what did they say?"

"She said something big had come up—"

"It was a woman?" Brian interrupted.

Mason nodded. "Yes. I think she told me her name, but I don't remember what it was."

"I suspect whatever it was, it wasn't her real name."

Mason let out a sigh. "I imagine it wasn't."

"So what did she tell you?"

"She said something really important had come up—something that could be potentially big for my charter service. She said Chris needed to talk to me before we took off in the morning, yet he couldn't get away. She said he was at his new office and was working on something really important, and asked if I could drop by to talk to him. She said I'd be glad I did."

"I imagine you were curious?"

"Yeah, stupid me. She told me Chris would be alone at the office headquarters, and if he didn't answer the door, to just walk in.

That's what I did. Next thing I know I was chained up in that damn basement."

"And you never saw anyone?" Brian asked.

Mason shook his head. "Not his face. I just remember walking down the hallway, calling out to Chris, and the next thing I know, some big guy has me from behind and is shoving a cloth over my face. And then someone sticks a needle in my arm, and the next thing I know I'm alone in that basement, chained up like some animal."

"Who did you discuss Chris with?"

Mason frowned. "What do you mean?"

"I suppose you told someone about your new big client. Someone piloted that airplane, and I imagine whoever did was connected to whoever attacked you and left you chained up. They obviously didn't want to kill you—after all, you had plenty of water and food."

"A case of granola bars," Mason said with a grunt. "If you call that food."

"My point being, they just wanted to get you out of the way while they hijacked your airplane—and passengers. And one very wealthy passenger. Who else knew Chris Johnson was going to be on your plane that day?"

Mason shook his head. "I didn't tell anyone. I mean, I might have mentioned my upcoming flight to a few people, but I never once mentioned Chris Glandon. I know I didn't."

Brian leaned back in the chair and crossed one leg over the opposing knee. "Oh, come on, no one? That was a mighty big client. Working for someone like Chris Glandon would mean never having to worry about booking future flights. He'd probably be willing to pay you a nice big salary to keep you on retainer. Isn't that how it works?"

"Which is why I didn't mention Chris's name to anyone. No one," Mason said emphatically. "Especially not anyone at the airport."

Brian frowned. "I don't understand?"

"To be honest, there are better charter planes out there—more luxurious ones. I really didn't want to risk another charter pilot approaching Chris, convincing him their charter was really the better one."

Brian considered Mason's answer for a moment and then asked,

"Okay, maybe you didn't brag about your new client around the airport. But are you sure you never mentioned Chris's upcoming trip to anyone—and perhaps dropped his name at the same time?"

Mason started to answer and then paused, his eyes widening. He began to shake his head. "But she wouldn't have had anything to do with any of this."

"Who is *she*?"

"Just a woman I know. But she wouldn't do something like this."

SEVEN

Sadie stood attentively on Cheerio watch. Each time one slipped from Evan's fingers, she rescued the crispy O and quickly gobbled it up. Walt didn't reprimand the dog. Instead, he sat on the chair across from the sofa, relieved Sadie was making the evidence disappear. When Joanne returned later that afternoon, he didn't want her finding cereal littered all over the parlor sofa—and it didn't appear the six-year-old was doing a very good job keeping the food in his mouth.

"I imagine that would taste better with milk," Walt noted.

"I eat it like this at home." Evan popped a fistful of Cheerios in his mouth and then asked, "Do you like Cheerios? It's my dad's favorite."

Walt leaned back comfortably in the chair, a cigar in one hand. "I've never had them."

Evan frowned. "Never had Cheerios?"

"In case you didn't know it—spirits don't eat food."

"You mean ghosts?" Evan popped more dry cereal into his mouth.

"I prefer spirit," Walt told him.

"What about when you were alive? You never had them then?" Evan dug his hand deeper into the box.

"I'm afraid Cheerios weren't around when I was alive."

"What did you have instead of Cheerios?"

"Instead of?" Walt considered the question a moment. "Well, we had oatmeal."

Evan wrinkled his nose. "I don't like oatmeal. My Aunt Sissy makes it, but I think it tastes like glue."

Walt chuckled. "We also had cornflakes."

"Cornflakes?"

Walt nodded.

"Cornflakes are okay." Evan set the now empty box next to him on the couch while Sadie eagerly sniffed the surrounding area for any stray Cheerios.

"Are you still hungry?" Walt asked.

Evan shook his head. "No. I'm fine."

"We need to get that box back in the pantry. I can't have Joanne finding it in the trash."

"Hey, Walt, if you can't eat, how come you can smoke?"

Walt shrugged. "I don't know. I just can."

"My dad says smoking is bad for you."

Walt eyed Evan seriously. "It is. I would recommend you never try it."

"Then how come you do it?"

Walt smiled. "Well, since I'm dead, it's really not an issue."

"It must be awesome to be dead. To be like you."

"Awesome?" Walt frowned. "I would much rather be alive like you."

"How come? You can walk through walls and spy on people and make stuff float through the air."

Walt studied Evan a moment and then asked, "Do you like ice cream?"

"Ice cream? Well, sure! Everyone likes ice cream."

"I liked ice cream too."

"They had ice cream when you were alive?" Evan asked.

Walt laughed. "Yes. In fact, we used to make our own using a hand-cranked ice cream maker. I wouldn't be surprised if it's still around here someplace. But my point was—I can never enjoy ice cream again. But it's not just food I can't enjoy—I can't go outside or have conversations with people like you can. No, trust me, Evan, I would take life over death any day."

"I don't think I'd like it if I couldn't have ice cream again."

Walt stood up. "That's just one of many things I miss now that I'm on this side. Now come, let's put that box in the pantry."

"I'm glad my dad is still alive. He really likes ice cream." Evan picked up the empty cereal box and climbed off the sofa. He followed Walt out of the parlor, heading for the kitchen, Sadie trotting along by his side.

"What are we going to do now?" Evan asked after he put the cereal box in its place in the pantry.

"At the moment, there's not much *we* can do. I'm going to keep trying to dream hop—but so far I haven't been successful. Then of course, we need to figure out some way to use that information to help bring them home. I feel horrible about your aunt and uncle—and even your brother."

"Horrible why?"

"I'm sure they're worried sick about you—plus they're also worried about your father. But whatever I find out will do no one any good if I can't communicate it to the outside world, and I need you for that."

"I want to do whatever I can to help! I'll stay here until we find my dad!"

Walt smiled at Evan and then looked to the kitchen door. "Why don't you go into the parlor and watch some television." Walt looked at Sadie. "And you stand guard. Let Evan know if Joanne drives up." He looked back to Evan. "And I'm going to go into the library and concentrate. It might be the middle of the afternoon, but maybe I can catch one of them sleeping."

Evan headed for the door. Just as he reached it, Walt called out his name. He turned and looked at Walt.

"Remember," Walt reminded him. "If Sadie starts barking, turn off the TV and hightail it to the closet in the downstairs bedroom. And don't make a mess—or else Joanne will know someone's here."

After Evan reached the parlor, he was about to turn on the television when he noticed the telephone. His father had made him and his brother memorize several phone numbers—one of them was his Aunt Sissy's. He remembered hearing her cry when she had talked to his uncle about his missing father. He hated the thought that she was probably crying now because of him.

Evan stood there a few more minutes, asking himself what he should do. What would it hurt? Evan wondered. All he wanted to do was let his aunt know he was okay. After all, he had taken off in the middle of the night, and she might think he was dead somewhere.

Glancing to the door leading to the hallway, Evan considered going to Walt and asking him if it was okay if he called his aunt. He wouldn't have to tell her where he was—just that he was okay. But then, Evan remembered Walt was trying to initiate a dream hop, and if he interrupted him, it might mess things up and prevent them from helping his dad.

Deciding he could make the decision by himself, Evan marched to the telephone sitting on the desk and called his aunt's house.

"Hello?" Aunt Sissy answered a moment later.

"Aunt Sissy, this is Evan."

"Evan! Oh my god, where are you?"

Evan could tell she was now crying. "I just called to tell you I'm okay."

"Evan, honey, tell me where you are, and I'll come get you. I'm not mad at you for leaving; I just want you to come home."

"I can't tell you. I just want you to know I'm okay. I promise. But Dad's alive, and I'm going to help bring him home."

"What are you talking about? Evan, where are you?"

"Don't worry, Aunt Sissy. I'm okay," Evan said before hanging up the phone.

BRIAN HADN'T BEEN BACK to the station for more than fifteen minutes when Adam Nichols walked through the office doorway and found him sitting at the chief's desk.

"Do you have a minute?" Adam asked when he walked in.

Brian looked up at Adam and leaned back in the chair. "Not really, but what's up?"

"I just talked to Bill. He told me about what he found in the basement at the Gusarov Estate." Adam took a seat and faced Brian.

"Yeah, well, I just got off the phone with the FBI."

"They're coming in on this one?" Adam asked.

"Looks like a kidnapping. We may no longer be looking for just the wreckage of a crash."

"I suppose that might be good news," Adam suggested.

"How so?"

"If someone hijacked the plane, then there's a good chance they're still alive."

"Regardless of the hijacking, someone saw that plane go down."

"Are they sure it was their plane?" Adam asked.

"It was where the plane should have been at the time it went down. And the witness was looking through binoculars. He described the painting on the side of the plane. It's a custom job. There isn't another plane that has it."

Adam started to say something and then paused. He looked at Brian and frowned. "If someone hijacked the plane in Oregon, why would they still be flying toward Texas?"

Brian shrugged. "I don't know. If it wasn't for the witness describing what he saw on the side of the plane, I'd be questioning if the downed plane was theirs."

"And there hasn't been any ransom request?"

"Not that I'm aware of, which is why I'm glad you stopped in."

"Why's that?"

"You're Chris's real estate broker, you must know something about his business—his personal finances—who would a kidnapper call to ask for a ransom?"

Adam shrugged. "I'm not really sure. I have no idea who his attorney is. And what makes you so sure the kidnapper—assuming this is a kidnapping—is targeting Chris?"

"Are you suggesting another target—Danielle maybe?"

"It's no secret she has money—you have to admit her story's been sensationalized, with the Missing Thorndike, the gold coins, not to mention the inheritances. As for Chris, it's not really public knowledge that he has money."

"The pilot knew," Brian said.

"He did?"

Brian nodded. "But he insists he didn't tell anyone—except for some girl he was seeing."

Adam shook his head and let out a heavy sigh. "It's always that one girl that brings a guy down."

Brian let out a snort. "Yeah, no kidding."

"As for Danielle, you might want to check the bank. That's where she has the Missing Thorndike. She doesn't have access to the coins yet, so if the kidnappers were looking for that, it's not going to happen."

"I have to admit I was pretty focused on Chris. It didn't even dawn on me that they might be targeting Danielle."

"And Lily, don't forget Lily," Adam noted.

"Lily?" Brian frowned.

"I know she got a hefty settlement from the Gusarov Estate, not sure how much exactly. I don't think it's anything like what Danielle has, but I'm pretty sure it was well over a million. Not sure who knows, but anyone who was following that case would assume she got something."

"Perhaps, but this is a pretty elaborate kidnapping if the target is someone like Lily—or even Danielle."

"Maybe it's all of them?" Adam suggested. "There's also Ian. He's pretty successful; a number of his books have been bestsellers and made into documentaries. I've no idea what he's worth, but I'd imagine it's more than Lily. Maybe even close to Danielle."

Brian picked up the phone.

"Who are you calling?"

"The bank. I want to make sure the Missing Thorndike is still there."

Adam glanced at his watch. "Are they still open? I know they close early on Saturday."

Brian didn't respond to the question because someone at the bank answered his call. When he got off the phone a few minutes later, he said, "It's still there. No action on any of her accounts."

"They told you that without a warrant?" Adam asked.

Brian smiled. "Susan Mitchell can be pretty accommodating." He leaned back in his chair and studied Adam.

"Susan answered the phone? Last time I spoke to her, she wasn't working Saturdays anymore."

"I imagine with Klein's death they've been moving people around," Brian said before asking, "Who controls Danielle's estate if she isn't here? Any idea?"

"Umm…you mean who would have access to her money?"

Brian nodded.

"The only one I know…my grandmother."

Brian sat up abruptly. "Your grandmother?"

"Yep. I know when Danielle had her last will drawn up, she listed three people who would have power of attorney in the event…well, in an event like this. Lily would be the primary one—and if she wasn't able to perform the duty, it would fall on Chris. And if Chris is unavailable, it then goes to my grandmother. Grandma showed me the papers after the plane went missing. So I suppose if a kidnapper was trying to contact someone with a ransom demand, they would have to go to her."

Before Brian could respond to Adam, the office phone rang. Putting up a hand to signify *hold that thought,* Brian answered the phone. Adam sat quietly, listening to Brian's side of the conversation.

"He what?…Did he say where he was?…Do you have that number?…It should be on the phone…damn…" Brian stood up abruptly, said a few more words, and then slammed down the phone.

"Everything okay?" Adam asked.

"Sissy heard from Evan. I need to go."

Adam stood up. "Sure, I understand. Hope the kid is okay. I'm going to head over to Grandma's and let her know what's going on. She needs to be prepared in case someone does contact her."

EIGHT

"I'm so stupid!" Sissy declared when she threw open the front door.

Wearing his Frederickport Police Department uniform, cap in hand, Brian stood on Sissy's front porch. Before he could ask what she meant, Sissy turned her back to him and marched to her living room, leaving the door wide open, a silent invitation for him to enter. Fitting the cap back on his head, Brian stepped into the house and closed the door behind him. He followed Sissy into the living room.

Stopping abruptly, she turned to face him. Clearly agitated, she said, "I didn't even think to trace the call. I just ran to get Bruce and tell him what happened, and then the phone rang. It was some stupid telemarketer, but then I couldn't trace it, it only tells you the number of the last person who called."

Brian glanced around. "Where is Bruce?"

"I had him take Eddy to the park. I didn't want him here when you showed up. The poor kid is so upset. Bruce and I told him this morning about his father—that his plane is missing—that we think it went down."

"It's gotten more complicated," Brian said, taking a seat on the sofa. He pulled off his cap again and tossed it on the cushion next to him.

"What do you mean?" Sissy sat down on a chair, facing Brian.

Brian quickly explained about finding the pilot and how they now believed the plane had been hijacked. He then turned the conversation back to Evan.

"He didn't give any clue as to where he was?" Brian asked.

She shook her head. "No. he just said not to worry, that he was okay. But that he was going to help bring his father home."

"Bring his father home?" Brian's first thought, *Is Evan with the kidnappers?* Not wanting to upset Sissy, he kept that thought to himself. He stood up. "I'm going to need a warrant. If you hear anything, call me immediately."

"Warrant?" Sissy frowned.

"The phone company should be able to give us the phone numbers of your incoming calls. For that, they'll want a warrant."

Sissy jumped to her feet. "You can find out where Evan is?"

"At least where he was when he called you—hopefully."

"Hopefully?"

"We don't know if he was calling from a landline or a cellphone. If someone handed him one of those throwaway phones to make a call, then there is really no way to trace him."

"DANIELLE'S BEEN KIDNAPPED?" Marie dropped her gardening trowel; it landed by her feet.

Adam bent down and picked up the trowel, handing it back to his grandmother. "Let's go in the house and discuss this."

With an anxious nod, Marie started following her grandson to the front walkway. They had just reached the door when a dark sedan pulled up in front of the property and stopped. Instead of going into the house, Adam and Marie paused and looked to the street. Two men, wearing sunglasses and dressed in dark suits, emerged from the vehicle and made their way to the front gate.

"Mrs. Nichols?" one of the men called out when he reached the gate, his companion at his side.

With a frown, Marie stepped from her porch back onto the walkway and looked at the men. "Yes?"

The man who had called out removed his identification from his pocket and flashed it at Marie. Even if she wasn't almost ninety-one years old, it would have been impossible for her to read it from where she stood. "I'm Special Agent Wilson with the FBI, and this is Special Agent Thomas. We need to talk to you—"

Before he finished his sentence, Marie had already shuffled to the gate, moving briskly for a woman her age. Agent Wilson was about to put his ID back in his pocket when Marie reached over the gate and snatched it from his hand, startling the agent.

"Goodness gracious, you don't expect me to be able to read this thing from all the way over there, do you?" she scolded. Squinting, she tried to read the identification badge.

"Ma'am, if we could just come in—" Wilson began, only to be cut off by Marie again.

Glancing over her shoulder, Marie used her hand—the one still holding the trowel—to wave Adam—who was already halfway down the walkway, coming in her direction—back to the front door. "Adam, run in the house and get my reading glasses. They're on the kitchen table." Marie paused a moment and then added, "Or maybe in my bedroom."

"Ma'am, can we please just go inside and talk?" Wilson asked impatiently.

Scowling at the agent, Marie shook her head defiantly. "Young man, I certainly did not get to be my age by letting strange men just march into my house." She turned to Adam, who was now at her side. "Adam, please, I need my glasses."

"Grandma, why don't you just let me see it." Adam reached for the ID in Marie's hand, only to be swatted away.

Clutching the ID to her breast, she frowned at Adam. "I'm perfectly capable of reading the man's identification. I just need my glasses!"

Rolling his eyes, Adam let out a sigh and shrugged apologetically at the two men before turning and heading to the house to retrieve his grandmother's glasses.

"And don't you be rolling your eyes at me, young man!" she called out to Adam.

A few minutes later, her reading glasses propped at the end of her nose, Marie closely examined the agent's identification. When she was sufficiently satisfied, she demanded to see the other agent's identification. Begrudgingly, he complied.

Standing behind her, Adam let out an exasperated sigh. Ignoring Adam, Marie handed the second agent his ID back.

"I know you just think I'm being a silly old lady," Marie said as she started to open the gate to let the men in her front yard. "But for all I know, you're the kidnappers who have Danielle and the rest of them."

Agent Thomas, who had just stepped onto the front walk leading to Marie's house, stopped a moment. "How do you know about the kidnapping?"

Marie let out a snort and said, "I'm old, I'm not clueless."

When they were in the house, Adam explained, "The man who works for me is the one who found the pilot. I stopped by the police station a little while ago and spoke to Brian Henderson—I assume that's the one who contacted you. We discussed the possibility of a kidnapping, which is why I'm here."

"You're the grandson?" Wilson asked.

Adam nodded and then put out his hand. "I'm afraid I haven't introduced myself. I'm Adam Nichols."

WALT STOOD at the door of the parlor, watching a strange cartoon character dance across the TV screen. Yellow and square with brown pants, black boots, and a large nose, Walt had absolutely no idea what it was supposed to be—but he was fairly certain the creature next to him was a starfish—one wearing flowered pants.

"What is that supposed to be?" Walt asked as he walked toward the television.

Evan looked up from the sofa, where he was spread out, watching the show. "SpongeBob SquarePants," he explained. He sat up and turned to Walt.

"It should be SpongeBob RectangularPants," Walt said.

Evan wrinkled his nose. "Huh?"

"Never mind." Walt snapped his fingers and the television turned off.

"Wow, you can turn the TV off by snapping your fingers!"

Walt shrug. "I don't actually need to snap my fingers to do it." To prove the point, the television turned on again and then off while Walt stood perfectly still. "It just looks more dramatic when I snap my fingers."

"Oh..." Evan got up from the couch. "Did you find my dad?"

"I'm afraid I wasn't successful in the dream hop. But I'll try again later—maybe I'll be more successful tonight. But for now, I was wondering if you're hungry?"

"Yeah, I am." Evan followed Walt out of the room and down the hall.

Once in the kitchen, Walt opened the refrigerator. "I'm afraid there isn't much in here. Danielle had Joanne clean it out before she left." He closed the refrigerator door and then opened the freezer. "There's some frozen meat in here, but I'm afraid that won't be of any use."

"Why not?" Evan stood by Walt and looked in the freezer.

"It will take hours for this to thaw."

"Don't you have a microwave?" Evan asked.

Walt glanced at the microwave on the counter. He remembered when Danielle had bought it. At the time, she had explained what it was, but he had never given it much attention. "Yes, but I have no idea how to use it."

"I do!" Evan said proudly.

Walt looked down at Evan and frowned. "You do?"

"Sure. My brother and I always help Dad make dinner. Dad lets me thaw the meat. He showed me how."

"Really? Interesting."

Evan nodded and then glanced around the kitchen, looking for the microwave. When he spied it, he walked over to have a closer look. "It is a little different from ours, but I think I can figure it out."

"Just as long as you don't burn the house down."

Evan smiled. "Dad told me never put foil or metal in the microwave because it'll blow up the house."

"Blow up?"

Evan shrugged. "Eddy said Dad only said that so I wouldn't put metal or foil in the microwave 'cause it might break it. He said the house won't really blow up; but I'm not sure."

"Well, let's not test it."

"But I did start a fire in it once when I made popcorn!" Evan said proudly.

"What happened?"

"Dad turned the microwave off and the fire went out. I was getting ready to spray it with water when he walked in the kitchen. We aren't allowed to have microwave popcorn anymore."

"Humm…then perhaps we should leave the microwave alone," Walt suggested.

"Oh, I've never started a fire when thawing meat. Promise!"

Unsure, Walt looked from Evan to the freezer. "Well, let's see what we have in here…" He pulled out a package of frozen hot dogs.

"I like hot dogs!" Evan announced when he saw the package.

"Then hot dogs it is." Walt closed the freezer and examined the package, looking for signs of metal or foil. Satisfied it was safe, he handed the frozen package to Evan and watched as the young boy put it in the microwave and turned on the appliance.

They stood there a few moments, watching the digital numbers tick away, when Sadie started barking.

"Oh no, that must be Joanne." Walt glanced at the clock. "She's earlier than I expected. Hurry, Evan, hide!"

With the microwave still running, Evan dashed from the kitchen and headed for the downstairs bedroom closet.

NINE

Forgetting the microwave for a moment, Walt followed Evan to the downstairs bedroom and made sure he was tucked safely in its closet. It wasn't until he heard Joanne open the front door did he remember about the microwave. In an instant he moved from one room to the next, appearing in front of the still-running appliance.

"I can do this," Walt mumbled under his breath. Looking over the controls of the microwave, he pushed the stop button. The microwave turned off. Walt smiled, proud of himself. "That wasn't so hard, was it?"

"Sadie, I'm happy to see you too!" Walt heard Joanne say as she entered the kitchen, Sadie jumping gleefully at her side.

Walt went to the kitchen table and sat down, watching Joanne, who was now refilling Sadie and Max's stainless steel water bowl at the kitchen sink. As she waited for the bowl to fill, her gaze wandered over to the nearby microwave. She cocked her head slightly, as if she was seeing something unexpected.

Walt frowned, wondering why she was staring at the microwave. He watched as she abruptly turned off the faucet—her gaze still fixed on the appliance—and abandoned the water bowl in the sink.

Absently wiping her hands on the sides of her jeans, she walked to the microwave and stood before it, staring. Walt got up from the table and walked to her, wondering what she was looking at. The light was off and the face of the door was dark. There was no way she could see the hot dogs still sitting inside the appliance.

In the next moment, Walt knew what had caught her attention. Normally, the numbers displayed on the microwave reflected the time—unless it was running. The digital number currently on the microwave reflected the remaining defrost time. Walt realized he had only paused the appliance; he hadn't cleared it.

Joanne reached for the microwave door and Walt panicked. If she found the partially frozen hot dogs inside, she would know someone was in the house.

"Sadie, quick, start barking and run to the front door—hurry!" Walt commanded. "And keep barking!"

The golden retriever started barking and ran from the kitchen. Joanne immediately abandoned the microwave and hurried after Sadie.

Walt followed Joanne to the door and watched her hurry down the hallway away from the kitchen. Satisfied she was momentarily distracted, he returned to the microwave and opened its door, removing the hot dogs and returning them to the freezer.

"DANI," Lily whispered in the darkness.

"Yeah?" Danielle turned to Lily. The two women lay together on the concrete floor of the dimly lit building, each with a foot securely shackled to a chain.

"Do you think we're going to get out of here?"

Danielle reached out and took her friend's hand and squeezed it. She didn't let go, but continued to hold it.

"We're still alive. If they wanted us dead, I think we'd be dead already. I'm just worried about Chris; he needs a real doctor."

"At least he has Carol Ann," Lily reminded her.

"I know, but she's not a doctor. He needs to get to a hospital."

"I feel sorry for the guys. At least you and me can talk about this without them hearing. Everything the guys say, they can probably hear."

"If they're listening," Danielle said.

"I'm sure they are."

"They obviously don't want to give the guys the opportunity to plot some escape, which will be kind of difficult if they have to shout while putting together a plan."

"It's a little insulting if you think about it," Lily said.

"What do you mean?"

"If they chose to separate us so it would be harder for us to formulate an escape plan, yet were forced to chain two of us together, it obviously means they felt you and I were less of a threat than the guys—or even Kelly."

Danielle chuckled.

"What is so funny? I don't think this is funny!"

"Think about it, Lily. Of all of us, we are the two who shouldn't have been put together. You and I have the ability to get a message to the outside world."

"You mean the dream hop?"

"Yes. I bet Walt will keep trying, and when he does, we can let him know what's going on. And if Percival comes back, maybe we'll have something useful to tell Walt."

"And exactly how is that going to help?" Lily asked. "Even if we knew where we were, how is Walt going to help us if he's stuck in Marlow House and can't communicate with the outside world?"

"Lily, that's why it's a good thing we're together—because we can devise a plan and come up with something. In fact, that's what I've been thinking about."

"Okay, so what have you come up with?"

"What are you two talking about?" Ian called out from the darkness.

"I hope it's a plan to get us out of here," came Kelly's voice.

"If they only knew," Danielle whispered.

"We're just wondering where we are," Lily called back.

"Lily!" Danielle scolded. "They might hear."

"So. They have no idea what we can do with the information."

"My guess is somewhere in the desert," the chief called out.

Danielle and Lily exchanged glances.

"Why do you say that?" Lily called back.

"Think about it. It's April—well, I guess it's May now," came Joe's loud voice. "Doesn't seem to be any air-conditioning or heating in here. If we were near home, it would be a lot colder in here at night."

A door opened, letting in a stream of light. "Quiet in there unless you want us to take your water away," a man's voice ordered. The door shut, cutting off the brief streak of sunlight.

"They don't want us to figure out where we are," Danielle whispered.

"Even if we do, how is Walt going to get that information to the right people?"

"He could write a note and leave it for Joanne," Danielle said with a snort.

"Right," Lily said dryly. "Like *that* would work."

"It would probably give poor Joanne a heart attack."

Silently, they each considered possible options. Finally, Lily blurted, "Heather!"

"Heather what?"

"Walt can get Heather to help us!" Lily suggested.

Danielle frowned. "Heather?"

"The only people I know who can see spirits—you, Chris, Heather, and Evan MacDonald. You and Chris are here. I don't really see a six-year-old boy being able to help. It would be possible for Walt to communicate with Evan via a dream hop. But seriously, what could Evan do? But Heather, she might be able to get the information to the right people."

"Heather sees spirits on occasion. Sure, her sensitivity has increased, but we don't even know if she'd be able to see and hear Walt. In the past, she's only seen flashes of him. Nothing more. And if he did reach out to her in a dream hop, she'd probably wake up in the morning thinking she had just been dreaming."

"I think we need to consider it, Dani. Heather might be our only link between Walt and help."

BRIAN HENDERSON WAS SITTING in his office, talking to the two FBI agents, Special Agents Thomas and Wilson, when he heard back from the phone company. The two agents sat quietly and listened while Brian took the call.

When he got off the phone, he looked at the agents and said, "That's interesting. The phone Evan MacDonald used to call his aunt, it's the landline at Marlow House."

"Marlow House?" Wilson frowned.

"It's the bed and breakfast—"

"Yes," Wilson interrupted. "We know what it is. If you'll recall, we went over there when we first interviewed Danielle Boatman about Baron Huxley."

"Ahh, that's right." Brian stood up. "I'm going to go over there. Hopefully Evan's still at the house."

Wilson and Thomas simultaneously stood up.

"We were led to believe the house is currently vacant," Thomas said. "Is whoever staying there in some way involved in the hijacking? Are they holding the boy hostage?"

"I have no idea why Evan would be there. But as far as I know, the only ones staying at the house are Max and Sadie."

"I think we need to learn a little more about Max and Sadie before we barge over there and put that boy in danger," Wilson said seriously.

"I agree," Thomas concurred.

Brian began to chuckle.

"I don't find this amusing," Wilson snapped.

With a sheepish grin, Brian said, "Max is Danielle's cat, and Sadie is Ian's golden retriever. They were left at the house. Joanne has been going over there several times a day to feed them and check on things. In fact, I need to call Joanne so she can let me into the house."

"NOW THAT I think about it, it's entirely possible Evan is in the house," Joanne told Brian and the two FBI agents. They stood by the gate leading to Marlow House.

"Why do you say that?" Brian asked.

"When I got here this morning, there was mud all over the kitchen porch and all over the outside of the doggy door. But neither Sadie or Max had any signs of having been in the mud. There was also a broken tree branch, which I suppose could have happened if he climbed the tree to get into the yard."

"Is this doggy door large enough for a boy to crawl through?" Wilson asked.

"Yes, someone Evan's size. I think he could easily get through it. But I can't imagine why he would come here."

"And you didn't see him when you were here earlier?" Thomas asked.

Joanne shook her head. "No. I've been here twice today, and never saw anything. But this is a big house. I didn't really go through it. Didn't see any reason to check all the rooms. But I still don't understand, why would he come here?"

"Hopefully he's still here and can tell us. One thing we do know, he made that call from this house," Brian said.

A few minutes later, Joanne handed Brian the house key. Instead of going inside, she waited in her car.

"This house is a little creepy," Wilson muttered as Brian unlocked the front door.

Brian laughed. "You have that right."

"What do you mean?" Thomas asked Brian. The door was now unlocked, but instead of entering immediately, the three men stood on the front porch of Marlow House.

"Just that I've witnessed some strange things here. If I didn't know better, I'd say the damn place is haunted."

Thomas and Wilson exchanged glances while Brian pushed the door open and stepped inside the darkened entry hall.

WALT HAD Evan once again tucked safely into the downstairs bedroom closet. It was Max who had signaled the alarm this time. Sadie had been sleeping soundly in the library, but Max was outside in a tree when he noticed company had arrived. He immediately dashed into the house to tell Walt, who in turn rushed Evan into hiding.

"What are they doing here?" Walt asked when the three men entered the house. He immediately recognized Brian—not one of his favorite people, although Danielle had insisted he had become much more friendly. As for the other two men—it took Walt several minutes for recognition to click into place.

"You're those G-men who were here a few weeks back, questioning Danielle."

"I'll go check the kitchen," Brian whispered. There's a door in there, and I don't want him taking off."

"I'll check this room." Thomas nodded to the parlor.

"I'll look in that one." Wilson motioned to the downstairs bedroom.

"No!" Walt shouted. "You really do not need to go in there."

In the next moment, Walt was in the closet with Evan. "I want you to be real quiet. Don't say a peep. I'll tell you when it's safe to come out."

Evan nodded, and in the next moment Walt vanished, reappearing in the bedroom outside the closet door. Wilson entered the room and looked around. Walt watched as the agent peeked under the bed and then looked in the adjoining bathroom before turning his attention to the closet.

Clutching the doorknob of the closet door, Wilson attempted to turn it, but it wouldn't budge.

"He wasn't in that front room or the living room," Thomas told Wilson when he entered the bedroom a few minutes later, only to find his partner wrestling with the closet door.

"What's the problem?" Thomas walked into the room.

"This won't budge, and it doesn't have a lock."

"He's not in the library or kitchen. I also checked the bathroom," Brian called from the doorway. Noticing Wilson struggling with the closet door, he stepped into the room. "What's the problem?"

"This damn door is stuck tighter than a drum!" Wilson cursed.

Walt realized he couldn't keep the door immobile indefinitely. It then dawned on him, *If Evan has to go home, I can still visit him in a dream hop. What was I thinking?*

Brian walked to the closet. "Evan? Are you in there, Evan? This is Brian Henderson. Come on, open the door."

"If he is in there, I certainly don't think he's holding the door shut!" Wilson snapped. "I seriously doubt a six-year-old is stronger than me!"

"Evan, it's going to be okay. I think you should go home, and we'll work this all out in a dream hop. Open the door and come out," Walt told him.

In the next instant Evan pushed open the closet door at the same time Wilson gave it another jerk, sending the special agent flying across the room into the dresser.

TEN

Slender and tall for his age, with delicate features, Evan sat on the parlor sofa, his brown eyes wide as Brian Henderson knelt before him. The two FBI agents hovered in the background, listening. By his side sat Walt, who flashed him reassuring smiles and an occasional wink, telling him everything was going to be okay.

"Why did you come here?" Brian asked for the second time.

Evan glanced at Walt, unsure how to answer.

Walt shrugged. "Tell him you were looking for your dad. You're six, you can get away with an excuse like that."

Evan frowned, but he said it anyway. "I was looking for my dad."

"Why did you think he would be here?" Brian asked.

Again Evan glanced at Walt.

With a wave of his hand Walt summoned a lit cigar. He took a puff and said, "Tell him you dreamt he was here. More believable than the truth."

"Notice how the kid keeps looking toward the door?" Wilson whispered to his partner as Evan continued to answer Brian's questions.

"Yeah, I noticed that too," Thomas whispered back.

Wilson sniffed the air. "I smell it again, cigar smoke. Someone else is here."

"We already looked through the house. No one else is here," Thomas said. "Remember, it's just how this creepy place smells."

Abruptly, Wilson stepped forward and threw a question at Evan. "Did someone tell you to come here?"

He didn't need to ask Walt for help on this one. "No. It was my idea." That was the truth.

"Why were you hiding?" Wilson asked.

Evan shrugged. "I didn't want to get in trouble."

"Not a bad answer," Walt said with a smile as he took another puff.

"My dad's alive," Evan blurted out. "I know you think the plane crashed and he's not coming home. But he's alive."

Walt cringed and took another puff.

Wilson asked in a serious tone, "How do you know that?"

Again, Evan glanced over to Walt.

"Stick to the dream story. And if you think about it, you're actually telling the truth—in a way. But it was Lily's dream—so to speak—not yours."

"I dreamt about it."

"Ask him what they know so far," Walt told Evan. "I want to know what's going on with the search—assuming there is one."

"Are you looking for my dad?"

"Yes." Wilson smiled.

Brian stood up. "I'm going to take Evan back to his aunt now."

"Hold your ground, kid. Refuse to budge until they give you some answers," Walt told him.

Grabbing hold of the sofa's arm, Evan held on tightly and looked up at Special Agent Wilson. "I'm not going until I find out what you know about my dad," he said stubbornly.

"You just need to go with Officer Henderson here, and we'll handle things," Wilson instructed.

"No!" Evan said stubbornly.

"Tell them you have a right to know," Walt told him.

"I have a right to know!"

"Whoa, Evan, calm down. Your dad would not like you talking to an adult like that," Brian chastised.

Evan glared at Brian. "You don't know what my dad would want."

Agent Thomas spoke up, his voice calm and soothing. "We think your father's plane was hijacked."

Evan looked at Thomas. "Hijacked?"

Thomas walked to Evan and took a place on the sofa—unfortunately it was Walt's place. Moving from where he had been sitting, Walt grumbled under his breath, but he didn't retaliate, considering Thomas's kind tone toward the boy and the fact he seemed to be willing to tell Evan what was going on.

"Do you know what that means?" Thomas asked.

Evan shook his head.

"The pilot they hired wasn't the one flying the plane that day. And we think whoever was flying the plane took it somewhere else." Thomas withheld the part about a witness seeing the plane go down.

"Ask them how they know that," Walt told him.

"How do you know that?" Evan asked.

Thomas glanced over at Brian and Wilson and then back to Evan. "Because we talked to the pilot they hired."

"From what I understand, the pilot owned the plane," Walt murmured. "Ask them what the pilot told them."

"What did the pilot tell you?"

"We found the man who was supposed to be flying the plane, tied up in an abandoned building. He's okay, so that's a good sign. We think whoever was flying that plane might have your dad and the rest of them," Thomas explained.

"Has anyone asked for a ransom?" Walt asked.

Evan looked at Walt, confused.

"Ask him if anyone has asked for money," Walt restated.

Evan looked back at Thomas. "Has anyone asked for money?"

"No. Not yet. But that's why we need you to go back to your aunt's house. We need to keep you safe while we figure this all out. And if a stranger approaches you—or even if someone you know tries to get you to leave with them without your aunt's permission, you need to tell your aunt immediately," Thomas told him.

"Go with Officer Henderson, Evan," Walt said gently. "After you go to sleep tonight, I'll come see you. I'll let you know if I find out anything about your dad. But this is a good thing. They're looking for the plane."

EVAN WAS JUST ABOUT to get into the backseat of Brian's

police car when he looked up to the attic window and saw Walt standing by the spotting scope, looking down at him. Without thought, Evan raised his hand and waved goodbye to Walt.

Brian glanced up to the attic window, half expecting to see Max sitting on the windowsill or Sadie looking down at them. But there was no one at the window. With a frown, he looked down at Evan while opening the car door for him.

"What were you waving at?"

"Walt," Evan said as he climbed into the car.

Brian glanced back at the attic window. "Walt?"

"I'm hungry. I hope Aunt Sissy will let me have something to eat."

With a shake of his head, Brian dismissed the boy's odd comment and slammed the door shut.

WALT STOOD at the window and watched the police car and dark sedan drive away. Alone in Marlow House again save for Max and Sadie, he walked over to the sofa bed and sat down. Closing his eyes, he leaned back and thought of Danielle. Imagining her sleeping, he focused his attention on her—attempting to enter her dream.

After ten minutes with no results, he turned his attention to Lily. Minutes went by—still no results. He then tried Chris, and after Chris, he focused on Evan's father, Police Chief MacDonald. Finding none of them sleeping—which he assumed must be the case—he decided to work on one of the other passengers. While they would just assume it was a dream, Walt hoped to glean some useful information. He would try Ian first. Between Ian, Joe, and Kelly, it was Ian Walt was most familiar with.

IAN OPENED his eyes and found himself sitting on the sofa in the library at Marlow House. He didn't remember the sofa being this hard. It felt as if he were sitting on a rock. *Danielle needs to get a new couch*, Ian thought as he tried to make himself more comfortable.

"Hello, Ian," Walt greeted him. He stood beside the life-size portraits of himself and his late wife.

Ian turned to the voice and found himself looking at a man who bore an uncanny resemblance to the man in the portrait. "You look just like Walt Marlow!"

"That's probably because I am Walt Marlow." Walt smiled and walked to the chair facing the sofa and sat down.

"That's impossible. Walt Marlow's been dead for almost a hundred years."

"Not so impossible considering this is a dream."

Ian frowned and looked around. "This doesn't feel like a dream."

"Why don't you tell me about the trip you're on. I understand Chris rented a charter plane. But I don't think you ended up where you were supposed to go, did you?"

Ian groaned. "Damn, this is a dream." Leaning his head back against the sofa, he closed his eyes. "Why did you have to ask me about the trip? It would have been nice to escape into a dream—at least for a while."

"What happened?" Walt asked.

"Why doesn't this feel like a regular dream? Weird."

"Where did they take you? Is everyone okay?"

Opening his eyes, Ian looked at Walt. "I wish I knew. I really do. I'm worried about Chris."

"What about Chris?"

"He's pretty bad. God, I hope he makes it." Ian closed his eyes again.

"Tell me where you are?" Walt asked.

Ian looked up at Walt and smiled. "I'm in the library at Marlow House."

"You're dreaming. We just talked about that. But when you wake up, where will you be?"

Ian shrugged. "Sleeping on a concrete floor in some old warehouse. Which probably explains why this sofa is so damn uncomfortable."

"Is Chris the only one who's hurt?"

Ian nodded. "We're all together—except for Chris. They took him away, along with Carol Ann."

"Carol Ann? Isn't that the chief's girlfriend?"

"Yeah. She's a nurse, and they're having her take care of Chris. I don't know what they plan to do if he dies. I think they intended to use us as hostages to get money out of Chris, but now that he's unconscious and barely hanging onto life, I'm not sure what that means for us if he dies."

"How are Danielle and Lily?"

"They're okay for now. But they have us chained up at opposite ends in a large storage building. No lights on, but during the day it's not pitch black; a little light comes in through the walls."

Before Walt could ask another question, Ian disappeared.

THE METAL SHACKLE cutting into the raw abrasion on his ankle woke Ian from his brief nap. Sitting up, he leaned down and repositioned the shackle. He could tell it was still daylight considering the beams of light cutting through some of the ill-fitting wallboards.

"Hey, Danielle," Ian called out.

"Yeah?" she answered.

"You'll never guess who I just dreamt about. Walt Marlow. Craziest dream, it felt so real. He kept quizzing me on where we are. I think he's worried about you."

ELEVEN

With nightfall came the evening breeze. Its intensity increased, sending the limbs of the taller trees along the north side of Danielle's property brushing against the eaves of Marlow House. Inside, Walt had abandoned his efforts to hop into another dream. He would wait until later in the evening and try it again. Instead, he made his way downstairs to do some reading.

The moment Walt entered the library, the overhead light turned on. He found Sadie napping on the sofa. She lifted her head and looked at him, her tail wagging. Walt only gave her a smile and shook his head, saying with a chuckle, "It's a good thing Joanne isn't here."

Sadie rested her chin back onto her front paws and closed her eyes. Walt walked to the bookshelf and perused the titles, looking for something to read. Since Danielle had entered his life, he had become something of a TV junkie, yet he hadn't abandoned his love of reading. After selecting a novel, he sat down on the chair facing the sofa and opened the book.

"What are you reading?" A male's voice came from the door leading to the hallway.

Walt looked up and to his surprise found Chris standing in the doorway, a cocky grin plastered on his face.

Standing abruptly, Walt's book fell through his body, landing on the chair. "Chris! Where's Danielle, Lily?"

Sadie lifted her head and looked at Chris. Her tail now wagging, she leapt off the sofa. But instead of rushing to him, she sat next to Walt and watched.

With a shrug, Chris walked into the room and looked around. "I don't know. I was hoping I'd find them here." He wandered over to an empty chair and sat down.

"What do you mean you hoped to find them here?" Walt quizzed.

"This is where they live, isn't it?" Chris leaned back in the chair and smiled.

Walt studied Chris, whose gaze wandered around the room as if he was unable to focus. He didn't have a good feeling about this. *What had Ian said? Something about Chris possibly dying…*

"Chris, look at me!"

Somewhat startled by the harsh demand, Chris looked at Walt and frowned. "What's your problem?"

"Chris, do you remember going on a trip with Danielle? Do you remember renting a plane?"

Furrowing his brows, he considered Walt's question, his gaze again wandering off.

"Oh…that's right." Chris looked back to Walt. "You weren't thrilled about that, were you?"

"It doesn't matter if I was happy about the trip or not. Do you remember going?"

Now frowning, Chris narrowed his eyes, considering the question. "I guess…but…"

"But what?" Walt snapped.

"Hey, why are you getting so crabby? Where's Danielle?"

Exasperated, Walt waved his hand, sending several dozen books falling from the shelves onto the floor.

Eyes wide, Chris looked from the books now littering the floor to Walt. "Why in the world did you do that? You better hope Danielle doesn't walk in here and see what you did."

"I don't think there's a risk of that!" Walt fumed.

Chris stood up. "Walt, why are you so worked up?"

"Focus, Chris, focus!"

"Focus on what?"

Letting out a deep breath, Walt closed his eyes for a moment. When he opened them again, he said, "Chris, do you remember getting on that airplane to leave for your trip?"

Chris sat back down. "Yeah, now that I think about it…I guess so. Why?"

Walt's gaze dropped momentarily to the chair he had been sitting in and the book now resting on its cushion. He stepped back from the chair and looked at Chris.

"Chris, maybe you'll have a better idea of what happened if you pick up that book for me."

"Pick up the book?" He looked over to the other books scattered on the floor. "What next, do you expect me to pick up all the books you just threw off the shelves? I don't think so."

"No. Just this one. Please pick it up for me. You'll understand why after you do."

Rolling his eyes, Chris stood up and reluctantly walked to the chair Walt had been sitting in. He leaned down to pick up the book. His fingers moved through it. He tried picking it up a second time and failed. And then a third time.

"Oh crap," Chris groaned. Combing his fingers through his hair, he shook his head and moaned, "Oh crap, am I dead?"

Walt shrugged. "That appears to be the case."

Chris considered the possibility and then shook his head in denial. He began pacing the room. "No. I'm not dead! I know it!"

"Well, the only time I saw someone unable to pick something up like that—and the person wasn't dead—was Lily."

"That's right! Danielle told me she initially thought Lily was dead—but she wasn't!"

Walt sat back down in his chair. "I believe Lily called it an out-of-body experience."

"I don't want to be dead." Chris plopped back down in his chair.

"No one wants to be dead," Walt reminded him. "I sure as hell didn't want to be."

"I'm too young!"

Walt let out a snort. "You're older than I was when I died."

"I've finally met a woman who I could spend my life with!"

Walt arched his brow and muttered, "You and me both, chump."

Chris turned abruptly to Walt. "No, seriously, this can't be happening. I must be having an out-of-body experience like Lily did!"

Walt shrugged. "There is one way to find out."

"How's that?"

"Go look in the mirror. Whereas I have no reflection, Lily had a faint one when she was lurking on—" Walt didn't get a chance to finish his sentence; Chris dashed out of the room.

Letting out a weary sigh, Walt stood up and followed Chris out to the dark hallway. Assuming Chris would be unable to turn on the light—considering he was either a newly departed spirit with unharnessed powers or a soul experiencing an out-of-body experience, with no powers—Walt glanced at the entry light and watched as it suddenly went on.

When Walt reached Chris, he looked in the mirror. Chris looked visibly relieved—at least the faint reflection in the mirror did.

"Does this mean I'm still alive?" Chris asked.

"I assume so. Do you think you can focus now so we can figure out what happened?"

"Yes. Should we go in the parlor?" Chris asked.

"No." The overhead light turned off, sending the hallway into darkness. "Not unless you want to sit in the dark. If someone drives by and sees the light on, I imagine we'll be getting another visit from the police."

"Another?"

"I'll explain later." Walt turned toward the library. "Come on. No one will see the light on in the library unless they climb over the side fence and come in the yard."

Once in the library, Chris took a seat on the sofa where Sadie had been sitting when he had first arrived. Yet Sadie didn't stay away for long. She jumped up on the sofa with Chris and insisted on sitting with him.

"Now do you remember what happened?" Walt asked after taking a seat across from Chris.

"I remember now—boarding the plane. I was told the pilot I'd hired had come down with the flu, and he arranged for a substitute."

"What happened on the flight?"

"That's kind of…blurry." Chris frowned.

"Sometimes it takes a while for things to come into focus. At least that's the case when you die. Yet, according to Lily, it was the same for her out-of-body experience. I remember when she showed up here—her soul, that is—it didn't even dawn on her how peculiar it was that she was here—when she was supposed to be back in

California at her teaching job. She forgot completely about her trip to Palm Springs—at least initially. But it came back to her. I suspect it will come back to you."

With a frown, Chris shook his head. "No. Not blurry like that. I remember sitting in the plane; we had just taken off. And I looked over at Carol Ann, and her head just dropped to one side, landing on Ed's shoulder."

"Ed?"

"Chief MacDonald."

"So now he's Ed?"

Chris shrugged. "Yeah."

"Go on…what about Carol Ann?"

"I remember finding it a little amusing that she'd nodded off so quickly—I mean, we hadn't been up in the air that long. I was going to say some smart-aleck crack to Ed about it, but then things got blurry, and the next thing I know I'm walking down some steps."

"Steps where?"

"I don't know. Everything was black. Not like I was in a dark room, but there was something wrapped around my head, like a scarf. There was someone on each side of me, clutching my arms, and then there wasn't. But I was going downs steps, and someone was behind me, holding onto my shoulder and telling me to keep going. I sort of freaked and tried to pull away, and the next thing I know I'm falling—and then—well, I'm here."

"I don't believe you just leapt from there to here. Try to focus—retrace your steps backwards from when you walked in here and asked me what I was reading. Concentrate."

Chris let out a sigh and closed his eyes. Leaning back on the sofa, he imagined himself standing at the door to the library. After a few minutes, he looked at Walt. "I remember something."

"What is it?"

"I remember standing by the plane—but I wasn't. I was lying on the ground—at least I think it was me. I had a blindfold on, and I really couldn't see my face. But it felt like it was me. The pilot was there and another man. A large man I had never seen before. They were standing over me, yelling at each other. I told myself to get up, and then I noticed it…" Chris stood up abruptly and began pacing the room, his right hand absently combing through his hair.

"You noticed what?" Walt asked.

"The blood. My hair was soaked in it." Chris paused a moment and touched his hair, searching for his head wound.

"There's no blood there now," Walt told him.

"Where's Danielle, Lily, the rest of them?"

"That's what I want to know. As best as I can figure out, the plane and all the passengers went missing. The pilot you hired, he was found tied up. From what I gathered, you were kidnapped."

"Kidnapped?"

Walt nodded and then went on to tell Chris about Evan's visit and what he had learned when Brian and the FBI agents had showed up at the house.

"After they left, I was able to visit Ian in a dream hop. Of course, he assumed it was a regular dream. But I managed to get him to tell me a little about what's going on. They have the others locked up in some warehouse. He knew you had been injured—he's even worried you might die. Focus, where did the plane land?"

Chris shook his head. "I can't remember anything but standing by the plane and looking at myself on the ground, unconscious—the men yelling at each other, and then the next thing I remember, I'm here—standing at the library door, watching you read."

"You must have wandered around first, seen your surroundings. Something that can help us find where they have the others."

"I'm sorry, Walt. I remember getting on the plane—watching Carol Ann nod off—everything getting blurry—waking up to darkness while I was being guided down some stairs—falling—" Chris winced and then said, "A hell of a pain on my forehead. There is something more—but it's just beyond my grasp. It's foggy…I can't explain exactly."

"Focus, Chris! Focus!"

Chris closed his eyes for a moment and tried to concentrate on what had happened after his mind stepped out of his body. When he opened his eyes again, he looked at Walt and said, "I was wandering around—trying to figure out where I was. But like I said, everything is foggy—out of focus. But I do remember wishing I was home, and then the next thing I know, here I am."

"Marlow House is not your home."

Chris frowned at Walt. "That's not a very kind thing to say, especially considering my current situation."

"None of you would be in this situation right now if you hadn't gotten that harebrained idea to rent a plane!"

TWELVE

THREE WEEKS EARLIER

When Danielle opened the front door, she found Chris standing on her porch, a bottle of wine in one hand. He handed the bottle to her and then stepped into the house. Now holding the wine, she glanced down at the bottle's distinctive red and gold chateau label and smiled.

"Oh my, what's the special occasion?" Danielle closed the door.

"Does it have to be a special occasion?" Chris asked with a grin.

"When you spend three hundred dollars on wine, one assumes it must be," Walt said when he appeared a moment later, standing in the entry hall with Danielle and Chris.

"Maybe it is a little bit." Chris shrugged. "Plus, that is damn good wine. I have to thank Adam for introducing us to it."

Wine bottle in hand, Danielle headed for the kitchen, Walt and Chris trailing behind her.

"Technically speaking, Baron Huxley introduced us to this wine," Danielle reminded him as she walked into the kitchen. "You want a glass now?"

"Definitely," Chris said as he took a seat at the table with Walt and watched Danielle remove the bottle's cork. Taking two wineglasses out of the overhead cabinet, she poured two glasses and brought them to the table. After handing one to Chris, she sat down.

Instead of a wineglass in his hand, Walt held a thin cigar. He took a puff while leaning back in the chair, watching Danielle take her first sip.

"This is the best wine," Danielle said a moment later.

"Well, Chris can afford it," Walt said before taking another puff.

"How's the heating project going?" Chris asked.

"They promise it'll be wrapped up next week—*finally*." Holding her stemmed wineglass in one hand, she swirled it slightly before lifting it to her nose and taking a deep breath.

"Do you know what you're doing?" Walt asked with a chuckle.

Danielle laughed. "Not really. But it almost smells as good as it tastes." She took a sip.

"So what are your plans after they finish putting in your new furnace?" Chris asked.

"An air conditioner," Danielle reminded him. "This place is moving into the twenty-first century."

"So what are you going to do?"

Danielle shrugged. "Our next reservation isn't until the first week in May. I really don't have any plans."

Lifting his glass in a toast, Chris said, "I think you should use the time to take a well-earned vacation." He took a drink of the wine.

"Yeah, Lily and I were talking about that. But it's sort of late in the game to plan something now. I wish I would have thought of it earlier."

"What do you think about dude ranches?" Chris asked.

"Dude ranches? I haven't given them much thought, why?"

"Oh, come on, don't you like horseback riding, eating barbecue, sitting under the stars?" Chris asked.

Danielle paused mid-sip and grinned across the table at Chris. "For some reason, I don't see you as the cowboy type."

Walt rolled his eyes and mumbled, "Oh brother…"

Shifting her glance to Walt, she wrinkled her nose at him and took a sip.

"Here's the deal," Chris began, setting his glass on the table. "A while back I bought tickets for this charity event. It's to raise money to save wild horses."

"I like wild horses," Danielle told him.

"It's being sponsored by a dude ranch in Texas. I have eight tickets. I never planned to go, but I was sorting through some of my papers at the office and I came across the information on the event and realized it's later this month. And I thought, why not go? How about it?"

Danielle set her glass on the table. "Are you asking me to go to Texas with you?"

"First, a man asks you to go to California for dinner, and now Chris wants you to go to Texas with him?" Walt scoffed.

"What's wrong with Danielle going to Texas with me?"

Walt glared at Chris. "Other than the obvious…you are not married."

Danielle chuckled. "Well, I'm not married either. So I don't see what the problem would be."

Walt turned his attention to Danielle. Arching his brow, he said, "You know what I mean."

"Actually, I don't," Danielle muttered just as Chris started to respond.

"If it makes you feel any better, it won't be just me and Danielle. Did I mention I have eight tickets?"

Danielle picked her glass up off the table. "Who were you thinking of inviting?"

"Lily and Ian, of course. And I was thinking Adam and whoever he wants to bring."

"Adam? Seriously? I would have to spend…wait a minute, how long would we be gone?"

"Four days."

"Okay…so I would have to spend four days with Adam?" Danielle groaned.

"Oh, come on. You like Adam," Chris teased.

"Well…I don't loathe him anymore. And he can be fun. But four days?"

Chris flashed Danielle a rebuking glance.

Rolling her eyes, she took a sip and said, "Okay, okay. Adam and a friend. I just wish Melony was here to go with him. I'm kind of afraid of what kind of woman he might show up with."

"Four days? You'll be gone four days? What will Ian do with Sadie?" Walt asked.

"I suppose she could stay here with you," Danielle suggested.

"I'm not sure Ian will be thrilled about that. It's not like Ian knows about Walt," Chris reminded her.

"True, but I can pay Joanne to come over several times a day to check on Sadie and Max. We have the doggy door, so it's not like she needs to come over and let her out. I think she'd be happier here than staying at a kennel."

"Maybe Ian would prefer leaving her with his sister," Chris suggested. "Of course, that's assuming he and Lily agree to go with us."

"I'll see if I can talk him into leaving Sadie here," Danielle said. "She'd be happier here." *And so would Walt.*

"You say you have eight tickets, who else are you intending to invite?" Walt asked.

"I was thinking the chief and his girlfriend."

"The chief?" Danielle asked.

"Yeah. I appreciate how much help he's been, keeping my true identity out of the press. I think if Joe or Brian had their way, my true name would be common knowledge."

"That would be fun, but what would it cost for us to fly? I'm not sure the chief can really afford that, and I doubt he'd appreciate it if I offered to pay for his and Carol Ann's ticket. I think he pretty much tapped out his vacation allowance with that trip to Hawaii this last October, and he mentioned to me he was saving money to take his kids to Disneyland in the summer."

"That won't be a problem," Chris announced. "I'm chartering a plane."

"Really?" Danielle asked.

Chris nodded. "I hooked up with a charter service. After my last trip to New York, I realized how much I hate all the airport crap you go through when you fly commercial. I figured why not do what everyone else does in my position, charter a plane."

"No, Chris. I think most people in your position own their own jet," Danielle teased.

Chris shook his head. "No, thank you. I have no desire to own a jet."

"Are you seriously thinking of going?" Walt asked Danielle.

She looked at Walt. "Why? You don't think I should?"

Walt studied Danielle a moment, ignoring Chris's eye roll commentary on his question. After a moment of contemplation, Walt reluctantly said, "You would probably have fun. I think you should go."

Danielle wrinkled her nose. "Really?"

Walt looked at Chris. "So what do they do at this dude ranch?"

"I just glanced over the brochure. I know they have horseback riding, cookouts, line dancing, oh, and I saw something about a massage."

"Massage?" Danielle perked up. "I'm so up for that!"

"Yes, according to the brochure."

Danielle looked at Walt. "I wish you could come."

Chris sat back in his chair and muttered under his breath, "That would be a little crowded."

"IT SOUNDS FUN," Adam told Chris the next morning. "But there's no one I'd want to take." He handed Chris back the dude ranch brochure. The two sat together in a booth at Lucy's Diner.

"So come alone," Chris said, tossing the brochure on the table.

Adam smiled. "I'm really flattered that you asked me. But I don't want to go along and be a fifth wheel."

"I told you Ian and Lily are coming, and I just talked to the chief. I'm pretty sure he's going, but he needs to talk to Carol Ann first, see if she can get the time off from the hospital. There will be a lot of people coming with us."

Adam shook his head. "You mean couples. Thanks, Chris, really. But I don't think so."

CHRIS STOPPED at Ian's house after he left Lucy's Diner. He found not only Lily and Danielle sitting at Ian's kitchen table, but Ian's sister, Kelly.

"Hi, Kelly. I thought that was your car out there," Chris greeted Ian's sister as he took a barstool at the kitchen counter and looked down at the table.

"Hi, Chris, they were just telling me about the trip you guys are taking, sounds fun." Kelly had her brother's eyes and coloring, and while there was a strong family resemblance, she was as feminine as her brother was masculine. "I offered to keep Sadie for him, but Danielle says she's going to stay at Marlow House."

"She'll probably be happy there with Max." Chris flashed Danielle a quick smile.

"I don't have much of a yard, so you're probably right," Kelly agreed.

"We need to buy cowboy boots," Lily said.

"Is that really necessary?" Ian asked with a chuckle.

"Yes, it is!" Kelly insisted. "You have to wear cowboy boots when you ride. I mean, it would just be wrong to wear another type of shoe to a dude ranch. Especially if you intend to go riding."

Ian smiled at his sister and then looked over at Chris. "My sister is quite the horsewoman. Growing up, she had a horse and used to do the horse-show thing."

"Horse-show *thing*," Kelly said dryly under her breath and then chuckled.

Danielle looked over to Kelly. "I always wanted a horse when I was growing up."

Kelly smiled. "I love horses. You guys are going to have a great time."

"Then why don't you come with us," Chris said impulsively.

"Thanks for the offer. But Ian told me you only have eight tickets."

Chris looked from Kelly to the others. "Adam's not going."

"Why not?" Danielle asked.

Chris shrugged. "He said he'd feel like a fifth wheel. There wasn't anyone he wanted to take." Chris looked at Kelly. "So the offer is still on. If you want to go with us, I have two other tickets."

Excited, Kelly jumped from her chair. "Oh really? You mean that?"

"Sure." Chris smiled.

"Oh my god, I've always wanted to go to a dude ranch! I haven't been riding in years. I'm going to go call Joe and see if he can get the time off." Kelly dashed from the kitchen, heading to the living room so she could make a private call on her cellphone.

"Awkward," Lily muttered under her breath.

Chris looked at Lily and frowned.

Ian chuckled. "I imagine Lily is referring to the fact Joe and Danielle once dated."

"Hey, it's okay. Really," Danielle insisted. "Joe and I are friends, and we only dated casually—*very casually*."

THIRTEEN

When Sergeant Joe Morelli arrived at the station later that morning, he found Brian and the chief standing by the front desk. The woman who was normally sitting there was nowhere in sight, and Joe assumed she was either in the restroom or had left for lunch.

Of the three men, Joe was the youngest, being in his thirties, while Brian was the oldest—old enough to be Joe's father. Brian's shortly cropped hair had already gone gray, while the chief's brown hair just showed streaks of it. There was no sign of aging in Joe's thick, wavy black hair.

"I understand you and Kelly will be going with us to the dude ranch," the chief greeted Joe.

Brian laughed and shook his head. "The chief was just telling me about the trip. Damn, you guys are sure rubbing shoulders with the rich and powerful these days."

Joe flashed Brian a frown and then turned his attention to the chief. "I don't know how I can go, but when Kelly called to tell me about it, it kind of threw me. I told her I would check with you and see if I can get the time off."

Edward MacDonald shrugged. "So why don't you think you can go?"

"For one thing, you're going to be gone then too. We both can't go."

"Why not? I checked the schedule. You're already off two of those days. I'm sure you can find someone willing to switch shifts with you. In fact, I heard Gary talking the other day about wanting to swap days with someone so he can attend his high school reunion without taking vacation days."

"I don't know..." Joe mumbled.

Brian laughed again. "Sounds like you're trying to wiggle out of this trip. What, you don't want to be obligated to someone who you'd rather see locked up? I suppose I can understand that."

MacDonald looked at Brian. "Oh, come on, do you two still have an issue with Chris? I thought you guys got over that."

Joe shrugged. "Brian heard Chris threaten that woman, and she disappeared. I have to admit that still bothers me."

"He has a point," Brian chimed in. "I'm the one who overheard that conversation, and I have to agree with Joe. There is something more there."

"I thought you told me the woman herself insisted you misunderstood," the chief reminded them.

The person they were discussing was a guest who had mysteriously showed up at Marlow House over Christmas. She was a young woman who had called herself Anna Williams. What Joe and Brian didn't know, Anna was really Trudy Ann—a spirit who had attached herself to Chris and in some way—which the chief still could not understand—had led those around her to believe she was in fact a flesh and blood woman. She wasn't, and when she suddenly vanished, the mystery of her disappearance continued to haunt Joe and Brian, especially considering the fact Brian had overheard Chris threatening the woman. Yet it was not a woman Chris threatened, it was a spirit. Edward MacDonald knew the truth.

The chief stood there a moment, again reminded that two of his officers seemed unable to let go of their suspicions. He decided the only thing he could do was lie. It seemed as if he had been doing a lot of that recently—ever since Danielle Boatman had come into his life.

"Do you guys trust me?" the chief asked.

Brian looked at his boss and frowned. "Of course we do. But I'm not sure what that has to do about our feelings concerning Chris Glandon—or as you prefer we call him, Chris Johnson."

"This has to stay between the three of us," the chief told them.

Curious, both Joe and Brian stared at the chief.

"Anna Williams is not dead. She's in witness protection. It has absolutely nothing to do with Chris."

"Witness protection?" Joe asked. "Why?"

"I can't say." *I prefer to keep my lies as simple as possible.*

"So Chris really had nothing to do with her disappearance?" Brian asked.

"Nothing. And like I said, you can't mention this to anyone. No one. If you do, it could endanger her life."

The three stood there a moment while Joe and Brian digested what they had just heard. Finally, Brian said, "Joe, I think you're going to a dude ranch."

"I suppose…" Joe muttered.

WHEN THE CHIEF returned to his office, he closed his door and called Danielle on the phone.

"She's in witness protection?" Danielle said with a laugh after MacDonald recounted his conversation with Joe and Brian.

"You go ahead and laugh. But I really hate lying."

"I understand. But trust me, if you tell them she was really a ghost who moved on to the next level, they might be going to your supervisor, demanding you undergo a psychiatric evaluation."

"I know. But I still hate it."

"Thanks for getting them off Chris's back. I guess this means Joe and Kelly are going with us?"

"Yes. Although, I was surprised Chris asked him in the first place, considering everything."

"To be honest, I think it was more of an impulsive invite. Had he thought about it for a moment—remembering that Kelly would be asking Joe to go—he probably wouldn't have asked. Or, knowing Chris, I suppose it's possible he would have. He might have seen it as his opportunity to win Joe over."

"Did you ask Chris why he invited her?"

"No. We were over at Ian's when he asked her, and he left before me. We really haven't had an opportunity to discuss it. I couldn't really ask him with Ian and Kelly standing there. Although Lily seemed to think it was amusing. But that was because I'd briefly dated Joe."

"You think Chris cares what Joe thinks about him?"

"It's not that he cares exactly—like wanting people to like you—but I know from personal experience, life tends to be easier when the local police aren't suspicious of your every move—especially for people like me and Chris."

"Understood."

"So is Carol Ann all excited about the trip?"

"I don't know how excited she is. But I know she's out buying cowboy boots right now."

SAMUEL HAYMAN'S JEWELRY STORE, located next door to the bank, had closed down during the summer. The jewelry store, originally founded by Samuel's grandfather, had been a regular fixture of Frederickport since the twenties. But now, Samuel was serving time after a plea deal for stealing the diamonds and emeralds from the Missing Thorndike, a valuable necklace owned by Danielle Boatman and currently housed in a safety deposit box in the bank next door to Samuel's former store.

What had once been the location of the Hayman jewelry store remained vacant for months, until a new business opened in the fall: West Portland Shoes. There were other shops in Frederickport that sold shoes, but West Portland was the only one that carried cowboy boots.

Beverly Klein, an attractive well-dressed woman in her forties, was on her way to the bank, where her husband had been manager—until his recent fatal fall off the Frederickport Pier after going into anaphylactic shock when he unfortunately ate tamales she had stuffed with crabmeat. Beverly hadn't intended to kill him—just to punish him for his inability to keep his pants zipped up. But now that he was gone, she was surprised she didn't miss him as much as she had expected she would.

Headed to the bank to pick up some personal items her late husband, Steve, had left there, her attention was distracted when she walked by West Portland's storefront window and noticed a cute little pair of red shoes. Instead of continuing to the bank, she made her way into the shoe store.

"Beverly, hi," a familiar voice called out when she entered the store. Turning in the direction of the voice, Beverly found Carol Ann Peterson sitting in a chair, trying on a pair of cowboy boots.

"Hello, Carol Ann." Beverly's gaze dropped to the boots Carol Ann was fitting onto her stockinged feet. "For some reason, I just never pictured you in cowboy boots."

Carol Ann laughed. "I think the last time I had a pair of cowboy boots was when I was in grade school. They were a birthday present, as I recall. Wore those shoes everywhere."

"Any special occasion for this pair? You taking up riding? Line dancing?" Beverly picked up one of the red shoes she had been admiring.

"I'm going to a dude ranch in Texas," Carol Ann said excitedly.

"Really?" Beverly sat down in the empty chair next to Carol Ann, still holding the red shoe.

"Yes. We're going the last week of this month."

"We? Who are you going with? Anyone I know?" Beverly smiled.

"Ed MacDonald." With the boots now on her feet, Carol Ann stood up and took several steps to test the fit.

Beverly arched her brows. "The chief? Really? I thought…"

Carol Ann waved her hand dismissively at Beverly and sat back down. "We worked everything out."

Beverly chuckled and muttered under her breath, "I bet."

"This trip was sort of a spur-of-the-moment thing."

"My, I didn't realize the police chief did so well. Didn't you two go to Hawaii a while back?"

Carol Ann shrugged. "Well, this trip really isn't costing us anything."

"Even better…" Beverly smirked.

"A friend of Ed's—Chris Johnson—he dates Danielle Boatman, I believe…"

"I didn't realize Danielle was seeing anyone."

"I just assume they must be dating since she's going with him. Eight of us are going—on a private charter plane."

"How did you swing that?"

"Chris recently got a job with some nonprofit organization that's opening its foundation offices in town—Glandon Foundation."

Beverly tossed the red shoe on the empty chair next to her and sat up a little straighter before leaning closer to Carol Ann. "Really?"

"Yeah. From what I understand, the foundation hired Chris to find a building—they bought the Gusarov Estate. He's been over there setting up the offices, and I guess he'll be managing it."

"The Glandon Foundation, you say?"

"Yes. I believe that's what it's called. In appreciation for all his hard work, they gave him eight tickets for a dude ranch in Texas. It's some kind of fundraiser for saving wild horses. They even chartered a plane for Chris and his guests. Nice perk, huh?"

"Interesting…We are talking about that very attractive man who bought a house on Beach Drive, not far from Marlow House? Amazing blue eyes, blondish hair, looks like he should be on the book cover of a romance novel?"

Carol Ann laughed. "Yes, that's him."

"I've met him. How in the world did he land a job like that? I thought he was some out-of-work beach bum."

Carol Ann shrugged. "He isn't out of work now."

"Hmm…" Curious, Beverly pulled her smartphone from her purse. Holding it in her hand, she started an Internet search. "Glandon, you say?"

"What are you looking up?" Carol Ann asked.

Instead of answering, Beverly continued to search. A moment later she began to laugh.

"What's so funny?"

Enlarging a photograph on the small screen, she handed the phone to Carol Ann.

Carol Ann looked at a picture of a young bearded man. "What am I looking at?"

"The reason Chris Johnson could land such a plum job. Does the guy look familiar?"

"A little…" Carol Ann narrowed her eyes and stared at the man's face.

"It's him, Chris Johnson. Take off the beard, and I bet you a new pair of cowboy boots it's the same man. There is no mistaking those eyes."

Carol Ann handed the phone back to Beverly. "I still don't understand."

"The man in the picture—the man with the beard—his name is Chris *Glandon*."

"Chris Glandon?"

Beverly laughed again. "I remember reading about the Glandon estate once. Worth billions. It all went to their adopted son after they died in some boating accident. He tries to stay out of the public limelight and is known for being something of a philanthropist."

"Are you saying Chris Johnson is really this Chris Glandon?"

"Appears so." Beverly dropped her phone back in her purse and picked up the red shoe. "Chris Johnson isn't working for Chris Glandon's foundation—he's working for his own foundation. And he's flying you to Texas."

FOURTEEN

Walt lounged on Danielle's bed, his stockinged feet up on the mattress while he leaned back against the headboard. At the foot of the bed was an open suitcase. Danielle filled the suitcase—carefully folding each item of clothing as Walt watched.

Glancing up from her packing, Danielle looked into Walt's blue eyes. "Are you going to miss me?"

He shrugged. "You won't even be gone a week."

"I suppose that means you won't," Danielle teased. She turned from the bed and went to her dresser, opening a drawer.

"Do you want me to miss you?" he asked, his expression unreadable.

"I'll probably miss you." She removed several pair of flannel pajama bottoms from the drawer.

Walt eyed the pajama bottoms. "Are you taking those?"

Danielle tossed them in the suitcase. "Yeah, why?"

Walt shrugged. "You and Chris are going away together, so I just assumed…"

Danielle frowned. "Just assumed what?"

"I'm learning to get used to your generation's loose morals—so I naturally assume when a woman goes away with a man, she takes more…attractive sleepwear."

Danielle rolled her eyes and slammed her suitcase shut. She

zipped it up. "Walt, I'm not going away on some clandestine rendezvous."

"You're going away with a man, Danielle," Walt reminded her.

"And six other people."

"Where will you be sleeping?" Walt asked.

Danielle snatched the suitcase off the bed and tossed it on the floor. "I suppose in a bed."

"I'm sorry," Walt said with a sigh. "It's none of my business. You are an adult, and you live in a different time than I did."

"Oh please," Danielle said with a snort. "You lived during the Roaring Twenties. Remember? Lord, you used to run moonshine!"

"I don't see what that has to do with anything. But like I said, it's none of my business." Walt looked to the window, his hand slightly twitching. He so wanted to conjure a cigar, yet he had promised Danielle he would not smoke in her room.

With a sigh, Danielle walked to the empty side of the bed and sat down. Pulling her feet up on the mattress, she leaned back on the pillows in front of the headboard and lay next to Walt.

"You don't have a problem with this trip, do you?" Danielle asked in a soft voice.

"Does it really matter what I think?"

Danielle shrugged. "I guess I care what you think."

"I told you, you should go," Walt said in an even softer voice. "And it really *doesn't* matter what I think. This is your life, Danielle. I understand that." *My life was over long ago.*

They both sat there a moment, each lost in his or her own private thoughts.

"Walt, is something bothering you? You've been out of sorts for days."

He considered her question a moment and then let out a heavy sigh. "I suppose I'm wondering how this trip will change everything."

Danielle frowned at Walt. "Change everything, how?"

"When you go away with someone—when you spend intimate time with them—the dynamics of that relationship, along with the relationships you have with anyone else, changes."

Pulling her knees up to her chest, Danielle wrapped her arms around her bent legs and looked into blank space. "I don't know if this trip is going to change the dynamics of Chris and my relationship. But I know it's not going to change how I feel about you.

You're important to me, Walt. I feel that I can talk to you about absolutely anything." She turned to him and smiled. "And I don't think I could give up our dream hops."

Walt, whose expression had been blank, broke into a smile as his eyes met Danielle's. "I'd miss them too. But I will refrain from any dream hops while you're gone."

Danielle grinned. "I guess that would be a good idea."

THEY FIRST STARTED CALLING him Sky when he was just a kid because that was where he longed to be—flying high above the rooftops with the birds. As an adult, they continued to call him Sky, now a man who could fly just about any type of aircraft.

Sitting on one of the two chairs in the motel room, he watched as Clay stood by the door, preparing to leave. Sky wasn't a small man, but next to Clay he always felt short and puny.

"The alarm is off, right? The last thing I need is for the cops to show up."

"It's off. I double-checked. He hasn't been using it since he started the remodel. He's lax on security. Which is good for us."

"Are you sure Glandon isn't going to be at his office? If he shows when the pilot does, then this whole thing falls apart," Clay asked.

"I told you he's not even in Frederickport. No one will be there. The office hasn't officially opened; he hasn't hired anyone. I checked ten minutes ago, and he's in Astoria right now. By the time he gets back to town, you'll have the pilot safely locked up in the basement, and we can move on to our next phase in the plan." Sky ran his hand over his clean-shaven face. The next step involved a fake beard.

Two hours later, Sky stood in the motel bathroom, looking into the mirror. Smiling, he pulled his sunglasses out of his shirt pocket and fitted them onto his face. Just as he did, he heard the door to his motel open. Stepping out of the bathroom into the bedroom area of the motel room, he watched as Clay walked through the door, a smile on his face.

Clay came to an abrupt stop when his eyes landed on Sky. Closing the door behind him, he let out a low whistle. "Damn, I don't think your own mother would recognize you."

Sky grinned broadly and removed the glasses. "Can I assume by your smile you took care of the pilot without any problems?"

"Piece of cake. He never heard me coming."

"You didn't have a problem getting him to the basement by yourself?"

Clay laughed. "Are you serious? That little guy?"

Sky had seen the pilot, and he didn't look that little to him. "Then I guess we're set?"

"I'M NOT GOING to be gone that long," Edward MacDonald told his six-year-old son, Evan, as he tucked him into bed that night.

"But what about the birthday party?"

Edward sat on the side of the mattress and gently tugged the covers upwards, tucking them below Evan's chin. The boy quickly moved his arms out from under the covers and placed them on top of the blanket. He looked up at his father.

"I told you I'll be back before the party. You'll have fun at Aunt Sissy's house."

"I wish I could go with you. I've never ridden a horse before."

Brushing one hand gently over his son's forehead, Edward smiled. "Maybe we can fix that after I get back. Don't forget, we're going to Disneyland this summer."

"Is Carol Ann going with us?"

"Why do you ask?"

Evan shrugged. "Whenever you take a trip, she goes with you."

Edward smiled. "Not really. This is only our second trip together. Do you want Carol Ann to go to Disneyland with us?"

Evan wrinkled his nose and shook his head. "No."

"Why not?"

"When you said we couldn't go with you on this trip, you said we'd be taking a family trip to Disneyland."

"Why would that mean you don't want Carol Ann to come with us?"

"Because she's not family."

Studying his son a moment, Edward rested his weight on his right arm as his right hand propped against the mattress. "Don't you like Carol Ann?"

Evan shrugged. "She's okay, I guess. But she isn't family."

"You know, Evan, I might decide to get married again someday. And if I do, my new wife will be part of our family."

"Are you going to marry Carol Ann?"

Edward smiled. Moving his right hand, he sat up, no longer leaning against his arm. "I don't know. Would that be such a bad thing?"

"Would I have to call her Mom?"

Edward gently brushed his hand over Evan's brow again. "Only if you want to."

"I wouldn't want to."

"WHAT TIME ARE you leaving in the morning?" Brian asked Joe. The two sat together at Pier Café, having dinner.

"They're going to pick me up at seven in the morning."

Just before popping a French fry in his mouth, Brian said, "You don't sound too excited about this trip."

"It just feels odd, going with Danielle and Chris. Especially knowing Chris is basically paying for the trip." Joe picked up his beer and took a drink.

"So why are you going?" Brian ate another French fry.

"Kelly is so excited. I'd sound like a jerk if I told her I wasn't going." Joe set the beer on the table and reached for his burger.

"Granted, I can see how it might be awkward, you and Danielle, considering everything. But you two seem to have gotten beyond all that, and you're with Kelly now. Not to mention the fact I don't see how you can avoid any of those people—not as long as you're with Kelly. So why not go on an all-expenses-paid trip?"

"I like Kelly's brother. I like Lily too. And yeah, you're right, no way I'm going to avoid Chris and Danielle, not as long as Lily is dating Ian, and I'm dating Ian's sister."

"Being with a woman can get complicated." Brian started to put another fry in his mouth, but paused. "So what about Chris? You okay with him now?"

"If you mean do I feel better knowing he didn't kill Anna Williams, certainly. Do I suddenly like him? If I give you the real answer, I'll sound like a major jerk, considering he's paying for this damn trip."

"I take that to mean you don't like him." Brian chuckled and then ate the French fry he had been holding.

"Something about the guy just rubs me the wrong way. I don't know what it is, but he irritates the hell out of me."

"It wouldn't have anything to do with the fact he's worth billions? That he never has to work a day in his life, yet can still afford to play big shot and charter a plane and take a bunch of his friends on a vacation?"

Joe took a bite of his burger and shook his head. After he swallowed his bite, he picked up a napkin and wiped off his mouth. "The thing is, while he rubs me the wrong way, I don't get the impression he is trying to play big shot. From what Kelly told me, he bought the tickets more as a donation, never intending to use them. But when Danielle had some free time, he thought it might be fun to go."

"So is it the fact he got the girl?"

"What do you mean?" Joe frowned.

"The reason he rubs you the wrong way. Is it because he got Danielle, and you didn't?"

"Are you suggesting I might be jealous," Joe asked incredulously.

Brian shrugged. "Maybe not jealous exactly. I know you're with Kelly now, and you two seem good together. But I also know your thing for Danielle lasted months. I know what it's like to be crazy about someone and then have them choose some rich guy over you."

"You're thinking of Darlene?" Joe asked in a quiet voice.

Brian nodded.

"It's not the same thing. I know you cared for Darlene, but she didn't choose Stoddard over you. She chose Stoddard's money over you. Danielle doesn't care about the money. She would have chosen Chris over me even if he was just an employee of the Glandon Foundation, like he now leads people to believe."

"I suppose that might actually be worse," Brian muttered.

FIFTEEN

"This is the first time I've really gone anywhere since I moved to Oregon," Danielle told Chris as she waited for him to remove their suitcases from the back of the vehicle. "Except for when I went to California for Cheryl's funeral. But that was hardly a vacation."

"I'm so excited!" Carol Ann gushed. "I've always wanted to go to a dude ranch." She stood between Danielle and Edward, next to Chris's vehicle.

Just as Chris pulled the first suitcase from the car, Ian drove into the parking spot next to them. With him were Lily, Kelly, and Joe.

"I didn't even know this little airport was here," Lily said as she got out of Ian's car, slamming the door shut behind her.

Ten minutes later they stood in the small office of the charter company. Yet instead of being greeted by the owner of the company, Chris found himself shaking hands with a bearded man wearing a pilot's uniform.

"You must be Chris Johnson? I'm Tom Brown. I'll be your pilot today."

Chris frowned. "I don't understand. I expected Mason Murdock to be here."

"Mason called me up late last night. He got sick about an hour after he went to bed. He's pretty sure it's food poisoning, but it might be the flu. Either way, he didn't think he would make it, so he asked me to take the flight. I want you to know I'm very familiar with Mason's plane. In fact, I may be the only pilot he has ever loaned it to. You'll be safe. Trust me."

After introductions were made, the pilot suggested they all use the restroom before takeoff, as they would not be able to use the onboard bathroom until the flight was well under way, which might be forty minutes or more.

THIRTY MINUTES LATER, the eight passengers had fastened their seatbelts and were prepared for takeoff. Instead of traditional airline bucket seats, two sofas provided the seating. There were two of them, facing each other and slightly curved to bend with the contour of the plane. There were no stewardesses or stewards asking them if they wanted a cocktail. The door to the cockpit was closed, but the pilot was able to communicate to them via intercom.

As the plane taxied down the runway, the passengers eagerly discussed their upcoming trip. Chris sat on the end of one sofa with Danielle next to him, Lily next to her, and Ian on the other end. Across from them sat the remaining four of their party, with the chief sitting directly across from Chris.

Chris was about to say something when he noticed Carol Ann yawn. "You aren't sleepy, are you?" he teased.

The next moment, Carol Ann's head dropped onto MacDonald's left shoulder, her eyes closed. Chris intended to say something in response to her impromptu nap, but his vision began to blur.

Twenty minutes later the pilot's voice came over the loudspeaker. "Is everyone okay back there? Hello?" The voice sounded somewhat garbled, yet if anyone was able to hear it, they would understand what he was saying.

No answer.

The pilot's voice then asked, "I showed you where the intercom is, someone please push it and let me know everything is okay back there."

Still no answer.

"Let's get this done," said the pilot's voice as he remained in the cockpit.

The bathroom door opened and out stepped Clay. He wore a gas mask; it covered his face. Looking into the passenger area, he was fairly certain everyone was unconscious. He would need to move fast. But first, he would check on Sky.

In the cockpit he found Sky, who also wore a gas mask.

"I'll take care of things back there," Clay said before heading to the passenger section of the plane. Like Sky's voice earlier, his was also somewhat garbled because of the gas mask.

He used handcuffs instead of tape to secure the hostages' wrists. For their feet he affixed shackles. When they were secure, he brought out the hypodermic needles.

"This will keep you out of our way," Clay said as he pushed the first needle into Chris's arm. After each hostage got a turn with a needle, he brought out the heavy scarves. He wrapped one around the head of each prisoner.

The plane changed course, taking a slight detour. Mindful of the airspace, Sky did what was necessary to reach his ultimate destination without attracting unwanted attention.

THE FIRST THING CHRIS WONDERED—*WHY are my hands behind my back?* He opened his eyes, but it was still dark. He knew instantly the darkness had nothing to do with a lack of lighting in the area, but because something was wrapped around his head, covering his eyes. When he tried to sit up, he felt metal weighing heavily on his ankles.

"Chris? Lily?" came Danielle's panicked voice in the darkness.

Over the next thirty minutes, voices called out as each of the hostages regained consciousness. Confusion and fear permeated the cabin space.

"Quiet!" an unfamiliar male voice called out. They all stopped talking.

"I want you to listen very carefully," Clay told them. "If you do exactly what you're told, no one will get hurt, and you'll be back in Frederickport before you know it."

"Who are you?" Carol Ann blurted out.

"Shut up," he snapped. "If anyone says another word—asks a single question—one of you will find the toe of my boot shoved in your gut. And you don't want to do that. I'm not exactly a small man. And I'll start with the nosey little blonde who just asked that question. You hear me? One question from anyone and the blonde gets the first taste of my boot."

They were so quiet, one might suspect a few were holding their breaths.

"That's better," Clay said. "So here's what's going to happen. As you might have suspected, we have already landed the plane. We will be removing you one by one. If you don't want to get hurt—if you don't want to get one of your companions hurt—then do as you're told and this will go smoothly."

The temptation to blurt out a question was unpalatable, but they each resisted.

"Each of you is blindfolded. It's for your own good. Once we get you to where you'll be staying while you're with us, we'll remove the blindfolds and handcuffs, but your ankles will remain shackled."

The hostages silently listened.

"As you might have already figured out, you have been kidnapped and we are holding you for ransom. As soon as your friend here—*Chris Glandon*—transfers fifty million dollars, you will all be free to go. But until then, keep your mouths shut and do as you're told."

In the next moment, Chris felt hands grasping his right and then left arm before being jerked violently to his feet.

"We're taking Glandon first. While I'm gone, don't anyone make a move or say anything. If you do, one of the other guys will introduce his boot to your friend."

Chris found himself being dragged across the plane, he assumed toward the door. It was difficult to walk with the shackles on his ankles, but he was afraid to complain or ask them to slow down, for fear Carol Ann would be punished for his request.

The moment he reached the doorway, he felt a shift in the air—as if the door was open and letting in some of the outside. Wherever they were, it felt sunny and warm. Not hot, but much warmer than it had been back in Frederickport.

Whoever was helping him down the stairway from the plane was no longer standing next to him, holding his arms. He could feel one of them behind him, gripping his shoulder while telling him to keep moving. Yet that was not as easy as his captor thought. With Chris's hands secured behind his back, he was unable to hold onto a handrail, much less maintain his balance, and with his feet shackled, it was impossible to maneuver the steps.

Chris was on the verge of telling them he was going to fall when he did just that. Stumbling headfirst toward the ground, the person behind Chris was unable to stop the fall. Before landing on the concrete—headfirst—Chris let out a panicked cry.

DANIELLE and the others heard Chris's scream. She felt as if her heart had literally stopped. No one asked what was going on, but she could hear two male voices in the distance. They were shouting at each other. She was fairly certain one of the voices was the pilot's, and she was positive the other voice belonged to the man who had threatened Carol Ann.

"What's going on?" Carol Ann dared ask. When there was no answer, she shouted the question.

"Your friend had a little trouble getting down those stairs. He fell, but he's going to be alright. Which one of you is the nurse?" came the pilot's voice.

"I am," Danielle heard Carol Ann say.

"Stand up. You're coming with me." The man didn't offer further explanations, yet by the sounds around her, Danielle guessed Carol Ann was being taken to Chris.

The minutes ticked away. Inside the plane it was deadly quiet. With Carol Ann no longer on board, Danielle dared to ask a question. If one of the kidnappers chose to kick her in the stomach, so be it.

"May I ask a question, please?" Danielle asked in a timid voice.

There was no answer.

She tried again. "Hello? Are you there?"

"I think we're on the plane alone," Lily said.

"Is everyone here?" Danielle asked.

"Quick roll call, say your name if you're here," MacDonald ordered in a low voice.

The responses came in whispers.

"Joe."

"Ian."

"Kelly."

"They're bound to be back any moment. Don't provoke them. But pay close attention to everything. What you hear, smell, feel," MacDonald told them.

After the kidnappers returned, they took the hostages from the plane—one by one. However, unlike with Chris, they removed the handcuffs from the remaining hostages when each one was taken off the plane. This allowed them to utilize the handrail while going down the steps. It was still a precarious exit, as the blindfolds and ankle shackles remained in place.

Once off the plane, they walked about ten feet and were led up several more steps before being told to sit down. The last thing Danielle remembered before everything went black was someone pushing a needle into one of her arms.

When Danielle regained consciousness, she was still wearing her blindfold, and someone was tugging on her arms, telling her to stand up. Still somewhat groggy, she managed to get to her feet and stumbled along with her captors, fearful that she might fall should they release hold of her arms. A few minutes later someone removed the blindfold, and she found herself standing in what appeared to be an empty warehouse. The others were with her, yet they were scattered around the large building. They had shackled her foot to a piece of bent rebar coming out of the concrete floor. She suspected her friends were similarly chained.

Lily was the last to be brought in. The two men with her each wore a ski mask. By his voice, Danielle was fairly certain one of the masked men was the pilot. She wondered why he bothered wearing a mask.

Danielle silently watched as the two men dragged Lily around the building. It appeared they were looking for something they couldn't find. She heard one of them curse. The one she suspected was the pilot pointed to her, and she watched as they pulled Lily in her direction. In the next minute the two friends were shackled together.

After the men left the building, Danielle and Lily quickly hugged.

"Have you heard what happened to Chris?" Lily whispered in Danielle's ear.

"No." Danielle couldn't help it; she began to cry.

An hour later, one of the men returned, bringing them each a supply of bottled water, boxes of granola bars, and a bucket.

"It shouldn't be too hard to figure out what to do with the bucket." The masked man laughed. Danielle thought his physique resembled that of a professional football player. By his voice she knew he was the one who had threatened Carol Ann.

"There's a bathroom over there." The man pointed to a door on the far side of the building. "You'll each have an opportunity to visit the bathroom twice a day. When you do, you can empty your bucket. If you try anything when it's your turn at the bathroom, you won't be punished, but one of the ladies will be." The man laughed.

Danielle, who had been holding Lily's hand, squeezed it tightly.

Their spring vacation had begun.

SIXTEEN

"I can't believe you let him fall!" Sky cursed at Clay. They stood together on the far side of the room, watching Carol Ann. She attentively cared for Chris, who lay unconscious on the cot.

"I told you we should remove the handcuffs so he could hold onto the rail," Clay countered.

"You were supposed to steer him down those steps. I thought you could keep hold of him."

"If you thought it would be so damn easy, then why didn't you do it?"

Carol Ann looked over at the arguing men. "He's alive, but he needs to go to the hospital."

"Just take care of him," Sky snapped. "We've come this far, you don't actually think we're going to drop him at some hospital and walk away."

"What are we going to do?" Clay asked Sky when Carol Ann turned her attention back to Chris.

"We wait until he comes to. He has to be conscious. I can't believe this is happening. Everything was going perfectly…and then this!" Sky kicked a nearby folding chair in frustration. It slammed against the wall and toppled to the floor. The unexpected sound made Carol Ann lurch.

She looked at the two men. "I need to see my friends. Let them know what's going on."

"You need to take care of him," Sky ordered.

"There's nothing I can do right now but wait and see. But I really do think we need to get him to the hospital," Carol Ann told them.

"That's not going to happen." Sky then turned to Clay and said, "Go ahead, take her to the others, but bring her back in fifteen minutes."

POLICE CHIEF EDWARD MACDONALD'S eyes had grown accustomed to the lack of light. He could see the others—at least their shadowy forms. Like him, they all sat on the concrete floor, each one chained and confined to a limited space.

Sunlight briefly cut through a portion of the warehouse when the door opened. Looking at the door, he saw two figures—the large man wearing a mask and a blindfolded woman. It was Carol Ann. Edward leapt to his feet; his chains rattled.

"You have fifteen minutes," the kidnapper said as he roughly shoved Carol Ann in Edward's direction. He turned and went back outside, shutting the door behind him and cutting off the incoming sunlight.

Carol Ann stood there a moment, the blindfold still covering her eyes. The others all called out to her. Her hands reached up and removed the blindfold. She looked around, trying to adjust to the darkness.

"Carol Ann!" Edward called out again.

"Ed!" She dropped the blindfold to the floor and ran to him, throwing herself into his outstretched arms.

When the hug finally ended, he placed his hands on her shoulders and looked into her eyes. "Are you okay?"

She nodded. "Yes. They haven't hurt me. I don't think they will. They need me to take care of Chris."

"How is he?"

Carol Ann shook her head. "He's unconscious. When he was getting off the plane, he fell and landed on his forehead."

"Do you think he's going to be okay?"

She shook her head again. "Honestly, I don't know. Head trauma can be fatal. Even if the person survives the initial fall."

"He needs to go to the hospital."

"They aren't going to allow that."

"How many of them are there?"

"At least four. But whenever I've seen them, they all have ski masks on."

"Do you have any idea where they have us?"

Carol Ann leaned into Edward, resting her head on his shoulder. "No. When they took me outside, they put a blindfold on me—like when they brought me here. I have no idea where we are. As far as we know, we could still be in Frederickport."

"We're not in Frederickport," the chief said.

Carol Ann pulled back and looked up into Edward's face. "Why do you say that?"

"Aside from the fact I don't know of any buildings like this in town, the temperature in here. If we were anywhere near the coast, it would be damp and cold, especially at night."

"I suppose you're right." Carol Ann leaned back into him again.

"They could have flown us anywhere. My guess, we're someplace like Nevada, Arizona, or maybe even Texas, where we were supposed to go."

"They're going to be back to get me. So I don't want to waste any time."

Edward hugged Carol Ann again.

When he let her go, she looked up into his eyes and said, "I don't want you to worry about me. From what I've gathered, they intend to hold us hostage until Chris transfers the ransom money, and then they'll let us go."

"How is he going to do that if he's unconscious?"

"Well…that's why they need me, to take care of him. I don't think they'll hurt me."

"Carol Ann, we need to figure out some way to get out of here. Even if Chris does come to and manages to transfer that money, there is no guarantee they'll just let us go. And what if he doesn't? Will they keep us here indefinitely?"

"As long as they let me take care of Chris, there's a chance I can get a message to the outside world. There's a telephone in the room they have Chris in. I don't know if it's hooked up or not, but if I could get to it somehow, even if it's only to dial 911…"

"If the phone's hooked up, I can't imagine they'd leave you alone in there."

"I understand that. So far, whenever I'm in the room with Chris, one of them is always in there, keeping an eye on us. But maybe… maybe they'll let their guard down and step out of the room for a moment, without thinking."

"You be careful!" Edward told her.

"I will be. I just don't want you to do anything crazy or impulsive. I don't think Chris is in any immediate danger, which means none of us is in immediate danger. I overheard them talking. They plan to keep you here and supply you with adequate food and water and give you access to the bathroom. I don't think there's any danger of them coming in here and randomly abusing any of us. I don't think that's on their agenda. They just want the ransom money."

"Unfortunately, Carol Ann, when men get desperate, when their plans go awry, they can behave erratically. I want you to be careful and pay attention to everything."

SKY SAT ALONE in the small room, thinking of the computer he had set up at the rental house. If Chris Glandon hadn't taken that tumble down the steps, they would have already cleared out of the rental house, and the hostages would be waiting for the police to find them.

Standing up, he gave the rusty office chair a shove as he walked to the window and looked outside. He had been planning this for over a year now. In the beginning, Andy thought he was crazy. But she went along with the planning—like she always went along with him. He suspected one reason was she didn't think it would ever get this far. And maybe it wouldn't have if she hadn't stumbled across the ideal mark.

The door to the office opened and in walked Andy and Clay.

"Is he any better?" Sky asked, turning from the window.

"He's the same," Andy told him. "He could die if we don't get him to a hospital. And you promised no one would get hurt."

Sky looked at Clay.

"It was an accident!" Clay said defensively.

"It doesn't matter. I don't know about you two, but if we get caught, I don't want murder charges on top of kidnapping, and not to mention the fact we took them across the state line," she told him.

"Andy, we've already gone this far. We can't turn back now," Sky insisted.

"When that plane doesn't show up in Texas, people are going to start looking for them. This was supposed to be over by now," she reminded him.

"They will never find us here. I made sure of that," Sky told her.

"How long are we going to have to stay here?" Clay asked. "Are we going to wait until Glandon wakes up—or until he dies? Then what? Like Andy says, then we could be facing murder charges."

"I can't believe you two! After all this, you want to give up?"

Andy walked over to a chair and sat down. "Maybe we need to turn our attention to one of the other hostages. Maybe one of them can pay our ransom."

"Are you saying one of them can give us fifty million bucks?" Sky asked.

"I don't know about that much. But Danielle Boatman has money," Andy told him.

"Danielle Boatman?" Clay asked.

"That's the one that was sitting next to Glandon on the plane," she explained. "I don't know how much money exactly, but she got two inheritances—one from her cousin, who reportedly was worth millions—and she was the one who inherited that necklace I told you about. The Missing Thorndike."

"I read about that," Clay piped up.

"And remember the article I showed you about the gold coins? The ones worth a fortune?" Andy asked.

Sky frowned. "What about it?"

"Danielle Boatman, she was the one in the article. The coins supposedly belonged to Walt Marlow—who left his estate to Danielle Boatman's great-aunt," Andy explained.

Clay let out a low whistle. "Damn. I thought Glandon was the only rich one in there."

"No, there are a couple," Andy told him. "I'm pretty sure Danielle Boatman's friend Lily Miller is worth at least a couple million. She's the one who won that lawsuit from the Gusarov Estate."

"Damn, what are we waiting for? What about the other ones?" Clay said excitedly.

"We won't get anything from the two cops. They're both squeaky clean. But the other guy, he might be worth something."

"Maybe we can consider them—later. If there's nothing we can do with Glandon," Sky said. "The plan was to keep this simple. Getting money from a couple of them would be complicated—and may not even be possible."

Andy stood up. "How about this. We give it a few more days. See if he wakes up. But if it looks as if he's taking a turn for the worse, maybe we should consider the possibility of one of the other hostages paying the ransom, and cut our losses and get out of here."

"Could we get fifty million from Boatman?" Clay asked.

"I doubt it," Andy said. "But we should be able to get something."

"Then I say we wait," Clay said. "I didn't come all this way to give up."

SEVENTEEN

What was supposed to be her first night at the dude ranch was spent sleeping on the concrete floor next to Lily. Although, to say she actually slept would be overstating how she had spent the evening. It wasn't until the wee hours of the morning did she finally manage to fall asleep, yet her brief slumber was interrupted several hours later when she woke to one of her captors jerking her by one arm, telling her to stand up.

They removed her ankle from the shackle, yet fit the blindfold back over her eyes. Overtired and achy, she stumbled in the darkness, led from the building by the masked man with the football-player physique.

When the blindfold was finally removed, Danielle found herself standing in the middle of what appeared to be a sparsely furnished, well-worn, single-wide mobile home. Sitting in front of her was a masked man, who lounged casually on a stained sofa, his gaze fixed on her. The man who had brought her left her side and walked from the room, leaving her alone with his partner. Silently, she glanced around. All the blinds were drawn, making it impossible to see outside.

"So you're Danielle Boatman?" the man on the sofa asked. By his voice, Danielle guessed he was the pilot.

"Can I see Chris?" Danielle asked.

"If you cooperate, that might be possible."

"How is he? I understand he was unconscious."

"He's alive—for now."

"What do you want from me?" she asked.

"I understand you are a very wealthy woman."

"I…I suppose I've been fortunate."

The man started to laugh and waved his hand, as if showing her the interior of the trailer. "Is this what you call fortunate? My, you do have low expectations."

When he stopped laughing, Danielle asked, "I suppose you want money. How much?"

"I would like it all," he said with a shrug. "But I suppose I can't be greedy. I understand you own the Missing Thorndike. I'm not especially thrilled with having to find a buyer for it, yet I suppose it's a start."

"If I give you the necklace, you'll let me and my friends go? You'll let us take Chris to a hospital?"

"Like I said…it's a start."

"The necklace is in a safe deposit box in Frederickport. I'd have to go to the bank to get it out."

He sat there quietly for a moment and then shook his head. "No. That wasn't part of the plan. It won't work. Have you cashed in those gold coins yet? Did you put the money in the bank?"

"Gold coins?"

"Don't play dumb!" he snapped. "I know about those gold coins. They're worth millions."

"I wasn't playing dumb…it's just that I don't have the gold coins yet, so I couldn't very well put any money from them in the bank."

"What are you talking about?" He sounded angry.

"That's still going through the legal process—there's no guarantee the court will decide I'm the rightful owner."

"But you do have your money from your inheritances? Substantial ones, I understand."

Danielle shuffled her feet. "Umm, yes…sort of."

"What do you mean sort of?" He stood up abruptly and began to pace in front of the sofa. "Do you want to get you and your friends killed?"

"I don't care about the money!" Danielle insisted. "If I had it all right here, including the necklace and gold coins, I would gladly hand them over to you. But I can't give you something I don't have."

He stopped pacing. Standing about six feet from her, he stared at her through the eye holes of his ski mask. "What did you mean you sort of have your inheritance money?"

Danielle let out a sigh and glanced over to a chair. She had been sitting on concrete for hours and the worn recliner looked inviting. "May I please sit down?"

Her kidnapper nodded and pointed to the recliner, and then he sat back down on the sofa. "Explain what you were talking about."

"My cousin, Cheryl, left me her estate. A portion of that—her house—was left in a trust to me. But the bulk of the estate was not in a trust and is going through probate. So really, I don't have access to that at the moment. At least, not until it finishes going through probate, and my attorney says that can take up to a year."

"What about the money your great-aunt left you?"

"Well…aside from Marlow House, which I still own, the money I eventually got—a significant portion of that—well—I gave it away."

"Gave it away?" he asked incredulously.

"I didn't really need that much money. And I thought Chris's foundation could do so much more with it than I could."

"Are you saying you gave your inheritance from your great-aunt away?"

"Well, not all of it…just most of it. And then there were the income taxes."

"Income taxes?"

"Well, yeah, on the gold coins and necklace. I might not have the gold coins yet, but I thought I might as well go ahead and pay the taxes on them, since the money was just sitting in the bank account. I figured if I didn't get the coins for some reason, I would just get a tax refund back."

"Just how much do you have left—or more accurately—how much do you have that's being kept in a bank account?"

"Umm…I did have almost forty thousand—well, I did until I put that new heating and air-conditioning unit in Marlow House. Maybe a little over thirty thousand." Danielle shrugged.

Jumping to his feet again, he shrieked, "Thirty thousand! What kind of nut gives away most of her inheritance?"

Danielle was tempted to remind him that she would be getting over ten million dollars after her cousin's estate was finally settled—as it turned out to be worth even more than what she was originally told, and donating a significant portion of the money from her aunt's estate to the Glandon Foundation helped alleviate some of the tax burden. She also owned the Missing Thorndike, and according to her attorney, he didn't doubt she would get the gold coins. But she thought it best to keep that to herself.

"I will be happy to give you whatever I have in my bank account," she told him.

"Get her out of here!" he shouted at the top of his lungs. The larger man who had brought her to the trailer walked back into the room from the hallway.

"Do I get to see Chris now?" she asked.

"No, you don't!"

Several minutes later Danielle found herself once again blindfolded and led back to the warehouse where her friends were being held captive.

"WHAT ARE YOU SO ANGRY ABOUT?" Andy asked Sky after Clay took Danielle back to the other prisoners.

"She doesn't have any money," he spat.

"What do you mean? Yes, she does," Andy insisted.

Sky went on to recount his conversation with Danielle Boatman.

"Oh my…" Andy muttered, taking a seat on the sofa.

Sky sat down on the recliner Danielle had been using earlier. He and Andy sat in silence for several moments, considering the turn of events.

Finally, Sky looked up at Andy and asked, "Do you think she's lying?"

Andy considered the question for a moment and then shook her head. "From what I've heard about her, I don't think so. I can't imagine she'd jeopardize her friends' lives, much less her own, by coming up with a story like that. From what I understand, money is not that important to her. So I can't imagine she'd concoct a lie like that to hold on to hers and risk getting everyone killed."

"Money not important? Why is it always people who have money that believe stupid crap like that?"

Clay walked back into the trailer just as Sky said, "Well, I sure as hell am not going to do all this for a measly thirty thousand bucks. What would we all end up with, less than seven thousand each? Sure as hell not worth the risk. This was supposed to be the big score."

"Seven thousand is better than nothing," Clay said as he took a seat on the sofa next to Andy.

"Don't you understand?" Sky shouted. "After I use the program to move the funds—the chances of getting it to work again are slim at best. Days after they realize what we did, that hole will be closed so tight. I certainly don't want to waste this on pocket change!"

Clay shrugged and shook his head. "I don't understand why we can't use it again."

Andy let out a weary sigh and turned to face Clay. "If Sky uses it to transfer money out of Danielle's account, the bank will eventually realize someone other than Danielle moved those funds. Once they look into it, they'll discover the vulnerability and it'll be corrected. I don't think this is something they'll keep to themselves. Sky's program is brilliant. But we only have one shot to use it."

"DID YOU SEE CHRIS?" Lily asked Danielle after she returned to the warehouse.

"No." Danielle picked up a granola bar packet and ripped it open.

"So what did they want?"

"Money. Ransom money. I would have been happy to give them what I have to get us out of here, but I'm afraid what I have in the bank isn't what they had in mind." Danielle bit off the end of the bar and started to chew.

"What I don't understand, they told us they'd let us go after Chris transferred fifty million dollars into their account. How would that even be possible? I mean, who keeps that kind of money in a bank?"

"Actually, Chris has that much money in one bank—the bank his family owns."

"He owns a bank?"

"Yeah, I guess it's his now—and the shareholders. His father started it."

Lily reached for a granola bar. As she opened it, she said, "I sure hope Chris is going to be okay."

Before popping the last bite of the granola bar in her mouth, Danielle said, "I'm just happy I haven't seen him. We have to figure out some way out of here. If only Walt was here to help us."

EIGHTEEN

When Danielle woke up the next morning, she wanted to weep. Not just because every muscle in her back cried out in pain from sleeping on the concrete floor—or the fact the shackle had rubbed her ankle raw—or that her stomach growled from hunger, and if she had to eat another granola bar, she was going to throw up—she wanted to weep because Walt hadn't visited her dreams. While he had promised not to intrude on her sleep while she was away with Chris, she desperately needed to talk to him. Not that he could actually do anything to help her, but talking to Walt always made her feel better.

Staring up at the ceiling rafters, she heard Lily say, "You're awake."

Dragging herself to a sitting position, Danielle combed her fingers through her tangled hair. "Does your back hurt as much as mine?"

"Probably. But I'm so glad you woke up; I have to pee so bad." Lily, who sat on the floor next to Danielle, began to stand up, rattling her chains.

"Why did my sleeping keep you from using your bucket? I certainly wasn't going to see anything." Danielle yawned and ran both set of fingers through her hair, attempting to tame her unruly curls.

"Because I didn't want to shout *privacy* and wake you up." Since being held captive, the group had come to an arrangement. When any of them needed to use their bucket, he or she would simply shout *privacy*, and the others would look away. It helped to preserve a modicum of their dignity. Fortunately, when nature called during the evening, the darkness of night provided the necessary privacy; therefore, it wasn't necessary to shout and wake anyone—not that anyone was getting any real sleep.

Just as Lily was about to shout *privacy*, the door opened, letting in the morning sunlight, along with two men. One man was the largest of the kidnappers—while the second man was someone Danielle had never seen before. What she found most troubling, he was not wearing a mask.

"Oh crap," Danielle muttered.

"No kidding!" Lily squirmed. "I can't very well pee now!"

"Bathroom break," the masked man shouted.

"Thank god," Lily mumbled under her breath. She then called out, "Can I go first?"

The large man shrugged and walked in her and Danielle's direction—his companion trailing behind him.

"This doesn't look good," Danielle whispered to Lily, her eyes never leaving the approaching men.

Lily muttered impatiently, "I just have to pee."

Danielle's gaze remained focused on the unmasked man. He now stood just a few feet away and smiled down at her while his companion unshackled Lily and led her—bucket in hand—to the bathroom. Danielle glanced at the pair and watched as Lily walked alone into the small bathroom, closing the door behind her, leaving the larger man standing guard just outside the door.

Looking back to the unmasked man, Danielle felt ill. *He has no problem showing us his face.*

While she had briefly seen the pilot's face that first day, she was fairly confident he was wearing a fake beard at the time and had colored his hair, not to mention the fact he wore large dark sunglasses. Danielle had felt she and her friends would be safe for as long as their kidnappers believed they would not be able to be identified. Yet, now that Danielle thought about it, the pilot—and she was fairly certain that was who the man was who had interrogated her about her financial situation had been—hadn't concealed his eyes from her the day before. She could see them through the eye holes of his ski mask—they were brown.

This man had blue eyes—icy blue eyes—and they stared at her with keen interest. The first two kidnappers each wore matching tan jumpsuits—reminding her of something a mechanic might wear. This man wore a suit that looked even more outdated than Walt's. On his head he wore—*What do they call those hats? Oh, I remember, a Bowler hat,* Danielle thought.

Pale complexioned, he wore a coal black pencil-thin mustache. She assumed it was the same color as his hair, which was hidden under the hat. If she was to hazard a guess at his age, she would say he was in his early fifties, which might mean some of the hair under the hat was more gray than black. She guessed he was no more than five feet seven inches tall, and she wouldn't describe him as thin or heavy—*an average build.* The way in which he examined her made her highly uncomfortable. She turned to where his partner waited outside the bathroom door for Lily.

"You look rather uncomfortable like that." To Danielle's surprise, the man had an English accent.

Danielle closed her eyes for a moment and took a deep breath, her back still to the man. She could feel the beating of her heart accelerate.

"You have lovely hair, although I imagine it could benefit from a good brushing," he said in his heavy accent. "I'd love to do that for you." He then chuckled. "Ahhh, or a warm bath. I bet that would feel good to you. I could scrub your lovely back—you'd like that, wouldn't you?"

A paralyzing chill moved down Danielle's spine. None of the kidnappers had made any sexual innuendos toward any of them—until now. She had a sick feeling he must be the ringleader—considering his manner of dress—which made her feel even more vulnerable. What terrified her most was the fact he brazenly allowed them to see his face. Clinging to her optimism was proving to be more and more difficult.

She continued to ignore his unwelcome comments and wondered if any of the others could hear what he was saying to her. He wasn't talking much louder than a whisper, and considering how spread out they all were, she suspected she was the only one who could hear what he was actually saying.

A few minutes later Lily returned from the bathroom, carrying an empty bucket. After setting the bucket down, she sat down quietly, waiting for the masked man to place the shackle back on her ankle.

"Can you please hook that to the other ankle?" Lily asked in a small voice.

"Why's it matter?" he snapped.

"My ankle is getting raw. It hurts…please?" Lily smiled pleadingly at her captor. He let out a snort, but honored her request.

"Oh, thank you!" Lily burst out, relieved not to have the shackle rub on her already sore skin.

Without another comment, the man locked the shackle and then moved to release Danielle's ankle. He knelt before her and slipped the key into the rusty lock. She glanced at the empty metal bucket Lily had just set down and thought how easy it would be to grab it and crack it over the man's head. If she could knock him out, all they would have to do is take his keys, secure the shackles around his ankles, free the rest, and escape. But there was only one problem—the guy with the English accent was standing there, and as far as she knew, he had a pistol in his pocket. Plus, she wasn't sure who was standing outside the door to the warehouse.

Ten minutes later, Danielle stepped out of the bathroom, carrying her now empty bucket. The man with the English accent was standing by Lily, and she wondered if he was taunting Lily in the same way he had taunted her. By all appearances, Lily was ignoring the man, just as she had.

"May I please see Chris?" Danielle pleaded before returning to her spot by Lily. "Just for a few minutes, please?"

The masked man shook his head. "No. Your friend is taking care of him."

"Please, can't I just see him?" she begged.

The masked man stared at her for a moment and then said, "I don't know. Maybe. I'll talk to the boss. See what he says."

Danielle glanced over to the man still standing by Lily and wondered, *Is that the boss?*

"Thank you. I would really appreciate that," she said in a small voice.

The man chuckled and then took Danielle by the arm and gave her a gentle shove in Lily's direction. "I have to say you two are the most damned polite hostages."

After he re-secured Danielle's shackle a few moments later, the masked kidnapper went to take Kelly to the bathroom. Instead of going with him, his English companion stayed by Lily and Danielle —both of whom were sitting side by side on the concrete floor.

"If I could help you ladies get out of here, I would," the man with the English accent said with a sigh.

Danielle resisted the temptation to look up at him, but stared blankly at the bathroom doorway, which Kelly had just gone through. The man in the Bowler hadn't spoken very loudly, so she doubted his companion had overheard what he had just said. She wondered, *Maybe he isn't the boss?* She assumed he must have made the same improper comments to Lily, which would explain why her friend was doing her best to ignore the man.

"I assume Chris is the one I saw in the bed—the one with his head all bandaged. I heard you ask about seeing him. Not sure what the point would be, he wouldn't even know you're there," the man told Danielle.

She reserved comment, yet sat quietly while the other man led her friends, one by one, to use the bathroom. The only one who wasn't there to use it was Carol Ann, who remained with Chris—wherever that might be.

"Looks like my friend is getting ready to leave," the maskless man said as he watched his companion chain up the last hostage who had used the bathroom.

With a sigh he turned from Danielle and Lily and started to the door, yet not before saying, "I do wish I could help you ladies."

After the two men left the building, shutting the door behind them, Danielle said, "Oh my god, what does this mean?"

Wrinkling her brow, Lily turned to Danielle. "What does what mean?"

"He didn't have a mask on! We can identify him."

Confused, Lily glanced from Danielle to the door leading to the outside and then back to Danielle. "What are you talking about? He had a mask on. And I thought it was rather decent of him to put that damn thing on my other ankle. I figure that's a good sign. He might be a kidnapper, but so far he doesn't seem sadistic."

"I'm talking about the other guy!"

"Other guy? What in the world are you talking about?" Again Lily glanced to the door and back to Danielle.

"The guy in the suit with the Bowler hat. With the English accent!"

Perplexed, Lily shook her head. "I seriously have no idea what you're talking about."

Danielle started to say something and then paused a moment and studied Lily's questioning expression. Finally, she pointed to the door leading to the outside and asked, "Tell me, how many men just walked out that door a minute ago?"

"How many men? Are you saying there was more than one?"

"Are you telling me there wasn't?" Danielle countered.

"I saw one. The same guy who comes in here every couple of hours to check on us. Are you saying you saw someone else?"

"I saw the guy who comes in here every few hours—and the guy who was with him."

"Guy that was with him?"

"Are you trying to be funny, Lily? I'm really not in the mood to be messed with. You know exactly who I mean. He was wearing a suit, Bowler hat, and had an English…" Danielle stopped midsentence and studied Lily. She knew her friend well enough to know she hadn't been messing with her.

"If you're saying you didn't see him…and I did…that means…"

Lily's eyes widened. "There was a ghost here?"

NINETEEN

"We would be going home today," Lily told Danielle the next morning when they woke up. It was the last Thursday in April.

"I wonder if Walt has any idea about what's going on?" Danielle sat up, rattling the chain hooked to the manacle securing her ankle. "Although I doubt it. If he did, I'm sure he would have come to me in a dream hop by now."

"I'm sure everyone back home knows our plane went missing, since we never arrived at the dude ranch. I suppose it's possible Walt saw something on the news—he does like to watch TV," Lily suggested. "Maybe he has tried a dream hop, but can't get through for some reason. It's not like either of us has gotten a decent night's sleep."

They sat in silence for a moment. Lily finally asked, "So do you have any idea who the ghost was?"

Danielle shook her head. "He was obviously British. And by what he was wearing, I'd have to say he died years ago…maybe the late 1800s."

"You think that could mean we're not in the United States anymore?" Lily asked.

"Why would you say that?"

Lily shrugged. "We could be anywhere. Who knows where that pilot flew us to."

"But like the chief says, we're probably in the desert, considering the evening temperature for this time of year."

"It just seems weird, a British ghost hanging around. Makes me wonder if we were flown out of the country."

"Lily, it's not like people from the UK didn't visit the US back in the late 1800s…" Danielle paused a moment and considered her words. "Was it called the UK back then?"

Lily nodded. "Yeah. I remember a lecture from one of my college history classes. What I recall, what we know as the United Kingdom was formed around 1800, so I wouldn't be surprised if it was called the UK by the end of that century."

"I wish I'd realized he was a ghost yesterday morning."

"I'm surprised he didn't stick around or come back to talk to you. Seems ghosts are always anxious to communicate with someone who can see and hear them."

"Yeah, but like I told you yesterday—I didn't acknowledge his presence. I'm really regretting that now. He said he was willing to help us."

"He also thought you were hot," Lily teased.

Danielle rolled her eyes. "Yeah, well, that. It freaked me out when I thought he was one of the kidnappers."

"But that's a good thing—I mean him finding you attractive. Maybe he'll come back to see you again. I know he's a ghost, but he was a man once."

"If he does come back, the most I can hope for is finding out more about our kidnappers—or where they're keeping us."

"Gee, Dani, why such low expectations? I was hoping we could use him to maybe steal the keys from our kidnappers so we can get out of this place."

Danielle shook her head. "I wish. But the fact is, if he's wandering around, I don't imagine he has any spare energy to move objects."

"But it is possible. I mean, perhaps he's confined to this area—which would mean, like Walt, he's capable of moving objects and helping us."

"Perhaps. But even if that's true, unless he comes back in here, there's no way for him to help us even if he can move objects." Danielle reminded her.

"WE CAN'T STAY HERE INDEFINITELY," Clay told Sky as he paced the living room of the single-wide mobile home.

Sky sat on the sofa, drinking a cup of coffee while watching his partner rant. "What do you suggest?"

"I say we take what we can get and then get the hell out of here!" Clay told him. "This was supposed to be done with on Monday. We take them, get Glandon to transfer that money before anyone even knows they're missing, and then we get the hell out of here."

Sky slammed his cup on the particle board table, sloshing lukewarm coffee on the already stained tabletop. "And whose fault is that?"

"I have an idea," Andy said as she entered the room. She had overheard their argument from the hallway.

"I hope it's a good one," Sky muttered as he picked up his cup and took a swig.

"We've been waiting for Chris to wake up—but that hasn't happened."

"Tell us something we don't know," Clay snapped.

"Shut up," Sky told him.

"What I'm suggesting, maybe we need to let Danielle come in here and talk to Chris." She turned to Clay. "You told us she wanted to see him, right?"

"Exactly how is that supposed to help us?" Clay asked.

"I've heard stories of people who were in a coma and came out of it after someone they cared about talked to them—encouraged them. Maybe he needs a familiar voice to bring him out of it."

"That's the stupidest thing I've ever heard." Clay flopped down in the easy chair.

"What do we have to lose?" Sky asked. "We sure as hell can't stay here indefinitely. The longer we stay here, the more our chances increase that we'll be caught."

"That's why I suggested we just cut our losses and take what we can get. What did Boatman say she had? Thirty grand? Hell of a lot better than what we're getting out of Glandon," Clay said.

"At least try," Andy urged. "Let her come see him. Give it one more night."

DANIELLE STOOD QUIETLY as one of her captors removed the blindfold. When she opened her eyes, she found herself standing at the foot of a bed—its occupant was Chris—who appeared to be sleeping, his head wrapped in a bloodied bandage.

"Chris!" Danielle gasped, rushing to his side. She sat on the edge of the mattress and reached out to gently touch his face. He didn't respond to her touch, yet she could tell he was breathing. She looked up to the man who had brought her to the room—the same man who came every day to let them use the bathroom.

"Where is Carol Ann?" she asked.

"We figured since you're here with him, we'd let her go back with the others. She's been nagging us to see her boyfriend. Maybe this'll shut her up."

Danielle watched as he turned from her and walked toward the door. Just as he was about to leave the room, he paused and looked at her. "I'll be in the hallway. And we have people outside those windows." He pointed to the bedroom windows; they were covered with foil. "Stay away from the windows, and don't try anything funny, or your little nurse friend won't be able to take care of your boyfriend." With that he walked out of the room, leaving Danielle alone.

"Oh, Chris, what are we going to do?" Danielle murmured as she gently stroked his cheek. She glanced around the room and took a deep breath and then wrinkled her nose; it smelled musty. Glancing overhead, she noticed a sagging ceiling with water stains.

"So they let you come see him," came an English voice.

Danielle looked to her right and found herself gazing into the face of the ghost she had seen the previous morning.

"You're still here," she said.

Startled, his eyes widened. "You can see me?"

"Yes," Danielle said calmly. "My name is Danielle, and I can see people like you."

"Dead people?" He sat down on the only chair in the room.

"So you know you're dead?"

He let out a snort and said, "Of course I know. Rather difficult to ignore that fact when I'm constantly walking through walls."

"Can you tell me your name?" Danielle asked.

"Excuse me. Very rude of me. Percival. Percival Clint."

"Nice to meet you, Percival Clint. Can you tell me where we are?"

"Where we are?" He glanced around. "It looks like some sort of bedroom to me."

Danielle let out a sigh. "I'm trying to figure out where they have us."

"Ahh, the people who've kidnapped you. I assume they're seeking ransom. Correct?"

"Yes." Danielle glanced down at Chris's lifeless body. "They intended to get it from Chris here, but there was an accident; he fell. Now they're not able to get the money. Although, I'm not really sure how they intended to do that in the first place."

"They do seem to be rather upset over your friend here. I believe that's why they brought you in to see him. They hope you can get him to wake up."

"Do you know anything about our kidnappers…their names maybe?"

"I haven't been here that long. But I did hear them call the gent who brought you here *Clay*. He was the one who I hitched a ride with when he was down by the bridge—to look at all the scantily dressed young women." Percival wiggled his eyebrows and smiled.

Danielle glanced at the closed door, wondering when they were going to come for her. "Can you move objects?"

"Move objects?" He frowned.

"Umm…can you move that chair you're sitting in?"

He began to chuckle. "That would be magnificent!"

Danielle let out a discouraged sigh. "Then perhaps you can tell me where we are."

"I told you, we're in a bedroom."

Frustrated, Danielle forced a smile. "Perhaps you can tell me about that bridge you just mentioned."

Percival uncrossed and recrossed his legs, shifting his position in the chair. "I watched them put that bridge up—twice." He laughed.

"Maybe you can tell me how you died?"

"You mean how I was murdered?"

"Who killed you? Do you know?"

"A scrawny little pickpocket who didn't have the good manners to shove off when I told him to keep his mitts out of my coat pocket. Stabbed me in the belly, left me there to die on the bridge."

"So you were murdered on the bridge?"

"Yes? Isn't that what I just said?"

"What city is the bridge located in? Do you remember that?"

"At the time, London."

Before Danielle could respond, one of the kidnappers walked into the room. He was still wearing the mask, but Danielle knew it was the same person who had brought her to the room earlier—the man Percival had called Clay.

"I was just checking to see if everything was okay." Clay glanced around the room. Even if he could see ghosts, he would not have seen one. Percival was no longer in the room. With a grunt, Clay turned to the doorway and walked back into the hallway, closing the door behind him and leaving Danielle alone with Chris.

"Percival?" Danielle called out in a loud whisper.

No answer.

"Percival?" She looked around the room. Still no answer.

Convinced the spirit was no longer nearby, Danielle looked down at Chris's still form.

"Chris, are you there?" she whispered before placing a light kiss on his forehead.

TWENTY

It was the first Sunday in May. Chris had spent the previous evening trying to recall how he had arrived back at Marlow House after his fall. He discovered Walt had been correct. Once he was aware of his true condition, the fog clouding his memory began to dissolve. Like mist fading away in a movie scene, he saw the airplane he had rented—and next to it at the foot of the steps leading down from the plane was an unconscious body—his. Excitedly, he began to tell Walt what he was remembering.

"I saw myself," Chris said as he paced the library while Walt sat on the sofa, watching. "Nasty gash on my head. Damn, those head wounds sure do bleed! Two men were shouting at each other; one of them was the pilot. Not the one I hired."

"No, your pilot was locked up in your basement."

Chris paused a moment and looked at Walt. He arched his brows. "I also remember waking up—and it wasn't when I was being led down those steps. It was right before that. We must have still been on the plane. I couldn't see anything; I was blindfolded. They said something about me giving them fifty million dollars." He resumed pacing.

"What else do you remember?"

"The pilot was angry that his partner let me fall."

"Do you have any idea where you were?"

Chris took a seat across from Walt. "I remember now; it was

somewhere in the desert. Mountains in the distance. Not green mountains. There was a dirt airstrip. No idea how they landed that thing out there, looked like the middle of nowhere. But the plane wasn't sitting outside, it was in a hangar of sorts—more like a Quonset hut, without any doors or walls on either end."

"Quonset hut?" Walt frowned. "What's that?"

"You know, a Quonset hut—" Chris paused and let out a sigh. "That's right, I don't think they were really a thing in the '20s. I believe they started making them during World War II. Sort of a semicircular structure made out of metal and steel. A prefab building, quick to put up. They were used extensively in the war."

"Ahh, you mean a Nissen hut," Walt said with a smile.

"Nissen hut?"

"Your Quonset hut sounds like the British's Nissen hut they used during World War I," Walt explained.

Chris shrugged. "Whatever it was, it was big enough for the airplane to fit under. The only other building I saw on the property was an old mobile home. But it was all boarded up, with keep out signs. I did go inside it, looking for help, but no one was around, and I didn't see any signs of life. There was only one vehicle, a motorhome. It was parked right outside the hangar area." Chris paused again and looked directly at Walt and asked, "You do know what a mobile home and motorhome are, don't you?"

Walt rolled his eyes. "Yes. I do watch television, you know. And it's not like we didn't have things like trailers back in my day." With a wave of his hand, Walt summoned a cigar. "What else did you see? Danielle, the others?"

Chris shook his head. "No. It's weird, but I knew that was me on the ground with all the blood—yet it didn't occur to me that I was dead, that my spirit was seeing myself. And I certainly didn't consider I was having some out-of-body experience. All I knew was that I needed to get help. So I ran first to the boarded-up mobile home, but when no one was there, I started running down the road, looking for someone to help me."

"You didn't try going back on the plane for Danielle and the others?"

"The two arguing men were blocking the stairs—"

"You could have walked right through them, and they wouldn't have known," Walt reminded him.

"I didn't realize that at the time. But the two men were yelling at each other; I knew they weren't on my side. All I wanted to do was get help. So I started running down the road. I was somewhat surprised they didn't try to stop me. I just wanted to get help."

"And you just ended up here?"

"No. I remember running down a long dirt road. I didn't see any other people, no cars, no buildings, nothing but open desert. And then—then—"

"Then you were here?" Walt asked.

Chris shook his head. "No. Then I was standing on the highway, looking at a sign. It said Seligman ten miles."

"Seligman?"

"That must have been where they landed the plane, somewhere outside of Seligman."

"Where in the world is Seligman?" Walt murmured.

Chris shrugged. "I have no idea. I've never heard of it before. But they must be near the plane."

After considering Chris's suggestion, Walt shook his head. "No. I don't think so. When I visited Ian in a dream, he told me they were being held in a warehouse. Do you think he might have mistaken the mobile home you went into for a warehouse?"

"No way. This means they took them somewhere else. Maybe they transported them in the motorhome I saw," Chris suggested.

"Did you see any warehouses in the area?" Walt asked.

Chris shook his head. "I don't remember seeing anything along the road. I'm not really sure how long I walked. But I do remember getting to the highway and seeing cars drive by. I tried to wave a few down, but they just drove by."

"They couldn't see you."

"And then I remember walking down the road, seeing the road sign…ten miles to Seligman…and then I remember wondering, *Why am I out here?*"

"You weren't wondering where is Danielle and the others?" Walt snapped.

Chris let out a sigh and turned to Walt. "I can remember now what I saw back then, and I also remember how hazy and confused everything seemed. When I was looking at that sign, for some reason I didn't quite grasp that I had left Danielle and the others back at the plane. In fact, when I stared at that road sign, all I could think about was *why was I out in the middle of nowhere?* I felt so confused, it was like I couldn't grasp anything tangible; my thoughts were erratic. And then Danielle's face popped into my head, and for a moment I didn't even know who it was. As cars whizzed by me on the highway, I closed my eyes and focused on her face, trying to comprehend who she was to me, and then I saw Marlow House, and I felt safe, and then, well, then I opened my eyes and found myself back here, looking at you reading a book."

After digesting what Chris was telling him, Walt silently took a puff off his cigar and then said, "At least we know where they landed the plane. That should help us find them."

"I'd try to go back there, but it would probably be a waste of time. I'm sure they've moved them. But maybe whoever owns that property is connected to the kidnapping."

"I agree. But now we need to figure out how we can get someone to help us. I don't believe Evan is really old enough to give us the help we need on this one." Walt flicked his hand and the cigar disappeared.

"I suppose I could see if I can find someone who we can use to help us."

"I assume you're talking about someone capable of seeing spirits and..." Walt looked Chris up and down and then added in a snort, "And whatever you are."

Standing up again, Chris began to pace. "Let me think about this—we need some way to communicate with the outside world."

Walt rolled his eyes. "Obviously."

Chris paused and turned to Walt. "How about a letter?"

"A letter?"

"It's one possibility. You can write a letter—you *are* capable of moving a pen over paper—and then you can put a stamp on it..."

"Exactly how do we get it to the mailbox?" Walt asked.

Chris shook his head and said, "Never mind. Stupid idea anyway. Even if we figured out who to send it to, it could take a couple days for the letter to arrive and they might think it's just a hoax, especially since I don't know where the plane actually is."

"You said it was near Seligman," Walt reminded him.

"Sure, but Seligman where? It was somewhere in the desert but where—California, Arizona, Nevada, Texas...anywhere."

"I suppose I could look it up in my atlas," Walt suggested.

"It would be much faster on a computer," Chris said.

Walt waved his hand dismissively. "I don't know anything about computers."

"Danielle left her laptop, didn't she?" Chris glanced around. "She said she wasn't going to take it with her."

"It's in the parlor. But I don't know how to use a computer."

"I do." Chris smiled.

"But you can't even pick up a pencil!"

"No, but I can tell you what keys to hit…" Chris suddenly smiled. "The computer! That would be better than a letter. We can use the Internet to get the message out—in an email or…" He paused a moment and then asked with a frown, "You don't happen to know her password, do you?"

"Password?"

"Yeah. She types in a password to get onto her computer. You don't know what it is?"

Walt frowned. "Why would I know? I don't know how to use a computer."

"Maybe you've seen Danielle type it in. I know you're always lurking around her."

"I do not lurk," Walt snapped.

"Fine. But we need to find out where Seligman is so we can tell the authorities where they can find the plane and, hopefully from there, track where the kidnappers are holding Danielle and the rest of them."

"Then perhaps we should first figure out who we're going to use to get this information to the right authorities."

Chris plopped back down in the chair. "You're right, of course."

"Naturally," Walt mumbled under his breath—that is, if ghosts could actually have a breath.

"We need to figure out who we can get to help us," Chris continued, ignoring Walt's mutter. "Without a password, the computer is out."

"I only see two choices here—Evan or—" Walt cringed. "Heather."

"She could also bring her laptop over here and help us figure out where Seligman is—use Google Earth. Maybe even figure out where that hut is by the pictures!" Chris added excitedly.

Walt furrowed his brows. "Google Earth?"

"Google is this search engine that…" Chris started to explain and then noticed Walt's confused expression. "I'm really surprised you haven't used Danielle's laptop before."

"Why would I?"

Chris shrugged. "I just am."

"So what is this Google Earth?"

"It's a website where you can see aerial photographs of earth. I'm thinking maybe we can figure out exactly where that Quonset hut is by looking in the area along the highway where the ten-mile sign is."

"Are you telling me someone has taken pictures of the entire earth? Close enough that you can actually see a highway or a building?"

"Yeah…pretty much."

Walt shook his head in disbelief.

"I suppose we'll have to use Heather. I can get her to bring her laptop with her," Chris suggested.

"Do you intend to just march over to her house and demand she come back here with you?"

"Seems like the only thing I can do. But I'm not sure I'll be marching exactly. You'll have to unlock the front door—do you think you can do that?"

"Of course I can do that. But perhaps we need to rethink Heather."

"What do you mean? You said yourself Evan is probably too young to help us."

"It's just that…it's Heather…"

Chris studied Walt for a moment and then asked, "So?"

Walt groaned and leaned back in his chair. "It's just that I'd prefer not to make myself known to her. But I suppose, if I have to—for Danielle."

TWENTY-ONE

Heather sat in the lotus position on the center of her sofa. Yet she was not in meditation. Propped on her lap was the Sunday newspaper open to the classified section. In her right hand she held a cup of steaming green tea while she scanned the help wanted advertisements. Periodically she would gently blow on the tea, attempting to cool it so she could take a sip, while her eyes never left the newsprint. She needed a job.

She hadn't had breakfast yet, and morning was slowly slipping into noon. But she wasn't especially hungry. Nor had she dressed for the day; she still wore the loosely fitting jogging pants and a T-shirt she had slept in. Her habit until recently was to sleep in her jogging clothes, rise early, run along the beach, and then return home and shower and dress for the day. Yet she hadn't been jogging on the beach for days. Repeatedly stepping over dead bodies or encountering ghosts along the beach had squelched her enthusiasm for early morning runs along the ocean.

Instead of the pigtails or traditional braids she normally wore, she had pulled her hair atop her head after getting out of bed that morning and had secured it with a rubber band in what she called her Pebbles look. Of course, unlike Pebbles her hair was coal black not red, and there was no bone stuck in the high-placed ponytail.

Turning the page of the newspaper, she sipped the tea and wiggled her toes, inadvertently forcing her right big toe to pop through and widen a hole in her sock. Looking from the paper to her right foot, she wiggled her toes again and sighed. The sock's hole grew larger and her big toe more visible.

"Sorry set of circumstances when I can't even afford to buy new socks," she said aloud. Leaning over the newspaper, she stretched toward the coffee table and set her teacup on the edge of the tabletop, carelessly splashing some of the tea on its surface. Instead of wiping up the liquid, she grabbed the felt-tip pen sitting next to the cup and leaned back. Turning her attention to the help wanted ads, she used the pen to circle several possible job opportunities.

A meow from the doorway caught Heather's attention. She looked up and spied her calico, Bella, strolling casually into the room, her tail wagging flag-like behind her. No longer a kitten, Bella had reached her full size, yet she still looked more kitten than full grown cat considering her delicate stature.

"So you finally decided to get up?" Heather asked Bella as she closed the newspaper and then tossed it on the sofa cushion next to her.

Ignoring the greeting, Bella strode to the living room window and jumped up onto the windowsill. She stared outside, her tail still swishing back and forth. A moment later she let out a loud meow.

"No, you can't go outside." Heather leaned forward, picked up her cup of tea from the coffee table, and took a sip. It had cooled and was now lukewarm. She leaned back on the sofa and uncrossed her legs. Propping her stockinged feet on the edge of the coffee table, her ankles crossed, she took another sip of the tea. From the window Bella let out a tortured cry; the intensity of her tail swishing back and forth increased.

Looking at the cat, Heather frowned. "What's your problem? Is Max out there teasing you?" Heather took another sip and Bella let out another cry, this one even louder and more demonic sounding than the last.

Heather rolled her eyes. "You can be such a drama queen!"

CHRIS STOOD in the flower planter outside of Heather's living room window, his gaze momentarily locked with Bella's. Glancing beyond the cat, he could see Heather sitting on her sofa, drinking what he assumed was her morning coffee.

When he had arrived at Heather's house a few minutes earlier, he had gone directly to the front door, something he would have done had he been dressed in his physical body. By habit, he had tried to ring the doorbell, only to have his finger and then hand disappear through the front wall of Heather's house. He immediately felt foolish for even trying to ring the bell—he knew better—and then he had glanced over his shoulder to see if anyone had witnessed his foolishness. The moment he looked, he felt ridiculous all over again—*No one can see me*, he reminded himself with disgust. *No one but Heather*. At least, he assumed Heather could see him.

Waving at the window, Chris tried to capture Heather's attention. Bella pawed at the window. Instead of looking his way, Heather set her cup on the coffee table and picked up the newspaper sitting next to her on the couch. Leaning back, she opened the paper and started to read, never looking to the window in spite of the fact her cat was repeatedly batting the windowpane with her front paw.

"I really did not want to have to do this," Chris said in exasperation before stepping through the window and wall and walking into Heather's house uninvited.

BELLA LET out another primal screech and leapt from the windowsill. Heather looked up in time to see the cat race from the room and disappear down the hallway. Shaking her head, she tossed the newspaper back onto the sofa, pulled her feet off the coffee table, and stood up. After walking to the window, she looked outside. But she didn't see anything unusual.

"What's your problem, Bella?" Heather mumbled under her breath as she turned from the window and headed for the kitchen. On her way there she halted abruptly, distracted by a flickering image of what appeared to be a man blocking her entrance into the kitchen. Blinking her eyes in confusion, she attempted to make out what she was seeing, yet it vanished before she could identify who or what it was. A chill traveled down her spine and she glanced over her shoulder. If she didn't know better, she would swear someone was using some sort of projector to cast an image—yet projectors cast images on screens or walls, not in doorways.

"Oh crap," Heather groaned. "Don't tell me some damn ghost is now lurking in my house? Can't I get any peace?"

"HEATHER? HEATHER?" Chris followed her as she angrily marched into the kitchen. Keeping by her side, he moved his hand in front of her eyes, only to have her walk through it. He didn't think she was ignoring him—however, he was certain she had seen him a moment earlier.

Frustrated, Chris watched as Heather opened an overhead cabinet and removed two small vials of essential oils and set them on the counter. She then took a diffuser from the cabinet, removed its lid, and walked to the sink.

Standing behind Heather, Chris yelled her name just as she turned on the water. Pausing a moment, Heather glanced over her shoulder and frowned. Chris looked into her eyes, but he saw no recognition coming from her. Heather turned back to the sink and filled the diffuser with water.

Taking a seat at the breakfast bar, he watched as she added several drops of oil from each vial to the water before placing the lid back on the diffuser.

"This should get rid of any spirits," Heather grumbled.

Chris followed Heather into the living room and watched as she set the diffuser on an end table and plugged its cord into a nearby socket. A thin trail of steam began wafting up from the hole in the center of the diffuser's lid.

With a satisfied smile on her face, Heather sat back down on the sofa and picked up the newspaper.

JOANNE HAD JUST PULLED up to Marlow House when Chris returned from Heather's. He followed her inside, while she never knew she had company. Sadie greeted them both when they walked into the house, but Joanne failed to notice Sadie's attention was not centered just on her. She made her way to the kitchen while Chris moved up to the attic. When coming down the street a few minutes earlier, he had spied Walt standing at the attic window, Max by his side.

"She couldn't see me," Chris announced when he walked into the attic.

Walt turned from the window to face Chris. "Are you sure?"

"Actually, I'm pretty sure she saw me—but only for a moment—when I first arrived. She even mentioned something about a ghost being in the house. I tried to get her attention, and one time when I screamed, she looked my way, but I don't think she understood what she was hearing."

"Interesting," Walt murmured. "Although, I shouldn't be surprised. Heather never saw me when she was staying here."

Chris took a seat on the sofa bed and looked up at Walt, who remained standing by the window. "Yes, but her gift has become stronger, she's seen and spoken to a number of spirits, and even you said she's become more aware of your presence—to the extent that you avoid being around when she comes over."

"True. But you're not a spirit. At least, not yet." Walt arched his brow and asked, "Have you looked in a mirror recently?"

Chris leaned back on the sofa and crossed his right leg over his left knee. "I glanced in the hall mirror after I got back from Heather's. I'm still there."

Walt took a seat on the end of the sofa. Max leapt down from the windowsill and joined them, taking a place on the center of the sofa between them.

"What now?" Chris asked.

"We still need Heather's help. I wonder if she'd be able to see me?" Walt leaned back on the couch, staring off into blank space.

"She saw glimpses of you before—and I think that's what she saw when I was over there—a glimpse."

HEATHER OPENED her wallet as the man at the ticket counter asked, "What movie?"

"*Age of Adaline.*" She slipped the money she had just pulled from her wallet through the slot in the window and waited for her ticket. Once she had it in her hand, she flashed the man a cool smile and headed for the door leading into the theater. Her first stop was the refreshment counter, where she waited in line behind several teenagers.

"Hello, Heather," came a woman's voice from behind her.

Heather turned and came face-to-face with Steve Klein's widow, Beverly. Heather had been the one to find Steve's body after it had washed up on shore, which was one reason Heather always felt awkward when she ran into Beverly around town. *What does one say to a grieving widow when you are the one who found the body?*

"Hello, Beverly, how are you doing?"

"I'm doing fine, thank you." Beverly smiled brightly and then said in a serious tone, "It is a shame about your neighbors. I rather liked Danielle and Lily. Sweet girls."

"I haven't given up hope on them," Heather insisted.

Beverly reached out and briefly patted Heather's hand. "I hope they come back too, but someone did see their plane go down. How long can they really survive out there in the wilderness? What has it been, a week already?" Beverly let out a sigh and added, "Oh my, I just realized this could mean you've lost three…no, four neighbors on your street. To think, tragedy striking that many homes on one street in Frederickport. A well-known author and that handsome young man…what was his name, Chris Johnson?"

Heather started to say something and then remembered the vision she'd seen earlier; she froze. *That image—that glimpse of a man—it was Chris!*

TWENTY-TWO

Sissy sat on the pier with her husband, Bruce, as they watched their nephews go into the ice cream shop.

Shaking her head wearily, Sissy said, "I still don't understand why Evan broke into Marlow House."

"He's just worried about his father. I don't understand what he thought he was going to accomplish, but it must have something to do with the fact two of the other people who went with Ed lived at Marlow House. Maybe he thought we weren't telling him the truth and that there would be someone at Marlow House that could tell him something," Bruce suggested.

Sissy shrugged. "I suppose. Makes more sense than anything I've been able to come up with."

Bruce let out a sigh and then said, "I hate to bring this up now, but we need to think about what we're going to do about the boys."

Sissy looked at her husband and frowned. "What do you mean?"

"If your brother—god forbid—doesn't come home, we need to figure out what we're going to do with them."

"What do you mean what we're going to do with them? They will stay with us, of course!"

Bruce shook his head. "Sissy, raising two boys is a tremendous responsibility. When we got married, we agreed we weren't going to have children. And it's not like the boys are orphans."

"What are you talking about?" She gasped. "A person is considered an orphan after losing just one parent—so tell me exactly how they wouldn't be orphans if they lost both parents?"

"Okay—I phrased that wrong."

"No kidding," she scoffed.

"I meant it's not like they don't have anyone. They have their grandparents in Portland. I'm sure they would love to have the boys."

"You think it would be better for my nephews to be forced to leave the only home they've ever lived in and move to Portland?"

"You certainly didn't imagine we would move into your brother's house."

"Of course not. But I meant forcing them to leave their hometown, their school, all their friends. You honestly believe that would be the better option?"

"It would be better for us," Bruce grumbled under his breath.

"I can't believe this! I thought you loved those boys!"

Bruce let out a frustrated sigh and turned to his wife. "I do love them. They're great kids. But I just don't want to step into their father's shoes. I'd rather stay the fun uncle. If I wanted to have kids that I had to worry about raising, I would have had my own. I didn't sign up for that, Sissy. And neither did you."

Tears filled her eyes. "I can't believe you're saying that!"

"It's not just that I don't want the responsibility, but, Sissy…and I don't mean to hurt your feelings…but the way you hover over those boys."

"You blame me for that? I may have lost my brother and now—"

"It's just that I've seen what happens to kids when their parents become overly—protective—controlling. I know you love them, and you'll still be in their lives, but I sincerely believe their mother's parents might be the best place for them. As I recall, they're not elderly and they raised a couple sons along with their daughter, and all their kids turned out great."

"But I can do this, Bruce! I know what you mean about how I can sometimes be controlling, but I can work on that!"

Sitting on the bench next to his wife, Bruce draped his arm around her shoulder and pulled her close. "Hey, let's not give up hope. It's always possible Ed will come home. But the boys are coming out of the ice cream shop, and you can't let them see you crying."

Wiping the corner of her eyes with the tip of her finger, Sissy looked to the ice cream shop. Eddy and Evan had just stepped out the door, each carrying a chocolate ice cream cone. They both started walking toward them when Evan apparently spied something to his right and took off in a run, stopping some ten feet away from where he had left his brother. Eddy ignored Evan's departure and continued walking toward his aunt and uncle.

"What is he doing?" Sissy watched as her youngest nephew stood by the railing, excitedly talking to—*a bird?*

"Is he talking to a seagull?" Bruce asked when he looked over at Evan.

CHRIS NEEDED to get out of Marlow House and think about what they should do next. He never imagined he would be running into Evan on the pier or that the young boy would be able to see him.

"Where's my dad!" Evan asked excitedly, unable to contain himself or the ice cream now dripping down his cone. "If you're back, that must mean he is too!"

Chris glanced down the pier and spied Evan's aunt and uncle sitting on a bench out of earshot—yet they were staring in his direction. He was fairly confident they couldn't see him, yet he imagined they were wondering who Evan was talking to.

"Evan, I don't want to scare you, but I'm not dead, I'm pretty sure your father is fine, but you are the only one who can see me. So please stop talking and start licking your ice cream before it melts all over the pier. Your aunt and uncle are staring, and I need to talk to you before they come over here," Chris ordered.

Evan frowned, but immediately started licking his ice cream cone, quickly cleaning up the melting mess. Before he had a chance to ask Chris any questions, they were joined by Eddy.

"Why are you talking to a bird?" Eddy asked. "You look dumb."

Evan glanced from Chris to Eddy. "Do you see him?"

"Well, duh, it's sitting right there."

"He's not sitting," Evan told his brother.

"Stop being weird. Aunt Sissy wants you to come over to where they are."

Evan looked up at Chris.

"Go with your brother. I'll tag along. I'll explain what's going on."

Evan silently nodded and then licked his cone. Eddy scowled at his brother and nudged him sharply with his elbow. "I said stop being weird!"

Instead of lashing out at his older brother for gouging him with an elbow, he silently trailed behind Eddy as they walked to their aunt and uncle. Next to Evan was Chris.

"I'm not sure how to explain this to you, Evan, but wherever my body is, I am very sick. But I'm not dead."

Evan picked up his step and glanced over at Eddy, whose attention was focused on his dwindling ice cream cone, and he paid no attention to Chris.

"What you see here isn't much different from what you see when you talk to Walt. The only difference, I hope I'm able to get back into my body before I die."

"Where's my dad?"

Eddy stopped walking and glared at his brother. "You sound like a baby when you ask me lame questions like that. You know I know as much as you do."

"You better not ask me any questions," Chris told him. "But Walt and I need your help."

"Evan, you have ice cream all over your shirt!" Sissy said when Evan got within arm's length of her. She reached out and pulled him to her and began wiping down his shirt with a tissue she had fished out of her purse. Evan remained silent, listening to Chris while allowing his aunt to hastily mop up the front of his shirt.

"I'm going to ask you some questions Evan. If the answer is yes, wiggle your nose." Chris paused a moment, studied Evan, and then asked, "Can you wiggle your nose?"

Evan smiled and wiggled his nose.

"Do you need a tissue, honey?" Sissy asked. She handed the dirty tissue to her husband, who reluctantly accepted it yet not before frowning down at the sticky wad of paper. Sissy then pulled a clean tissue from her purse and handed it to Evan. He silently accepted it and then stepped several feet away from the bench, staring out at the ocean, his back to his aunt, uncle, and brother.

"Do you know who Heather Donovan is?" Chris asked.

Evan glanced up to Chris but did not wrinkle his nose. Behind him he could hear his uncle talking to Eddy while his aunt occasionally chimed in. Ignoring what they were saying, he focused his attention on Chris.

"I will take that to mean no. Heather Donovan lives near Marlow House. She's about Danielle's age and has black hair she always wears in braids, sometimes ponytails. She has a calico cat named Bella—"

Before Chris could start the next sentence, Evan began wiggling his nose furiously.

Chris chuckled. "I take that to mean you know who she is."

Evan smiled and wiggled his nose, this time not as exuberantly.

"Heather is like Danielle, you, and me. She—"

Before Chris could finish the sentence, Evan started wiggling his nose again.

"You know about Heather's gift?"

Without thought, Evan nodded.

"Here's the thing, Evan, we need Heather to help us bring your dad and the others home. We need her to go over to Marlow House so she can talk to Walt. He can explain to her what we need. But the problem, Walt can't leave Marlow House, and it seems Heather's gift doesn't extend to seeing…well…whatever I am."

With his ice cream all gone, Evan bit down on the crunchy cone.

"Do you understand what I'm saying?"

Taking another bite from the cone, Evan glanced up at Chris and wiggled his nose again.

"I tried talking to Heather myself just this morning. I'm sure she saw me. She was just walking into the kitchen, and I pretty much jumped in front of her. But then, she couldn't see me anymore. I tried yelling at her, and she looked in my direction, but I got the feeling she didn't understand. Before I left her, she mumbled something about seeing ghosts, but I don't think she understood I was there."

Evan shoved the last bit of ice cream cone in his mouth and chewed.

"I'm just not sure how you can get her to go to Marlow House. I don't imagine your aunt and uncle are letting you wander around alone, especially after you snuck out of their house on Friday night."

Evan's eyes widened. He stared at Chris.

Chris smiled. "Walt told me about it."

Licking the last residue of ice cream off his lips, Evan glanced over his shoulder. Eddy had also finished his ice cream cone and now stood by their uncle.

"Why don't you boys help me get the fishing equipment," Bruce suggested.

"Can I see someone real quick? I'll be right back," Evan blurted.

"See who?" Sissy asked while Bruce stood by Eddy, listening to what Evan had to say.

"It's for my class's fundraiser. We're selling magazines. Miss Donovan told me she wanted to order something. I need to get her order."

"Fundraiser?" Sissy frowned and looked from Evan to Eddy, who only shrugged, unaware of any fundraiser.

"She just lives down the street. Dad's let me walk there alone."

Again, Sissy looked from Evan to Eddy.

"Yeah, Dad has let Evan walk down to Marlow House from the pier before."

Sissy turned to Evan and said, "You are not to go to Marlow House!"

"Oh, I don't want to go all the way to Marlow House." Evan smiled innocently. "Miss Donovan's house is before that."

Sissy looked up to her husband.

"I don't think it's a big deal. We know where he'll be. It's something your brother would let him do," Bruce said with a shrug.

Sissy looked uncertainly from her husband to Evan, who stood anxiously waiting for her to give him permission to leave. Hesitantly she suggested, "Maybe Eddy should go with him?"

Eddy groaned, clearly not thrilled with the idea, and Evan looked anxiously to Chris. But in the next second his uncle spoke up.

"Don't be silly. I know who Heather Donovan is. A little odd but not dangerous. And I need Eddy to help me get the fishing equipment."

"I suppose I could go with him," Sissy muttered, "while you get the fishing equipment."

"Sissy, this is what I was talking about earlier," Bruce snapped.

TWENTY-THREE

"That was a close one," Chris said as he walked with Evan off the pier and headed up the street to Heather's house. "I was afraid your aunt was going to come with us."

"What happened to you?" Evan asked as he glanced over to Chris while still walking.

"I fell when getting off the plane. Wherever my body is, I'm probably unconscious."

"What's unconscious?" Evan frowned.

"It's sort of like being asleep and not being able to wake up."

"I always thought that was being dead."

"Evan, you more than anyone should know death isn't like that. When someone dies, their spirit moves out of their body, leaving it behind. Like Walt."

"But isn't that what you did?"

Chris chuckled. "Good point. But in my case, I should be able to move back into my body. That's not something Walt can do."

When they arrived at Heather's house they went immediately to the front door. Evan rang the bell. There was no answer. Several minutes later, he rang the bell again. Still no answer.

"You stay here. I'll be right back," Chris told Evan before he walked through the door, disappearing into Heather's house. A few minutes later he returned.

"Where is she?" Evan asked.

"I can't believe this. She isn't home!" Chris groaned.

"What are we going to do?"

The next moment Evan's question was moot when Heather pulled into her driveway and parked her car.

"Evan? Evan MacDonald?" Heather asked when she got out of the car and slammed the door shut behind her.

"Hello, Miss Donovan," Evan said brightly. "I was afraid you weren't here."

"I'm just getting back from the movies. What are you doing here? Does your aunt know where you are?" Heather stepped onto the front porch and unlocked the door.

"Yes. They're down at the pier, fishing with my brother. They think I'm trying to sell you magazines for school."

The front door now open and purse in hand, Heather turned to face the young boy. "And you aren't?"

Evan shook his head. "No. I only told them that so they would let me come see you."

Heather arched her brow. "Really? And what is the real reason you wanted to see me?"

"It's about my dad."

Heather's expression softened. She reached out and placed one hand on his shoulder, giving it a brief squeeze. "I'm so sorry about your father."

"He's alive," Evan insisted.

Heather bit her lower lip, resisting the temptation to disagree with him. After her encounter with Beverly at the theater, she began thinking of the brief apparition she had encountered in her house. While she hadn't seen him clearly—and she was fairly certain it was male—the more she thought about it, the more she realized it resembled Chris. Considering his plane had disappeared—believed to have crashed in the middle of a forest a week earlier—it was highly possible it was Chris's spirit that had reached out from the grave.

Not grave exactly, Heather reminded herself. *Until he is found, he can't be buried. But if Chris is dead, chances are the others are too, including this poor boy's father.*

"I know you want to believe that," she said softly. "But why are you here?"

"I need you to help my dad."

Still standing on her front porch, the door open, Heather

glanced down the street toward the pier where Evan said his aunt, uncle, and brother were waiting. She looked back to Evan. "I don't understand."

"Tell her you know she can see ghosts. And that you know she saw something in her house this morning when she was going into her kitchen," Chris urged.

"I know you can see ghosts," Evan blurted.

Dropping her hand from the doorknob, she turned to Evan, her expression guarded. "What are you talking about?"

"I can see ghosts too. But my dad told me I can't tell people that, because they won't understand. I know you saw something in your house this morning—when you were going into the kitchen. It was Chris, who my dad went on the trip with."

Glancing around nervously, Heather snatched Evan by the forearm and dragged him into her house, slamming the door behind them. Tossing her purse on the floor, she kneeled down and placed her hands on Evan's shoulders while looking him in the eyes. "How do you know that?"

"Because Chris told me. He's here with me."

Heather jumped up and looked around. "I don't see him."

Evan shrugged. "But you did this morning, didn't you?"

Restlessly brushing her hands through her bangs, she glanced around warily. "I saw something earlier, but I didn't know what it was."

"It was Chris, but he's not dead. He…" Evan turned to where Chris stood and frowned, uncertain what to say.

"Tell her I'm having an out-of-body experience."

"Chris says he's having an out-of-body experiment."

Heather frowned. "What?"

"No, *experience*," Chris corrected.

"Experience, he said, not experiment," Evan clarified.

Hands now on hips, she looked down at Evan. "You're telling me Chris is here, now, in this room? But he isn't dead, he's having some out-of-body experience?"

Evan nodded.

"Ask Chris what my favorite ice cream is," Heather demanded.

"Huh?" Evan frowned.

Heather smiled. "Chris and I both lived at Marlow House for a time. I'm sure he will remember…if he's really here."

Chris chuckled and said, "Vanilla."

Evan wrinkled his nose and turned to Chris—yet to Heather it looked as if he was looking at an empty spot in her entry hall. "Vanilla? How can anyone like vanilla better than chocolate?"

With a gasp, her right hand flying up to cover her mouth, Heather took a step backwards and warily eyed the room.

"Do you believe me now? Will you help my dad?"

Fifteen minutes later Evan sat with Heather in her kitchen, each eating a slice of chocolate cake. The fact Evan had finished an ice cream cone less than thirty minutes earlier didn't seem a sufficient reason to turn down an offer of cake. Heather silently ate her piece while Evan explained all that he knew regarding his father's fateful trip and his unusual relationship with Walt.

"I knew I saw Walt Marlow when I was staying at Marlow House," Heather muttered as she popped another bite of cake in her mouth.

"So will you help us?" Evan asked.

Setting her fork on her plate, Heather picked up a napkin and dabbed the corners of her mouth. "Certainly. I hope I can. It's pretty obvious your experience with Walt Marlow's ghost has been much different than mine. I've only seen a flickering image of him —very sporadic. Kind of like what I saw of Chris." She turned to where she believed Chris stood. "I hope you're right, Chris, and we can get you back in your body."

The next moment the doorbell rang.

Heather stood up. "I wonder who that is? Stay here. I'll be right back."

Evan finished up his cake as Heather went to the door. He had just taken the last bite when she hurried back into the kitchen.

"It's your aunt. She's probably wondering what's taking you so long."

"Oh crud." Evan stood up. "What did she say?"

"I haven't answered the door yet." Heather picked up a napkin and wiped off Evan's mouth. "You told her you're selling me magazines, for school? Right?"

Evan nodded his head.

"Okay. Don't worry. You go with your aunt and I'll figure out some way to get in Marlow House."

"Tell her she needs to bring her laptop to Marlow House. She needs to go to the front door. I'll have Walt unlock it," Chris said.

"Chris says to go to the front door of Marlow House. Walt will let you in," Evan said as he walked with Heather to the front door. "And you have to bring your laptop."

"Why?" Heather glanced down at Evan.

He shrugged. "That's what Chris said."

"Okay, my laptop."

"Thank you," Evan said just as Heather reached to open the door.

Turning briefly to Evan, Heather gave him a wink and then looked back to the door, forcing herself to smile brightly as she swung it open. "Well, hello. I imagine you're here for your nephew. He was just leaving."

Sissy smiled, looking slightly embarrassed, and reached for Evan's hand. "I was getting a little worried. I didn't think he was going to be gone this long. She gently jerked him out the doorway by the hand, pulling him to her side.

Heather managed to tousle Evan's hair as he was pulled to his aunt's side. "You have quite the little salesman there." Heather flashed Evan a smile.

"I hope he wasn't being a nuisance."

"Nuisance? Certainly not. Evan is always a little gentleman; you can be proud of him. His father has done a terrific job with this boy."

Sissy relaxed, gentling her hold on Evan's hand. She glanced down at the child. "Yes, he's a good boy."

After saying their final goodbyes, Heather stood in the doorway, absently twisting the tip of her right braid while watching Sissy lead her nephew down the walkway and to the sidewalk. Periodically, Evan would glance back at Heather, seeking a reassuring sign. Still twisting her braid, she nodded silently and smiled.

"If you're still here, Chris, let's go." Walking back into her house, she grabbed her house keys and then snatched her laptop off her kitchen counter before stepping outside again. After locking her front door, she slipped her keys in her pocket and headed for Marlow House, carrying her laptop under one arm.

"I sure hope you'll be able to see and hear Walt," Chris said as he walked alongside Heather. "If not, I'm not exactly sure how you're going to help us if we can't communicate with you."

If Heather could hear his words, she made no sign; she continued walking in the direction of Marlow House.

"But I know you saw me earlier. You admitted it to Evan."

Impulsively Chris leapt in front of Heather, raised his hands over his head, and shouted, "I'm here!"

Heather stopped abruptly, her eyes wide.

"You can see me, can't you?" Chris asked excitedly, still standing in front of Heather.

Furrowing her brow into a frown, Heather reached out, attempting to touch something that she imagined might be there. Lowering her hand to her side, she glanced around. "Where did you go, Chris?"

"I'm right here!" Chris shouted in response.

Narrowing her eyes, she glanced around and let out an angry huff. "I don't know where you went, but stop jumping in front of me like that if you're just going to disappear. It's annoying!" She glanced around again before stepping through Chris and continuing on her way.

Chris, who remained standing in the same place, glanced down at his body, which Heather had just passed through. "I suppose it isn't actually my body. But I still don't like how it felt," Chris muttered. "I suppose I deserved this considering the times I teased Walt…oh, Walt!" Chris turned abruptly and hurried to Marlow House, passing Heather along the way. He needed to tell Walt to unlock the front door.

A few moments later Heather stood on the front porch of Marlow House. She was about to knock on the front door when it opened—ever so slowly—reminding her of a scene out of an old thriller. The unsettling sensation in the pit of her stomach brought back the memory of how she had felt when approaching Presley House some six months earlier.

Taking a deep breath, she stepped into the dimly lit entry hall. The door closed behind her, seemingly by itself. Glancing around uneasily, she called out, "Hello? Is anyone here?"

A moment later she heard a bark and the sound of a dog racing down the stairs in her direction.

TWENTY-FOUR

"Well, damn, how is this going to help if she can't see or hear us?" Walt asked impatiently. He stood with Chris in the entry hall and watched as Heather hesitantly wandered down the hall, Sadie by her side, tail wagging. Heather peeked in doorways and called out, "Hello, is anyone here?"

"I was certain she'd be able to see you. She's seen—and talked to—other ghosts." Chris walked with Walt down the hall, trailing behind Heather, who continued to search for some sign of their presence.

"If I have to listen to you call me a ghost, I need to come up with an equally annoying term for what you are," Walt grumbled. "But first…" Walt vanished from Chris's side and placed himself directly in Heather's path, focusing all his energy in her direction.

HEATHER WAS JUST COMING to the doorway leading to the library when the area directly in front of her flickered and sparkled with random rays of light. Sadie let out a bark, her tail still wagging, and then plopped her butt on the floor, as if someone had just given her the command to sit. In turn, Heather abruptly stopped. Her eyes still focused on the emerging apparition, she absently reached to her side and patted Sadie—a silent bid for support. Heather watched as the portion of light began to flutter and then twirl, gradually revealing a faint image. Her eyes widened. She watched as the image grew clearer, no longer faint and abstract. She let out a gasp. Standing before her was Walt Marlow, who—if she had seen him walking on the beach—she would assume he was just a regular man—one wearing a vintage suit of the 1920s.

"Walt Marlow!" she gasped, her hand briefly touching her lips.

"So you can see me now?" he asked impatiently.

Heather nodded in response.

"I assume that means you can hear me too?" he asked.

"I always knew you were here!" she said excitedly.

"We have no time to waste. Come, follow me." Walt turned and headed for the library.

"How long have you been here?" Heather asked as she followed him.

Still walking, Walt glanced over his shoulder at her. "You mean in this house?"

"Yes. Have you always haunted it? Or do you…I don't know… wander the streets of Frederickport?"

Chris chuckled. "Wandering the streets of Frederickport? What, and rattling chains as you go?"

Ignoring Chris, Walt said, "I've been here since I died."

"Danielle knows about you, doesn't she?"

"Of course."

"I knew it," Heather muttered under her breath and then asked, "Were you hiding from me before?"

Now in the library, Walt turned to face Heather. "Hiding from you? What do you mean?"

"I stayed here for weeks, and I never saw you like you are now. Oh, I caught glimpses of you. Like with Chris." Heather frowned and glanced around. "Where is Chris, by the way? I thought he'd be here with you."

"He is. You obviously can't see him, but he's standing over there." Walt pointed to the doorway and then paused a moment and studied Heather. "You really can't see him?"

Heather shook her head. "No. I mean, I saw him like a brief flash. Once in my house, and then again when I was walking here. I think I heard him shout something at me. But nothing tangible. Why couldn't I see you before, yet I can now?"

Walt shrugged. "I have no idea. But we need to—"

"I've seen other ghosts, why not you?"

"Would you please not call me that."

"Aren't you a ghost?" Heather asked.

Chris sat on the desk chair and snickered. "Yes, Walt, aren't you a ghost?"

"I prefer spirit," Walt said shortly, flashing Chris a glare.

"Isn't that the same thing?" she asked.

"Ghost just sound so…" Walt searched for the right word. Finally, he said, "Ghoulish." He considered his choice of word a moment and then nodded his approval. "Yes, ghoulish. As if I'm jumping out at people and yelling boo."

"I've encountered a number of—ghosts—and none of them jumped out at me and said boo. Although, I think Chris did that to me outside."

Walt turned to Chris and arched his brows. "You didn't?"

Chris shrugged. "I was just trying to get her attention."

"But I think you're being rather silly," Heather told Walt.

Walt frowned. "Silly?"

Heather nodded. "If you're a ghost, just own it. I mean, really, what's the big deal?"

"Can we just get on with what we have to do?" Walt said impatiently.

Heather shrugged and then headed for the desk. "I assume you need me to use the computer for some reason. Evan told me Chris wanted me to bring it."

Before Chris could move, he found Heather sitting on him. Leaping from the chair, Chris let out a curse. Glancing over to Walt, he was met with a snicker.

"Fair enough," Chris conceded. "I suppose I deserved that." Chris brushed off the illusion of his pants, as if in some way that might remove the uncomfortable sensation of Heather's body moving through his. "How do you ever get used to that?"

"One just does." Walt shrugged.

"One does what?" Heather asked.

"Nothing important, I was just talking to Chris."

Heather glanced around. "Why can't I see him? Evan was able to."

"It's obvious Evan's gift is stronger than yours; although yours seems to be intensifying. You're able to see and hear me now."

"I suppose," Heather muttered as she opened the laptop. "So why did you need me to bring my computer?"

"I need you to look up something. We need to find out where Seligman is," Walt explained.

"Why?"

"I assume Evan told you about the plane being hijacked?" Walt asked.

"I'd read that in the newspaper, about the pilot they found tied up at the Gusarov Estate. Evan said something about the plane landing and how everyone is still alive, but Chris got hurt."

"Chris remembers where the plane landed. It was somewhere near Seligman. The only problem, we don't know where that is."

"Are you saying the kidnappers have Danielle and Lily and the rest of them somewhere near Seligman?"

"We just know the plane landed there. If we can find the airstrip on the computer, and if the plane's still there, then we're closer to finding them."

Heather turned on her laptop. "I hope Danielle hasn't changed the Wi-Fi password."

"Wi-Fi password?" Walt looked at Chris and frowned. "I thought that's why you wanted Heather to bring her computer because you didn't know Danielle's password?"

"Different password, Walt," Chris explained.

"How many passwords does one need to use a computer?"

Ignoring Walt's exchange with Chris, Heather watched as her laptop powered on. A moment later she said, "Doesn't look like she changed it. So what do you want me to look up?"

"Seligman," Chris said, and then spelled it out.

"See what you can find out about Seligman," Walt suggested before spelling it out as Chris had.

Chris and Walt stood behind Heather as she ran a search for Seligman.

"Looks like there's a Seligman in Arizona and Nevada." Heather glanced up to Walt.

"Two Seligmans? Seriously?" Chris groaned.

"According to Chris, it was desert terrain," Walt told her.

"Considering both Arizona and Nevada have plenty of desert, I suppose it could be either one." Heather glanced back at the computer and refined her search. "Although the Nevada Seligman is in some area called White Pine. That might be the mountains; after all, Nevada also has forested areas like Tahoe…says here it's a ghost town."

"Try the Arizona Seligman," Chris said.

"Chris wants you to look at the Arizona Seligman. Earlier he said something about being able to get pictures of the area…" Walt glanced at Chris.

"Google Earth," Chris told Walt. "Tell her to check Google Earth."

"I bet Chris wants me to check Google Earth," Heather said before Walt could convey Chris's words to her. Walt and Chris exchanged glances.

"I wonder if she guessed that or…" Chris muttered.

Several minutes later Heather pulled up Google Earth and was able to locate the area along the highway that Chris had remembered—some ten miles from the exit to Seligman.

"That's where I was," Chris said excitedly. Looking over Heather's shoulder, he pointed to the computer screen.

"Chris said that's where he was," Walt told her, pointing to the section Chris had indicated. "Wherever he was, he was out in the middle of nowhere, and he walked a long dirt road and ended up along the highway."

Heather glanced up to Walt. "We can follow the dirt roads along this stretch of highway, but what are we looking for?"

"According to Chris, they parked the plane under a Nissen hut. Which would be a considerable size."

"Nissen hut?" Heather frowned. "What's that?"

"Tell her a Quonset hut. That's what most people know them as," Chris told Walt.

"Quonset hut, I mean," Walt corrected.

"And tell her there's a trailer near the Quonset hut," Chris added.

Before Walt could convey Chris's information, Sadie began to bark from the hallway.

"Oh damn," Walt cursed. "I forgot all about Joanne."

Heather looked up from the computer. "Joanne?"

"She's here to feed Sadie and Max. She comes at least twice a day," Walt explained.

From the hallway they could hear Sadie barking again and Joanne's voice.

"Oh crap," Heather muttered, slamming her laptop shut. "What am I going to do?" she asked in a loud whisper.

"She needs to hide somewhere," Chris called out from where he now stood in the doorway. "Joanne is coming this way, and she's looking in all the rooms."

Walt glanced around the library; there was nowhere to hide. "Stay here. I'll see if I can get Sadie to distract her."

"Where else am I going to go?" Heather said under her breath. She looked around frantically, yet like Walt, she couldn't see any place to hide. So she did the only thing she could do, she sat back down at the desk and opened her laptop and turned it on.

In the hallway, Sadie—with Walt's instruction—did her best to distract Joanne and nudge her to the kitchen, yet the light coming from the open door leading to the library caught Joanne's attention.

"In a minute, Sadie," Joanne said absently as she shoved Sadie aside and continued down the hall. "I don't remember leaving that light on."

When Joanne reached the open library door, she glanced in the room and was surprised to find Heather Donovan sitting at the desk, working on a laptop computer.

"Heather?" Joanne asked in surprise.

Heather looked up from the laptop and smiled cheerfully. "Joanne, hi! I thought I heard you coming in."

Wearing a frown of confusion, Joanne asked, "What are you doing here?"

"I'm using Danielle's Wi-Fi. Didn't she tell you?"

Still frowning, Joanne entered the room and glanced down at the laptop sitting on the desk. It didn't belong to Danielle. "I don't understand."

"I've been having problems with my router—and since I can't really afford to buy a new one, Danielle told me I could borrow her Wi-Fi when she was gone if I had a problem again." Heather smiled brightly.

"How did you get in here?" Joanne glanced around. Nothing seemed to be out of place.

"Danielle gave me a key, of course." Heather let out a sigh and seemingly turned her attention back to her laptop, ignoring Joanne.

Joanne stood there a moment and stared. Finally, she said, "When you leave, can you make sure you turn the lights off?"

Heather glanced up from the computer and flashed Joanne a smile. "Sure. No problem."

TWENTY-FIVE

"Joanne's in the kitchen, feeding Sadie and Max," Walt told Heather a moment later. "Did you find anything? Chris wanted me to tell you there's a trailer and dirt airstrip near the Nissen—I mean Quonset hut."

Focusing her attention on the monitor, Heather's fingertips tapped away on the keyboard. "I just hope Joanne doesn't ask for the key back, since I don't have one."

"If she does, tell her you set it down somewhere when you came in and can't find it now. Danielle and Lily do that often enough," Walt told her.

Heather glanced up at him from the computer. "Is Chris in here?"

"No, he's watching Joanne in the kitchen. He'll tell us when she's coming this way."

"I think I found it. If I'm not mistaken, this long road out in the middle of nowhere has a wind sock on one end—at least I think it's a wind sock—and those other two buildings have to be your Quonset hut and trailer."

"I'll be right back," Walt said before disappearing.

Walt returned a few moments later with Chris, while leaving Sadie to keep track of where Joanne was in the house.

"That's it!" Chris said excitedly as he looked over Heather's shoulder. "I'm positive!"

"You found it," Walt told Heather. "Now all we have to do is get this information to the right person."

A few minutes later, Joanne showed up at the doorway to the library. "Are you going to be much longer?"

"Umm…I'm not sure. Is there a problem?" Heather asked innocently.

Joanne didn't answer immediately—she just stared at Heather as if she couldn't quite understand why Danielle's neighbor and onetime tenant was in the house yet didn't feel comfortable coming out and challenging her story.

Sensing Joanne's conflict, Heather searched for something to say to normalize the situation. She glanced over at Walt and then back to Joanne and asked, "Is there anything new about the plane?"

Joanne shook her head. "Not that I know of. I'm sure you read in the paper about the witness who saw the plane go down. I know they're still looking for it, but it's in a heavily forested area."

Fidgeting with the corner of her laptop's case, Heather drew her forehead into a frown. She thought about the information passed on to her via Chris: there had been no crash. At least, none that he could recall. "How do they know it was the same plane?"

"I guess the witness described the mural along the side of the aircraft. From what I understand, it had some custom painting on one side—an eagle or something."

"Must have been some large eagle for the witness to see it from the ground."

Joanne shrugged. "I guess it was." Joanne glanced at her watch. "I need to get going. I have to be somewhere in about fifteen minutes. Are you going to be much longer?"

"I don't know…you see, I'm looking for a job. And it gets a little frustrating searching and having the Internet cut out."

"I didn't know you were looking for a job."

Heather shrugged. "Well, things here didn't work out quite like I thought when I moved in. I suppose you might say I need to get back to the real world." She looked over at Walt, who silently listened, resisting the temptation to break into laughter over the bizarre nature of her own words—discussing the real world while looking at a ghost.

"I hope you find what you're looking for."

"Thanks. You know, Joanne, if you need me to come over here to check on the animals, feed them or anything, I would be happy to. I'm just down the street. It's the least I can do to help out Danielle for all she's done for me."

"That's really nice of you. I might take you up on that. I'll let you know."

Heather flashed Joanne a smile. "No problem. You have my phone number, don't you?"

Joanne nodded and patted her purse. "It's in my phone."

Heather flashed Joanne another smile and then turned her attention back to her laptop. "I guess I should get back to what I was doing so I can get out of here."

Joanne glanced at Sadie, who had come into the library with her and was now curled up by Heather's feet. "I suppose Sadie's happy to have the company. I imagine she gets rather lonely over here."

After Joanne left a few minutes later, Heather opened the top drawer of the library desk and took out a pen and pad of paper. She began jotting down notes on the paper, occasionally looking up at the monitor.

"What are you doing?" Walt asked.

"I need to remember what to tell them," Heather explained.

"The question now—who is them?" Chris said as he walked in the room. A moment earlier he had followed Joanne to the front door and watched from the window as she walked to her car and got in before driving off.

"Chris is wondering who you should call," Walt explained.

Heather stopped writing on the notepad. "Well, we better figure that out before I leave here." Considering the question a moment, she absently twisted the end of one braid around her finger.

"There were those G-Men," Walt suggested.

Heather stopped twisting her hair a moment and looked up at Walt. "What G-men?"

"They came over here with Brian when they were looking for Evan."

"How exactly did they know Evan was here? He didn't tell me."

"According to what he told me, he called his aunt to tell her he was okay, and they traced the call," Chris explained.

After Walt recounted what Chris had just said, Heather let out a sigh, released hold of her hair, and glanced at the phone sitting on the desktop. "I suppose that means I can't use this phone to give my tip. It wouldn't have been such a big deal had Joanne not found me here."

"Do you know how to get ahold of the G-Men?" Walt asked.

Heather stood up and shut her laptop. "No. But I'll start with Brian Henderson first. Sounds like he's keeping in touch with all the agencies involved with this thing. I just wish there was some way I could find out if he's following up on my tip or discounting it as some crackpot."

"I'll take care of that," Chris offered. "I can go down to the police station and see what Brian does."

Walt nodded. "Good idea."

Heather picked up the laptop. "What's a good idea?"

"Chris is going down to the police station to keep an eye on Brian, see how he handles your information."

Heather put her laptop back on the desk. "Then I suppose I better leave this here to give me an excuse to come back over. If Brian doesn't follow up on the information, I'll have to figure out something else. I just wish I had a key so I didn't have to rely on you to unlock the door."

Just as Heather stepped from the desk, one of its bottom drawers slid open, seemingly of its own volition. From the drawer a key floated up, hovering just inches from Heather's face. Her eyes crossed from the unexpected closely placed object. She lurched back and laughed and then snatched the key from midair and said, "Thanks. Why didn't you give this to me before, when I was afraid Joanne might ask for the key back?"

"WHY DIDN'T YOU, WALT?" Chris asked after Heather left. The two had moved up to the attic.

"Why didn't I what?" Walt looked out the window and watched Heather disappear down the street.

"Give her the key when she first mentioned it?"

Walt shrugged. "I'm not sure how I feel about Heather coming and going at will."

"Well, for Heather, she seemed rather—*normal* today. And I do appreciate her helping us."

Still staring out the window, Walt let out a sigh. "Me too."

BRIAN HENDERSON HUNG up the telephone after talking to Mason Murdock. According to the pilot, the hospital would be releasing him in the morning. In the meantime, Murdock kept insisting the woman he had been dating—the woman whom he had discussed Chris's true identity with—would never have been involved in a hijacking and kidnapping scheme. Unfortunately, the woman, Andrea Banner, could not be located for questioning. According to one of her neighbors, she had taken off last Sunday—the day before the hijacking, and no one seemed to know where exactly she had gone.

Just as Brian was about to stand up from the desk, the phone began to ring. He sat down and answered the call.

"Someone's on the phone, insisting she—at least I think it's a she—knows where Chris Johnson's plane landed," the receptionist told Brian.

"Put her on. It's probably a crank call, but let me hear what she has to say."

Unbeknownst to Brian, he was no longer alone in the chief's office. Sitting in the chair facing the desk was Chris Johnson.

"I think it's a shame I don't have some of Walt's powers," Chris muttered as he leaned back in the chair. He propped one ankle over the opposing knee and glanced around the room before turning his attention to Brian and his phone conversation.

"Is this Brian Henderson?" came a raspy whisper on the other end of the line. Something crackled, as if whomever was on the phone was speaking through a piece of paper while it was being crinkled.

"Yes. I understand this has to do with the plane that was hijacked?"

"Yes. It didn't crash. It landed a few miles from Seligman, Arizona, on a dirt airstrip. The plane is hidden inside a Quonset hut."

"Who is this?" Brian asked.

"I can't tell you that. But you need to check it out," the raspy voice urged.

"It is illegal to make crank calls," Brian said sternly.

"I know Chris Johnson is really Chris Glandon."

Brian froze for a moment and then sat up straighter in the chair. Holding the phone to his ear, he said in a low and serious voice, "Go on."

Chris was unable to hear what Heather was telling Brian, yet he was fairly certain that's who was on the phone with him. He just hoped Brian would take the call seriously.

When Brian hung up a few minutes later, he picked up the phone again and made a call.

"This is Brian Henderson from the Frederickport Police Department. I have a lead on the missing plane…no, not at the location where the witness claimed it went down, but outside Seligman, Arizona…Yes, you heard me right. Seligman."

Chris continued to listen to Brian's side of the phone conversation. When he was confident they were going to investigate the area where he remembered the plane landing, Chris stood up and disappeared.

A few minutes later, Chris reappeared in Marlow House. He found Walt still in the attic, looking out the spotting scope.

Turning from the window to face Chris, Walt asked, "Well?"

"She called him. At first, I didn't think he was going to listen to her, but she must have said something to change his mind. As soon as he got off the phone with her, he called someone else and gave them the location of the airstrip and Quonset hut."

"But will they be able to find Danielle and the rest?"

FROM A DISTANCE SAM spied the dust cloud; it barreled up the lonely dirt road leading to Shafer's property. Bringing the quad to a stop, Sam took out a compact binocular set from his coat pocket. Unfolding the pair, he put them to his eyes for a closer look. The vehicle kicking up the dust was an SUV. Adjusting the binoculars for a clearer view, he caught a glimpse of the logo along the side of the car. It wasn't just any SUV—it was a Yavapai Sheriff's Department vehicle.

"I wonder why the sheriff's heading up to Shafer's place?" Sam muttered as he shoved his binoculars back in his pocket.

TWENTY-SIX

Opening her eyes, Danielle stared into a blazing fire. It was not a fire of destruction but of comfort. Blinking, she brought the scene into focus and found herself looking at the fireplace in her bedroom at Marlow House—*she was home!*

"Danielle?" came Walt's soft inquiry.

Turning to her right, Danielle realized she was sitting on her bedroom sofa next to Walt. Without thought she threw her arms around him. He held her tightly as she started to cry.

Stroking her back reassuringly, Walt whispered, "Please stop crying. You'll wake up, and we may not get another chance to talk tonight."

With a sniffle, Danielle stopped crying. She sat up and wiped off the tears with the back of her hand, her face damp.

"That's better," Walt said with a warm smile. He leaned to her and briefly kissed her lips.

Blinking away the tears, Danielle studied Walt. "Why is it I can actually feel you hold me—kiss me—during a dream hop?"

"I suppose that's because when we dream, anything is possible."

Danielle's solemn expression broke into a grin. "I've heard that before, but I have a feeling whoever originally said it, didn't mean it in quite the same way. Damn, I've missed you."

"So tell me where you are so we can get you home. And Lily, is Lily okay? And the others?"

Danielle took hold of Walt's hand and held it as she leaned back against the sofa's arm and studied his face. "Chris's the only one who is hurt. I'm worried about him."

"Chris is alive—but he is here. He's like Lily was."

Danielle glanced around and then looked back at Walt, still holding his hand. "Chris is here?"

"Well, not here exactly. Not in the dream hop. But he's back at Marlow House. He showed up there on Saturday night. Like Lily, he was a little confused at first, but his memory is returning."

"Has he looked in a mirror?"

Walt nodded. "Yes. He has a faint reflection. But we need to find you—find Chris's body—get him to a hospital."

Danielle's grin widened. "Aww, you do care about Chris!"

Walt rolled his eyes and leaned forward, placing a quick kiss on Danielle's lips. "I care more about you, but I suppose he isn't a bad guy, and I sure don't want him moving over to my side permanently. At least not yet."

Danielle cocked her head and smiled at Walt. "You just kissed me again. You kissed me twice, in fact. You don't normally do that."

"I've been worried sick about you. You have no idea how happy I am to be talking to you right now."

Danielle blushed and squeezed Walt's hand.

"We don't have any time to lose," Walt told her. "Have you figured out where you are yet?"

Danielle shook her head. "No. Ian thinks we're somewhere in the desert, because of the weather. They're holding us in this big old metal building, like a warehouse. There doesn't appear to be any electricity on in the building. They never turn the lights on, and we never hear any air or heating turn on or off. But it's fairly comfortable, even at night. Gets a little warm during the day."

"Ian is probably right. You're probably somewhere in the Arizona desert."

"Arizona? Why do you say that?"

"Chris remembers leaving his body. His body was unconscious on the ground while two of the kidnappers argued. He remembers a motorhome parked nearby and a trailer. There was a dirt airstrip and the plane was parked under a…Quonset hut."

"Are you telling me they landed a jet on a dirt airstrip?"

"Apparently."

"I guess the pilot really thought he was going to score big if he was willing to risk his jet," Danielle murmured.

"The owner of the plane was not involved—at least the authorities don't think so. They found him tied up in the basement of Chris's new business office. Apparently the kidnappers lured him over there. He thought he was going to talk to Chris."

"Is he okay?"

Walt nodded. "From what I understand."

"Just how are you getting all this information? From the television?"

"Listening to what people say."

"I guess that means people have been coming over to Marlow House," Danielle murmured.

"By the way, the authorities have found the plane. After Chris wandered off from the landing site, he found himself on a highway outside of Seligman, Arizona. We were able to get that information to Brian, and he in turn got it to the right people. I'm hoping this leads to finding you."

"How in the world did you get that information to Brian?" Danielle's eyes widened. "Heather?"

"Long story. I'll explain later. But first, is there anything you can tell me that can help them find you? Anything you remember or noticed?"

"Well…I met another ghost."

"The place is haunted?"

Danielle considered the question a moment and then shook her head. "No. But now that I think about it, knowing the plane went down in Seligman, Arizona, makes me feel a lot better."

"Why do you say that?"

"Because I was starting to wonder if the kidnappers took us to England. But unless they changed planes—which I seriously doubt—it sounds like we're still in the US."

"Why would you think you were in England?" Walt asked.

"My ghost. He's very British. And he's probably old enough to be your grandfather."

"What's he doing in the Arizona desert?" Walt asked.

"I have no idea. This is, of course, assuming the kidnappers are still in the general area of the airplane. After they took us off the plane, we were put in some sort of vehicle. It might have been a van."

"Chris noticed a motorhome parked near the plane," Walt told her.

Danielle shrugged. "It could have been a motorhome. We were blindfolded, and right after I sat down, someone shoved a needle in my arm. They sat someone next to me, but I didn't know who it was. We weren't allowed to talk. I think it was some sort of bench seat, so it may have been a motorhome. I remember the engine turning on, and we were driving down a bumpy road."

"A dirt road," Walt noted.

"Sounds about right. But after that, everything went black."

"They must have drugged you."

"Yes. They also drugged us on the plane."

"Back to the British guy. Can't he help you?"

Danielle shook her head. "Not really. He doesn't seem to have any powers. I think it's because he just wanders around, not really haunting any specific place."

"Can't he at least tell you where you are?"

"That sounds easier than it is. Percival tends to be rather cryptic."

Walt arched his brows. "Percival?"

"Percival Clint. Apparently he was murdered on some bridge over in London."

"So what's he doing in Arizona?" Walt asked.

"He said—" Danielle's eyes widened. "I know where we are!"

"Where?"

"Lake Havasu City, Arizona. That has to be it! The kidnappers have us somewhere in Havasu!" Excitedly, Danielle leapt from the sofa, dropping hold of Walt's hand. Anxiously, she began pacing back and forth between the sofa and lit fireplace.

"Where is Lake Havasu City? I've never heard of it," Walt asked.

"It wasn't around in your day. Relatively speaking, it's a fairly new town located on Lake Havasu."

"I don't think I've ever heard of Lake Havasu." Walt leaned back on the sofa and watched Danielle pace.

"Lake Havasu is actually a portion of the Colorado River, made after the dams were built. The lake itself is located on the border between California and Arizona," Danielle explained.

"I don't understand. Why is it you think they have you there? Is it next to Seligman?"

Danielle shook her head. "I don't think so. From what I remember, I think Seligman is a couple hours from Havasu."

"So why Havasu?" Walt asked again.

Danielle was just about to answer his question when she vanished.

Walt stood abruptly. "Danielle!"

WALT FOUND Chris sitting alone in the kitchen.

"When did you get back?" Walt asked.

"A few minutes ago. I'll go back down to the police station in the morning, see what's going on now that they've found the plane."

"I saw Danielle," Walt told Chris as he took a seat at the table.

Chris straightened in the chair and focused his entire attention on Walt. "And? Is she okay?"

"For now. She thinks they're being kept someplace called Lake Havasu City, Arizona." Walt then went on to tell Chris about the dream hop—omitting the part about him kissing Danielle—twice.

"The ghost was British?" Chris murmured. "And he was murdered on a bridge in London?"

"That's what he told Danielle. But I still don't understand why she's now convinced they're in Lake Havasu City. I just wish she hadn't woken up when she did."

Chris smiled knowingly and leaned back in his chair. "Well, I know why."

"Why?"

"The London Bridge," Chris told him.

"What are you talking about?"

"The London Bridge. Back in the late 1960s the founder of Lake Havasu City bought the London Bridge as some huge publicity stunt for his new town. They dismantled it, shipped it over to the US, and reassembled it in the middle of the desert."

"You're kidding me?"

Chris shook his head. "No. From what I understand, it's quite the spring break attraction."

"What's spring break?" Walt asked.

"I don't know if you had it when you went to school—Christmas break, Easter break, when school gets out for a week or so for vacation. These days Easter break has been turned into spring break, and it takes place over a number of weeks. One school might have one week off, while another has a different week. Havasu's been one of the places where the students like to flock to. Rather a party spot."

"Interesting…" Walt murmured.

"It would explain a British ghost. There are stories the London Bridge is haunted—that some of the spirits attached to the site came over with the bridge when they reassembled it in Arizona. If this Percival dude was murdered on the bridge back in his day, it is possible he traveled with it to its new home."

"I would assume this means the kidnappers have Danielle and the others near the bridge," Walt speculated. "I suppose we need Heather's help again?"

"She was able to get them to go check on the plane. If she calls Brian again and he recognizes her voice, then I think he'll take her tip seriously, especially now, since they found the plane."

TWENTY-SEVEN

"I can't believe it was really there," Brian muttered for the hundredth time. Or perhaps it hadn't actually been that many, it just seemed that way to Chris, who had spent much of the previous evening—and now Monday morning—in the company of Brian Henderson. Chris had left several times, once to update Walt and tell him the plane had been found, and another to check in, right after Walt had returned from his dream hop with Danielle. But he had returned again to see if there was any news about his friends—and his own unconscious body.

Brian had just welcomed Special Agents Thomas and Wilson from the FBI into the office. From what Chris managed to overhear, the property where the plane was found was owned by longtime Frederickport resident Herman Shafer.

"I just can't see Herman being involved in any of this," Brian told Thomas and Wilson as they each took a seat.

"What do you know about Shafer?" Thomas asked.

"He used to be the bank manager before Steve Klein. He's been retired for a number of years. His wife died about a year ago. She was pretty sick, in and out of the hospital for over a year. I ran into Herman about two months before his wife died, and he sounded pretty optimistic about her recovery, but then a month later their only child was killed in a car accident and I think she just gave up. She died not long after their son was killed."

"Doesn't sound like a man who has much to lose," Thomas noted.

Brian shrugged. "Maybe not, but he really doesn't need the money. I remember seeing him once, a few months after his wife died, and he said something about how some people think he was lucky that they had good medical insurance, but that it really didn't matter to him, since he had lost both his wife and son. From what I understand, he had a pretty good retirement from the bank, he lives in a nice home, and I just don't see him doing something like this for the money."

Thomas flipped open a small notebook and read a page and then looked up at Brian. "I assume James Shafer was his son?"

Brian nodded. "Yes. I remember Jim; he grew up in Frederickport. After college he moved to Southern California and got a job. Can't recall what he did, from what I heard about him back then, I got the idea he did pretty well."

"The property where we found the plane used to belong to James Shafer. His parents inherited it after he died, along with some other real estate he owned."

The desk phone rang and the men stopped talking. Brian answered it, said a few words to the caller, and then hung up.

"Herman is here. They've shown him to the interrogation room. You can talk to him there," Brian told them.

When Agent Thomas walked alone into the interrogation room a few minutes later, he found Herman Shafer waiting for him. Thomas knew the man was nearing his eighties, yet he looked closer to late sixties, with a thick head of snow white hair and a slight hunch to his back.

Using his cane to help him stand, Shafer managed to shake the agent's hand during the brief introduction. When he sat back down again, he let the cane drop to the floor by his feet. If the elderly man was annoyed at being called down to the local police department for questioning, he didn't show it.

"So what is this all about?" Herman asked curiously.

"I understand you own property in Seligman, Arizona," Thomas began.

Herman leaned closer so he could better hear. "Yes. Has something happened to it?"

"Happened? What do you imagine might have happened to your property there?"

"This is about an airplane, isn't it?"

Thomas arched his brow and leaned back in the chair. "Yes. Yes, it is. Why don't you tell me what you know about the airplane."

Herman raised a fist and angrily slammed it on the desktop while shouting, "Gall-dammit. I knew I should have sold that property. Or at least removed the damned wind sock. Was anyone killed?"

"Killed?"

"In the plane crash. Was anyone killed?" Herman asked.

"There was no plane crash."

Herman frowned. "I don't understand. Then why are you here? You said this had to do with a plane and the Seligman property."

"I assume you've heard about the hijacked plane—"

"You mean the one with Chief MacDonald on it?" Herman finished for him.

Thomas nodded. "Yes."

"Well, sure. That's all everyone in town is talking about. But what does that have to do with the Seligman property?"

"We found the plane. It was parked under the Quonset hut on your property."

Herman frowned. "Nahh. No way would that plane—I read about what kind it was in the paper—would fit under some Quonset hut. And what would it be doing there? I heard it went down in the mountains."

"That's a pretty large Quonset hut," Thomas said.

Herman shrugged. "Must be."

"Mr. Shafer, have you ever been to the property before?"

"No. It belonged to my boy, Jimmy. He planned to build a cabin up there. Something about living off the grid." Herman shook his head sadly. "He learned to fly and always talked about getting his own plane. When he found the property, he got all excited because it had its own airstrip. I had no idea it was big enough to land that size plane."

"If you've never been up there, do you have anyone who is watching the property?"

Herman started to answer but then paused, considering something. With a frown he asked, "Are you telling me that airplane that was hijacked—the one that had the police chief on it and all those other people—ended up on my property in Seligman?"

"Yes."

"Does this mean the police chief is back?" Herman glanced around, as if he expected Edward MacDonald to come walking into the interrogation room.

"We just found the plane. We still haven't found the passengers —or the pilot."

"What is the plane doing in Seligman, on my property?"

"That's what we'd like to know. So back to my original question, do you have anyone watching the property?"

"What's to watch? Nothing really out there but an old trailer and that Quonset hut. Wasn't even Jimmy's trailer. It was on the property when he bought it. From what I understand, when he'd go out there, he'd stay in his motorhome."

"So basically, that property's been abandoned since you inherited it?"

"I wouldn't say abandoned exactly. I pay taxes on it. Although now you tell me someone used the airstrip, I need to have that damn wind sock taken down. All I need is for a plane to crash-land and get sued."

"How many people know about your Seligman property and what's out there?" Thomas asked.

Herman frowned. "You mean people I know personally?"

"Yes."

"I don't know. I've talked about it with friends."

"Don't you find it a little odd, a plane full of Frederickport residents are kidnapped, and the plane they were on is found on your property?"

"You certainly don't think I had anything to do with the hijacking, do you? I don't even know how to fly."

"Whoever took that plane obviously knew about the airstrip, and they knew the plane would fit under the Quonset hut."

"I didn't even know it would fit under it. I figured it was something Jimmy parked his motorhome under." Herman shifted uncomfortably in the seat.

"Someone knew. I don't think the plane randomly landed there. Has anyone asked you questions about the property in the last few months?"

"Why just the last few months?"

"Because Chris Johnson didn't approach the airplane's owner until a little over a month ago," Thomas explained.

Herman shook his head. "No. I can't remember talking about

the Seligman property to anyone in the last few months."

"Okay, how about before that? Can you remember anyone taking a special interest in the property—asking you about the airstrip, anything?"

Furrowing his brow, Herman considered the question for a few moments. Finally, he shook his head and let out a sigh. "I really haven't had it that long. Not really. Jimmy's been gone almost a year now, but I've never been to the property—never intended to. I just figured I'd sell it, but never got around to taking the time to call a real estate agent. But I suppose I should."

"You say you've talked about the property with some friends?"

"Yes, but mostly that Jimmy left us some property."

"Did you ever discuss the fact there was an airstrip on it?"

"Well…not to everyone. I mostly said Jimmy had some property in Arizona he left us. That I needed to sell it. That's about it."

"So you never discussed the airstrip with anyone?"

Once again, Herman considered the question. "I suppose I mentioned it to a couple people."

"Please try to remember," Thomas urged.

"I remember talking about the property when my wife was in the hospital. Jimmy had just died, and I found out about it. It was the last thing I wanted to deal with. Of course, it had to go through probate, so it wasn't as if I could just turn around and sell it anyway."

"Who did you talk to about it then?"

"It was the nurse who had been taking care of my wife. Really sweet gal. She had just gotten off her shift and was heading home when she ran into me in the waiting room. I was pretty upset, dealing with my son's death and having to tell my wife. I remember asking the nurse, *What do I need with an airstrip in the middle of nowhere? I want my son and wife.* I started to cry, and she sat down with me. We talked for a couple hours. I always thought that was really sweet of her."

"Anyone else?" Thomas asked.

"I think I mentioned the airstrip to Ben Smith. He's an old friend of mine. We work at the museum together sometimes when I do docent duty. And I remember mentioning it to Steve and Beverly not long after my wife died. They took me out to dinner, and we discussed the property. Of course, Steve is dead now. That's Steve Klein; he was the manager at the bank after me."

"Anyone else?"

Looking off into space, Herman focused on the question yet drew a blank. He looked back up at the agent and shook his head. "I'm sorry. I really can't think of anyone else. And I don't imagine any of the people I mentioned had anything to do with the hijacking. Maybe it's just a bizarre coincidence."

"I don't believe in coincidences."

After Herman left the station, Thomas returned to the chief's office to talk to Brian and Wilson.

"There was one thing he said that I found strange," Brian said as he took a seat behind the chief's desk.

"What was that?" Wilson asked.

"He said he had to wait for the property to go through probate until he could do anything with it."

"What's so strange about that?" Thomas asked.

"After I found out about them landing in Seligman, I did a little search on the property. Jimmy paid less than fifty thousand for it. From what I remember a friend telling me after her mother died and left them some Arizona property, it didn't need to go through regular probate because her estate was worth less than seventy thousand. I doubt the Seligman property has increased that much in value."

Wilson shrugged. "He obviously left his dad more than just the Seligman property."

A phone call interrupted their conversation. Brian answered it, and when he was finished with the call, he hung up the phone and looked from Thomas to Wilson. "When you were interviewing Herman, I sent one of our men down to check out the payphone on the pier."

Wilson arched his brows. "Why?"

"We found out, that's where the tip came from."

"Are there any security cameras down there?" Wilson asked.

"Yes, that's why I sent him down there. But according to the officer who checked it out, whoever made the call must have been aware of the camera. It was moved slightly and didn't show the payphone."

"Did it catch anyone walking in the area? The possible caller?"

Brian shook his head. "No. Whoever it was could have gotten onto the pier, used the phone, and left without being detected. They're questioning possible witnesses, but I don't expect to come up with much. If the caller was savvy enough to mess with the right security camera, I don't imagine she's going to allow herself to be seen by a witness. But we'll see."

TWENTY-EIGHT

Herman Shafer pored over the menu at Lucy's diner, waiting for his lunch companion to arrive. Being hard of hearing, he failed to notice her walk up to the table. It wasn't until she placed a soft kiss on his cheek did he realize he wasn't alone.

Placing the menu on the tabletop, Herman looked up at Beverly and smiled. She gave him a friendly pat on the left shoulder and then sat down across from him in the booth. Tossing her purse on the empty space next to her, she flashed him a smile.

"You look lovely as always," Herman told her. He reached across the table and patted her hand.

"You are looking rather chipper yourself, Herman. I'm so glad you called to ask me for lunch. It's been ages. Well, aside from seeing you at Steve's funeral, but that was hardly a happy time." Beverly let out a sigh and picked up a menu and opened it.

"How are you doing, Beverly? I've been worried about you."

Beverly shrugged and closed the menu, setting it back on the table. Before she had time to respond, the server showed up at their table and took their order. When they were alone again, Herman repeated the question.

"Taking one day at a time," Beverly told him. "But then you know how it is."

Herman let out a sigh and gave her a weary nod. He then sat up straighter in the seat and said, "Although something interesting happened today."

"What's that?" Beverly reached for her water glass and then took a sip.

"You know that airplane that was hijacked? The one with the police chief on it?"

Beverly arched her brows and slowly set the glass back on the table. "Yes. What about it?"

"They found the plane last night."

Licking her lips, Beverly cocked her head ever so slightly. "They did?"

Herman nodded. "Unfortunately, they still haven't found the passengers. Still no word on the chief. But you'll never believe where they found the plane."

"Where?"

"On my property in Seligman, Arizona. The property Jimmy left me."

"Really?" Beverly picked up her glass again and took another sip.

"Surprised the hell out of me. From what I read, the plane was actually a small jet. I had no idea something like that could land on a dirt airstrip. Especially considering nothing has been done to that airstrip in years."

"I imagine it was a rocky landing. So they didn't find any of the passengers or crew?" Beverly asked.

He shook his head. "No. Just the plane."

"How did they find the plane? From what I remember you telling me, that's a rather remote area."

"I really don't know. They didn't tell me. From what I understand, it was partially hidden. I guess the hijackers managed to park the jet under the Quonset hut out there. I had no idea something like that would fit under it."

Beverly shrugged. "I remember you telling us Jimmy said the Quonset hut was over a hundred feet wide, so it doesn't really surprise me. So who talked to you about this? Surely they don't think you had something to do with the hijacking?"

"Some guy from the FBI. I don't know what they're thinking. But the fact a hijacking from our area ends up on property I own in Arizona has the FBI looking closer at me—and whoever I know who I told about the property. Especially the fact it had an airstrip."

"And the Quonset hut," Beverly muttered.

"I suppose you're right. I imagine the FBI is watching the area to see who comes back for the plane. Actually, I was told not to say anything about them finding it."

Beverly smiled and reached over the table, gently patting Herman's hand. "You can trust me. We've been friends a long time. Your secret is safe with me."

"I imagine they figure the chief and the rest of them are in the general area. I hope they're able to find them before anyone gets hurt."

"Umm…did they ask you anything about the other property Jimmy left you?"

"No. Why would they?"

Beverly shrugged. "Oh, I don't know. Just wondered." She stood up and grabbed her purse off the seat next to her. "If you'll excuse me, I think I'll run to the lady's room before they bring our food."

HEATHER WAS DYING to know if Brian had followed up on her phone tip. For a brief moment she considered going back to Marlow House—she now had a key—to see what Walt knew, yet then she remembered he was unable to venture beyond Marlow House. So chances were he would know less than she did. That was why he needed her.

While it was always possible Chris had found out something and relayed that information back to Walt, Heather decided to go directly to the source: Brian Henderson.

Twenty minutes later she found herself standing at the doorway leading to Chief MacDonald's office. Brian sat behind the chief's desk, papers spread across the desktop.

Heather stepped into the office and glanced around. "Wow, you've already moved into the chief's office. I wonder how he'll feel about that."

Setting his pen on a stack of papers, Brian looked up at Heather. "They told me you wanted to see me. But I'm very busy. I can only give you a minute. What's this about?"

"I just wanted to see if you've heard anything new about Danielle and the rest of them." Heather took a seat facing Brian and dropped her purse to the floor.

"Nothing I'm at liberty to discuss."

"So you do know something?" Heather prodded.

"As I said, nothing I'm at liberty to discuss."

"I read in the paper a witness saw the plane go down in a forested area. Have they found the wreckage?"

"Heather, I really can't discuss this with you."

SOME MEN ARE QUITE FORGETTABLE. Morton Simmons was such a man. More average looking than average looking, nondescript with nothing notable one might mention about him should the need arise—which it never seemed to—he moved through his life gathering no attention. Not an especially difficult task, considering the fact he lived in a trailer behind his gas station, miles from his closest neighbor.

People who passed through called the area a dead spot—there was no Internet service, no cell service. Morton didn't really care. He had never learned how to use a computer, and he had a landline and saw no reason to pay extra for a cellphone. There was no one he wanted to call. Some people thought he was crazy to live in such an isolated area. The nearest store was thirty minutes away. But Morton didn't care. He enjoyed his solitude, and he made a decent living selling gas.

When the dark sedan pulled into the station, it didn't park by a pump. Morton figured whoever it was just wanted to use his restroom or ask directions. He didn't mind giving directions, but it annoyed the hell out of him when someone used his bathroom without buying gas.

Standing in the doorway to the small station, Morton watched as two men in dark suits and sunglasses stepped out of the vehicle. He continued to watch as they approached him.

"We're looking for Morton Simmons," one of the men said as he removed his sunglasses.

"You found him," Morton replied.

"Mr. Simmons, I'm Special Agent Thomas from the FBI, and this is Special Agent Wilson."

"Wow…the FBI? What do you want with me?"

"We understand you were the one who reported seeing a plane going down?" the one identified as Wilson said.

"Umm…yeah…" Morton shifted nervously from foot to foot.

"Can you tell us where you saw it exactly?"

Absently scratching his head, Morton stepped out from the doorway leading into the station and looked to his right, where the road weaved higher into the mountains. "Umm…I was taking a little drive. Stopped at the view point a mile or so from here. That's when I saw this jet fly over. Real close like."

"It was a jet?" Wilson asked.

"Umm…yeah. Pretty sure. I guess it was. It was an airplane."

"But you said it was a jet," Wilson reminded him.

"Jet, airplane…does it matter?"

"Then what happened?" Thomas asked.

"Well, after it sort of skimmed over the treetops—like some daredevil—it went up in the sky. I thought it was going to just take off and then fly away. I watched it for a bit, and then the strangest thing happened, it just did a nosedive, like it was out of control. Smoke coming out of its tail. Just disappeared in the distance, in the trees. I guess they haven't found it yet?"

"Why do you say that?" Thomas asked.

Morton shrugged. "I don't know. Hadn't heard anything about finding it yet."

"According to the police report, you didn't report it until the next day. Why did you wait so long?"

"I…I figured other people had to have seen it. But when I didn't hear anything about it on the news the next day, I called in."

"You described the mural on the side of the plane," Thomas began.

"You mean that big old painting on the side of it?" Morton asked.

"Yes." Wilson pulled a photograph from his coat pocket and handed it to Morton. "Is this the same plane?"

Morton stared at the photograph for a few moments and then handed it back to Wilson. "I guess so. Looks like what I saw."

"Did you know that is a one-of-a-kind painting? According to the jet's owner, there isn't another plane out there with that mural on it." Wilson returned the photograph to his pocket.

"Umm…so?"

"We're just wondering, if you saw that plane going down in a heavily forested area, why is it we found the plane—intact—hundreds of miles from here? Just last night?"

Morton stared dumbly at Wilson.

"I think you better explain what you really saw," Thomas told him.

Licking his lips nervously, Morton looked from Thomas to Wilson and back to Thomas. "Am I under arrest?"

"It depends what you tell us," Wilson told him.

Ten minutes later, Morton sat in the small office of his filling station with Special Agents Thomas and Wilson.

"They paid me a thousand bucks," Morton explained.

"Who paid you?" Wilson asked.

Morton shrugged. "I don't know. I'd never seen him before. He gave me cash. Told me all I had to do is call the police on the last Tuesday of the month and report the accident. Say I saw it go down the day before."

"Did he tell you what to say about why you didn't report the crash on the day you supposedly saw it?"

"Yes. He said it wasn't like anyone was actually going to get hurt. Said some guy was just trying to disappear. He gave me five hundred up front and promised me the rest after he heard about the report on the news."

"Did you get the rest of the money yet?"

Morton shook his head. "No. I think the guy stiffed me. He promised I'd have it the next day. But it's been almost a week now, and I haven't heard anything."

TWENTY-NINE

Chris had a new appreciation for all those frustrated spirits who had reached out to him over the years. He recalled all those times he had tried to ignore a spirit's request, and when he had helped a spirit, it was often done begrudgingly.

"This is karma," Chris muttered to himself. "Serves me right for being such an insensitive jackass." Of course, Chris was being overly harsh on himself. There were numerous times he had gone out of his way to do the right thing and help a spirit who had reached out. Yet it was those times that he was less than enthusiastic in helping that now plagued him, considering his current state of being.

He had spent Monday afternoon and evening vying for Heather's attention. While he knew she was unable to see him as she had Walt, he knew she had caught glimpses of his presence, which was why he spent a good portion of the day leaping out at her, jumping in her tracks and shouting as loud as possible. He figured if she noticed him, she would then understand it was a sign to go see Walt. Walt needed to tell Heather about what Danielle had told him in the dream hop, and Heather needed to make another anonymous tip.

When Chris's outrageous antics provided no results, he decided his only course of action was to approach the one person whom he could communicate with: Evan MacDonald. Chris figured he could at least get Evan to call Heather on the telephone and give her the message. Unfortunately, he couldn't find Evan. He was not at his aunt's house and he was not at school. The only remaining option, Walt would need to visit Heather or Evan in a dream hop—which was what he did.

On Monday night, after Chris returned to Marlow House without Heather, Walt waited for the evening to move on so he could leap into Heather's or Evan's dream. He tried Heather first, and it proved a success.

EARLY TUESDAY MORNING, Heather waited for Joanne's car to drive away. While she had convinced Joanne Danielle had given her a key and permission to use her Wi-Fi, she felt uncomfortable going to Marlow House while the housekeeper was there. Plus, it would be impossible to hold a conversation with Walt Marlow while Joanne was in the house.

Walt Marlow—Heather smiled at the thought. She had to admit, he was much better looking than his portrait. She wondered what it was like for Danielle to have a resident ghost. He was vastly different from the ghost of Presley House—who visited just once a year and who was so immersed in issues that he proved not only unstable, but dangerous to have around. But since Presley House was no more, it had burned to the ground, she assumed Harvey had either moved on or had found somewhere else to haunt. In either case, Heather wouldn't mind having a resident ghost—providing he was more like Walt and nothing like Harvey.

Heather sat on her front porch, Bella on her lap, an empty coffee mug sitting next to her, waiting for Joanne to leave Marlow House. She had been sitting on the porch for thirty minutes now. Just as Heather was about to get up and refill her cup, Joanne's car drove by.

"About time," Heather muttered. Tossing Bella into the house, Heather headed to Marlow House, its house key in her pocket.

"Did you call Brian Henderson?" Walt asked Heather the moment she walked into Marlow House.

"So that really was you in my dream?" Heather asked, closing the door behind her. She glanced around. "Is Chris here?"

"No. He's down at the police station. So did you call him?"

Before Heather could answer the question, Sadie raced into the room, tail wagging. Dropping to her knees, Heather greeted an exuberant Sadie and then glanced up at Walt. "I haven't yet. I wasn't sure that was really you in my dream last night—or just a dream."

"You're wasting time!" Walt said impatiently. "Their lives are in danger."

"Hey, I'm sorry." Heather stood up and gently pushed Sadie away. "I really didn't want to call in a tip and find out I had dreamed it up."

"Fine," Walt said with an impatient sigh, Sadie now sitting by his side. "But do it now."

Absently twirling one of her braids, she said, "I'm not sure where I can make the call."

"Where did you make it before?"

"At the pier. But I had to move the security camera, and I'm sure they know by now where that call came from. Even Frederickport isn't that backwards when it comes to tracing phone calls. So I wouldn't be surprised if they have someone keeping an eye on that phone."

"Then use your own phone," Walt suggested.

Heather rolled her eyes. "Seriously? Don't you know anything about cellphones?" She paused a moment and then shrugged. "Never mind, silly question. I obviously don't want them tracing the call back to me."

"Use the phone here," Walt suggested.

"Here? But they'll be able to trace it."

"So? No one is here."

"I am."

"No one knows you're here. Leave out the back door if you don't want anyone to see you. As it is half of the people on this street were on that plane."

"Well, not half…but you have a point."

"Heather, we're wasting time. Please. Call."

BRIAN STARED at the drawing of a man Agent Thomas had handed him minutes earlier. Sitting behind the chief's desk, he glanced up from the drawing to the agents now sitting on the two chairs facing him.

"Do you recognize the man?" Wilson asked.

Standing up, Brian leaned across the desk and handed the drawing back to Thomas. "No. If I've ever seen him before, I don't remember him."

Standing beside the desk, Chris leaned over to look at the picture as it was being passed around. "That was the guy arguing with the pilot!" Chris told deaf ears. "From what they were saying, I think he was the one responsible for my fall."

Accepting the drawing back from Brian, Thomas glanced at it briefly before setting it on his lap. "Simmons says he's the one who paid him to call in the false report. Claims he didn't know him. Paid him in cash."

"Do you trust it's a good likeness?" Brian asked.

"Looks damn good to me," Chris muttered, annoyed that no one could see or hear him.

"After Simmons finished with the artist and he looked at the drawing, he swore it looked just like the man who paid him. But so far we haven't come up with anything on the guy's identity."

"We're watching the Shafer property, and hopefully the kidnappers will be back there to check on the plane," Wilson said. "Unfortunately, with the good weather they've been having in Seligman, it's going to be difficult to keep the off-road vehicles out of the area, and someone is bound to see that jet and start talking. Not every day you see a jet like that parked in the middle of nowhere. Fortunately, it's partially concealed under the Quonset hut."

"I was hoping we'd be closer to finding them," Brian said with a sigh. "I've been talking to the family members all morning."

"How are they holding up?" Thomas asked.

"As to be expected. But I did tell them we no longer believe the plane went down, which was comforting." Brian leaned forward and propped his elbows on the table. "Of course, they all know now that their love ones have been kidnaped, so that gives them something else to worry about."

"We've been taking a closer look at all of them," Wilson noted.

"Are you serious?" Chris snapped. "None of my friends had anything to do with this. Would you focus on finding the real culprits and get us all home!"

"You don't think one of the hostages has ties to the kidnappers, do you?" Brian asked. "I know all those people; there is no way anyone would be involved."

"Maybe you're too close to the situation," Wilson suggested.

"I've had my issues with Danielle Boatman, and there was a time I wouldn't have been opposed to locking her up, but there is no way she'd be involved in hijacking a plane for profit. The same goes for Lily Miller. And I would trust the chief or Joe with my life."

"Considering Danielle just gave my foundation a considerable chunk of her inheritance, I seriously doubt she'd be involved," Chris scoffed. "Idiots."

"What about the Bartleys?" Wilson asked.

"Ian? Kelly? Sheesh…" Annoyed, Chris paced the room.

"I know Ian got pretty close to both the Missing Thorndike and the gold coins found in his house, and he didn't seem interested in claiming ownership of either one."

"But did he really have a case?" Wilson asked. "Maybe he figures it's time for him to get his share."

"Ian was the only one who knew the Thorndikes left the necklace to Marlow," Brian explained. "He had a good reason to believe the necklace was hidden in the house. He had ample opportunity to find it, and when Danielle did find it and thought it was fake, Ian was the one to insist it was real and urged her to take it to a jeweler to have it appraised. If Ian was so mercenary, that would have been his chance to get his hands on the necklace, when Danielle thought the stones were just paste. No, I don't see Ian being part of this—his sister either."

"That leaves MacDonald's girlfriend," Thomas said.

Brian shook his head. "I don't think so. Carol Ann is a nice woman who takes care of people for a living. The passengers are the victims here. I don't believe for a minute any of them are involved."

"For once you and I agree on something," Chris told Brian—who, of course, could not hear him.

The conversation was interrupted when the phone rang. Moments after answering it, Brian raised his hand frantically and waved the agents over to his desk to listen.

"Would you repeat what you said," Brian told the caller as he held the phone out so they could all listen.

"I know where the kidnapped victims are—from the hijacked plane," came the raspy voice.

"Where?" Brian asked.

"They're being held in a warehouse in or near Lake Havasu City, Arizona."

"Who is this?" Brian asked.

"Just someone who doesn't want to see anyone else get hurt. When you find them, have an ambulance ready. Chris Glandon fell on the day of the hijacking, and he has been unconscious since then. You need to move fast so he doesn't die—and so no one else gets hurt."

"Where in Lake Havasu City?" Brian asked.

"I'm not sure. But not too far from the London Bridge. I don't think there is any electricity hooked up in the warehouse where they're keeping them—but I could be wrong about that."

"Why should I believe you?" Brian asked.

"I was right about the airplane, wasn't I?" The call ended. Hanging up the phone, Brian looked from Wilson to Thomas.

"Was that the same person who called in about the plane?" Thomas asked.

Brian nodded. "I'm pretty sure. Sounded just like her. Where do we even start to look?"

"There's one place we need to check first," Thomas said as he removed his phone from his pocket.

"Where?" Brian frowned.

Wilson looked at his partner and nodded. He then looked back to Brian. "When we were looking into the owner of the Seligman property, we discovered that wasn't the only property his son left him."

"Shafer inherited property in Lake Havasu City?" Brian asked.

Wilson nodded. "Not in the city exactly, but an area they call Donkey Acres, on the outskirts of town."

THIRTY

The snowbirds had begun heading home several months earlier; many had crossed paths with the party-hardy spring breakers, who had more recently said their goodbyes. Lake Havasu was now gearing up for its next big holiday, Memorial Day, which was just weeks away. That was when jet skiers, boaters, and water sports enthusiasts would be showing up. Many had already arrived, clogging the Channel with their boats and paddleboards while enjoying the last remnants of the spring-summer.

Sky was noticing the shift in the weather. It had been April when they had taken off from Oregon, and the plan had been to be out of Havasu before May's arrival. Although they had only been in town for a little over a week, he already noticed the spike in temperature. In a few days the captives might find the afternoon heat unbearable in the warehouse. But that was not going to be his problem. By then he planned to be back in Washington.

Sky pulled the car up to the trailer and got out. Slamming the door shut, he hurried inside, where he found Andy and Clay.

"It's over," Sky announced.

Clay stood up from the table. "What are you talking about?"

"They found the plane," Sky told them.

"Are you sure?" Andy asked.

"Positive. It's only a matter of time before they come here." He looked at Andy. "You know what you have to do."

"How much time do we have?" Andy asked.

"We should have been gone yesterday." Absently he combed his gloved hand through his hair and then paused. He looked down at his leathered palm. "Great. We've been careful not to leave fingerprints, and here I am practically yanking out my hair and leaving my DNA all over the place."

Andy stood up. "If it's really over, then let's get it done before the police come driving up."

CAROL ANN CHECKED Chris's vitals. He hadn't shown any improvement.

Leaning over his still body, she whispered in his ear, "Come on, Chris, you can't die. Please wake up. Please."

After taking a deep breath, Carol Ann exhaled slowly and turned from his bed. She walked to the door and grabbed the doorknob, trying to turn it. But it wouldn't budge. It was locked. Returning to Chris's bedside, she sat down on a nearby chair. Through the thin walls she heard a car engine turn on. The engine revved, and then she heard the vehicle barrel down the drive, away from the trailer.

WHEN THEY TURNED onto South McCulloch Boulevard, Sky slowed the car. Coming in his direction were four Lake Havasu Police vehicles. After they passed, he glanced in his rearview mirror and watched as they turned off South McCulloch Boulevard and headed in the direction from where he had just come.

Sky had one stop to make before heading out of town, the vacation house he had rented two weeks earlier. He didn't want to chance parking James Shafer's car anywhere near the rental, should the police start looking for it. His plan was to leave it in the Safeway parking lot and walk to the rental house.

The rental—which they had obtained online through a private party—had the necessary Internet for the transaction—a transaction that had never taken place. In its garage their getaway car waited. It had been purchased when Sky had visited two weeks earlier, when checking out the Seligman airstrip and the Havasu site.

He had flown in then, which had saved considerable traveling time, but he didn't want to risk flying when leaving Havasu, should something go wrong—which it had. He didn't want the police to start checking out the local airport.

The getaway vehicle had been purchased from a private party two weeks earlier. Sky intended to dump it in California and take a bus the rest of the way home. The last thing he wanted to do was show up back home driving a car with Arizona plates. He had expected they would be incredibly rich when this was all over—but instead, they were out about ten thousand dollars. Sky was not happy.

"I SURVIVED MY OUT-OF-BODY EXPERIENCE. Chris will too. I sincerely believe that," Lily whispered to Danielle as she stared up at the ceiling. Sunlight slipping through random spots in the poorly insulated building provided dim lighting. The two friends lay side by side on the concrete, each pillowing their heads on towels Carol Ann had talked the kidnappers into giving them.

"I hope you're right, Lily. But the thing that bothers me, you had real doctors looking after you. I know Carol Ann is trying, but she isn't a doctor, and she doesn't have any medical supplies aside from basic first aid."

They were both quiet for a few minutes when Lily asked in a hushed voice, "Do you think any of us are really going to get out of here alive?"

Before Danielle had a chance to answer the question, Percival's face appeared overhead—floating in the air a few feet over hers. He smiled down and said in his English accent, "Good'day. I believe your incarceration is about to come to an end."

Startled, Danielle sat up abruptly. No longer hovering over Danielle, Percival now sat by her side while laughing heartily. "I wish I could do that with everyone!"

"Is everything okay, Danielle, Lily?" the chief called out after hearing the startled gasp come from their direction.

Lily sat up and looked at Danielle. "What's going on?"

"We're fine," Danielle called out to the chief. She then whispered to Lily, "Percival's here."

Lily glanced around. "Where?"

Danielle pointed to the empty spot next to her and then asked Percival, "What did you mean just now?"

"I'm talking about the automobiles surrounding your little prison."

Danielle frowned. "What automobiles?"

"And your kidnappers, they ran right over me. If I wasn't already dead, I surely would be now."

"What are you talking about?" Danielle asked.

"Your kidnappers took off in a hurry. And now there's a number of bobbies milling about."

"What do you mean bobbies milling about?" Danielle frowned.

"What are you two talking about?" Lily asked.

"I'm not sure. Percival said something about bobbies—"

"Are you talking about police?" Lily interrupted excitedly. "Are there police here?"

Danielle didn't need to answer the question. In the next moment the door to the warehouse burst open and a number of Lake Havasu police officers, each wearing riot gear, flooded inside. At least, Lily thought it looked like riot gear.

Everyone started talking at once—the hostages jumped to their feet—chains rattled—Kelly began to cry, and Danielle wanted to. In the midst of the commotion Percival silently slipped away, returning to the bridge he normally haunted.

After the officers secured the crime scene, Carol Ann was reunited with her friends and Chris was whisked off to the hospital. The hospital was where they all eventually went after their initial interview with the police. There they were interrogated again, but this time by agents from the FBI.

It wasn't until the next day that they were able to leave the hospital. Danielle was anxious to return to Oregon, but she couldn't leave Chris; the doctors didn't feel it was safe to move him quite yet. To help her friends get home quickly, she hired a plane to take them back to Oregon—yet first she asked the FBI agents to check out the pilot. Her friends were all a little gun-shy when it came to chartered planes.

"I wish you were coming home with us," Lily told Danielle as she gave her a hug goodbye. The two friends were alone together in the hallway outside Chris's hospital room.

"I can't leave Chris. As soon as I can arrange the transportation and the doctors say it's safe to move him, I'll come home. We need to get him in a hospital near us. According to Walt, his spirit is back in Frederickport, and if we get him with his body again, maybe it'll work like it did for you."

"Dani, are the doctors going to listen to you? I mean, you're not his wife or anything."

Danielle smiled. "Remember when I donated that money to Chris's foundation, and I was revising my will?"

"I know you gave me the power of attorney and then named Chris after me, but that doesn't work in reverse."

"I never mentioned it to you, but Chris also gave me his power of attorney. He's like me, he doesn't have any family."

Lily reached out and squeezed Danielle's hand. "It really doesn't surprise me. I'm glad he has you to watch over him."

"I called his attorney this morning. He's helping me make some of the arrangements, and he faxed the hospital the necessary papers."

"It's funny the kidnappers didn't seem to take anything out of our purses—aside from our money."

"It would have been nice had they left our cellphones," Danielle grumbled.

"Oh…that's right! What are you going to do about a cellphone? How will I call you?"

"I'll run over to K-Mart after you leave and pick up a few things, including a throwaway phone. I'll call you on the landline at Marlow House."

"What are you going to use for money? I thought you cancelled your credit cards this morning when I did mine."

"Yes, although I was tempted not to when I found out they hadn't used them. But like the chief reminded us, they still had our numbers and could sell them online."

"So what are you going to use for money?"

"They didn't touch my checkbook, and there's a couple of banks within walking distance of the hospital."

"You think they'll cash an out-of-state check?"

Danielle shrugged. "I'll ask to speak to the manager and work out something. And then I'll go to K-Mart and pick up a phone and some other things I'll need."

"Who knows, maybe our cellphones are still on the plane with our suitcases," Lily said.

Down the hallway, past the nurses' station, the elevator opened and out stepped Edward, Joe, Ian, Kelly, and Carol Ann. The weary travelers made their way towards Chris's room.

"Our ride's here," Ian said as he approached Lily and Danielle. "I wish you were coming with us."

"I do too, Ian. But I need to stay."

"I understand," Ian said as he wrapped his arms around Danielle and pulled her close. After kissing her forehead, he whispered words of encouragement in one ear. Just as the embrace ended, the rest of her friends moved in to give her a final goodbye hug, even Joe. No longer able to hold back the tears, Danielle let them slide down her face unfettered.

THIRTY-ONE

"I'm so sorry about this," Kelly told Joe as she snapped on her seatbelt. She sat next to him in the private plane. In the seats behind them were Lily and Ian, and behind them, Carol Ann and Edward. Turning in his seat to face Kelly, Joe reached out and cupped her face in his hand. Their eyes met—hers watered from unshed tears.

"Sorry about what?" he asked in a whisper.

She looked into his dark brown eyes—so caring. That was one thing she adored about Joe—aside from the fact she found him utterly sexy with his dark good looks. "You wouldn't have spent the last week in hell if I hadn't talked you into this trip. I know you really didn't want to go."

Joe leaned to Kelly and brushed his lips over hers. He smiled softly. "Kelly, don't be silly. None of this was your fault. And while I might have been a little hesitant at first, I was looking forward to going."

The pilot interrupted their conversation and reminded the passengers to buckle up.

After checking his seatbelt one last time, Joe reached over and took Kelly's hand in his. He held it tightly and leaned back in the seat as the plane taxied down the airstrip.

"I have to admit I'm a little nervous," Kelly whispered.

"You mean because we have to fly?" Joe gave her hand a gentle, reassuring squeeze.

"Yes." Kelly leaned toward Joe and rested her head on his shoulder. "I really thought we might all be killed. I wonder why the kidnappers just left us."

"Considering they didn't leave anything behind—other than us—my guess, someone or something tipped them off. They knew the police were on the way. Hopefully, they left behind some fingerprints—or something. Difficult to spend that much time living in such a small space and not leave some DNA behind."

"You know what's funny, Joe?"

He let out a snort. "Not a damn thing."

"Oh, I don't mean funny ha-ha."

Joe briefly squeezed her hand again. "I'm sorry. Go on."

"This is the most we've talked since we took off last Monday. Well, aside from at the hospital. I guess we talked a lot then."

"I know what you mean."

"It was a very peculiar—isolation," Kelly told him. "We were all in the same building—but other than the chief's twice-a-day roll call, we never were able to talk. I envied Danielle and Lily having each other."

"I felt pretty damn helpless," Joe grumbled.

"I heard my brother and the chief say the same thing. Ian is my big brother, and he has always felt that he needs to take care of me. And considering your profession, as well as the chief, I can see how it'd be especially frustrating for you."

"The one thing I kept holding onto was the fact we hadn't seen their faces."

"We saw the pilot's," Kelly reminded him.

"True. But after I thought about it for a while—and we had lots of time to think—my guess, it was a fake beard and hair color. I imagine if we ran into the guy now, he would be clean shaven with shorter hair and a different color. I doubt we'd recognize him."

"I would recognize his voice," Kelly insisted.

THE PLANE WAS up in the air and had already crossed into Nevada airspace.

Lily, who sat directly behind Kelly, tilted her seat back and purred, "I never thought I'd say this, but this seat is sooooooo comfortable."

Ian chuckled. "I have to agree. Compared to where we've been sitting—sleeping this past week, it's damn comfortable."

"My butt is bruised."

"Really? Can I see?" Ian teased.

Lily laughed and swatted his arm. "Maybe. But first I'm going to eat a steak dinner when we get home."

"I'll buy it for you."

"And a baked potato. With butter, sour cream, and chives. Oh… and that yummy bread they serve at Pearl Cove. Maybe I'll get lobster with it…"

Ian laughed.

"Oh, and that volcano chocolate cake they make!"

Ian leaned over and kissed Lily's nose. "It sounds delicious. And I'll be happy to see you get it." He then settled back in his seat and stared ahead.

"You're too good to me, Ian," Lily playfully quipped.

"Yeah, I take you on amazing vacations," he said with a snort.

"I think this was our first real vacation, and it sorta sucked."

"Yeah, sorta," he said dryly.

"The only thing that's marring our homecoming…"

"Chris?" Ian asked in a whisper.

"Yes. I wish he and Dani were on the plane with us."

"On the bright side, so far the tests that've come back on him look good. I'm just glad he's in a hospital with real doctors."

"Carol Ann tried to do her best," Lily whispered, glancing behind her to see if Carol Ann had overheard what Ian had just said.

"I understand that. But even she would agree with me."

"I suppose you're right. She seemed pretty happy to get Chris in the hospital." Lily let out a sigh.

"She has been by his side all week. Not surprising she feels protective of him, especially considering her profession."

"Ian…do you think Chris is still in danger? Aside from his obvious medical issue."

"Why do you ask that?"

"They haven't caught the kidnappers. When he gets out of the hospital, do you think they'll try it again, to get the money out of him?"

"I'm still trying to figure out how they thought they'd transfer that kind of money. And if it was a transfer, I have to assume they intended to use a computer to make it."

"According to the chief, there was no electricity hooked up to the place where they kept us. Just a few solar panels that helped run some of the lights in the trailer. Of course, a laptop doesn't need electricity if it has a charged battery."

"It needs Internet," Ian reminded her.

Reaching to her waist, Lily unhooked her seatbelt and then turned in the seat, sitting up on her knees so she could look over the seat at the chief.

"Hey, Lily," MacDonald greeted her when he looked up and noticed Lily peering over at him.

"Did those FBI guys or cops mention anything about that place having Internet?"

"When I talked to them, they said all the power was turned off; so I assume that included Internet." He glanced at Carol Ann. "Do you know if they had Internet service in the trailer?"

Carol Ann frowned. "I never saw anyone using a computer."

"We have to assume they intended to use the Internet in some way to transfer that money of Chris's," Lily explained.

Carol Ann shrugged. "I don't know. They pretty much kept me in the room with Chris with the door locked. I don't really know what they had in the trailer."

Lily flashed Carol Ann a smile and then sat back down in her seat. She looked over at Ian. "I don't think they had Internet there, which leads me to believe they must have been using another location in Havasu."

THE FLIGHT HAD BEEN under way for over an hour. Next to the chief sat Carol Ann, who silently stared absently into space. He reached over and gently touched her knee. Unprepared for the physical gesture, she lurched in surprise.

"I'm sorry," Edward quickly apologized, his hand still on her knee.

Carol Ann smiled sadly at him and patted his hand. With a

weary sigh she said, "No, I'm sorry. I shouldn't be this jumpy."

"You're just tired; we all are. This has been…well…traumatic seems too tame. But I worry about you. Are you sure you're okay… nothing happened? Because if anything did, you need to know I'm here for you."

Placing her hand over his, Carol Ann looked into Edward's eyes and smiled. "No. Nothing happened, at least, nothing like that. Like I told Lily, I really never saw much of the kidnappers. I spent my time locked in the bedroom with Chris. They were actually very polite. I don't believe they ever intended to hurt us."

"Carol Ann, they did hurt one of us."

"Yes…yes, I know. But I heard them arguing about that. They were very upset Chris got hurt."

"Sure they were upset," Ed scoffed. "With Chris unconscious, he couldn't give them what they wanted. But I don't believe for a minute if a bullet in Chris's—or any of our heads would have gotten them what they wanted, we would all be dead now."

Carol Ann shook her head. "No. I mean, they were wrong. And yes…criminal. But I don't believe they were killers. Look, they let us go, didn't they?"

"Carol Ann, one thing I love about you, you always try to see the good in people."

Her eyes widened. "Did you just say you love me?"

He smiled. "Umm…yes. I guess I did."

Smiling, Carol Ann leaned to him, placing a kiss on his cheek. "I'm so glad you're okay."

He returned her smile and said, "The feeling's mutual."

They each leaned back in their seats and looked toward the window. Clouds obscured the view below.

"You think your brother's going to meet us at the airport?" Ed asked.

"No. I told him not to bother coming down. There's really no reason to."

Ed turned to Carol Ann. "I'd think you'd want support from your family, considering all you've been through."

"No. It really isn't necessary. All I want to do is get home."

"Considering how close you two are, I wouldn't be surprised if he is waiting at the airport."

Carol reached over and patted his hand. She then took it in hers and held it. "I bet you're excited to see your boys."

"You have no idea. I was hoping they didn't know what was going on, but I guess our being missing was the talk in Frederickport, and there was really no way to keep it from the boys." Ed let out a weary sigh and looked blankly at the seat ahead of him.

"Oh no…you didn't tell me that." Carol turned in her seat and studied Ed's face. He continued to stare forward.

"There was so much going on when we got to the hospital. With all the questions and then everyone calling their families, and getting this plane arranged. I just didn't want to mention it before. I figured we all had enough on our plate."

"Oh, Ed, I feel horrible that the boys thought something had happened to their father. I absolutely hate that."

"That's why I didn't say anything before. I remember when you told me how difficult it was for you when your dad died, because you'd already lost your mother."

"And I wasn't even as young as your poor boys. They must have been terrified."

"At least now they know I'm alright and coming home. So I guess that's the important thing."

THIRTY-TWO

From the entry hall came a repetitive thumping sound, as if something was being dragged down the staircase. Getting up from the sofa in the living room, where she waited with her husband and eldest nephew, Sissy walked to the foot of the staircase and looked up. It was Evan, wearing his pajamas, and in one hand was his suitcase.

"What are you doing?" Sissy asked.

"I'm bringing my suitcase downstairs."

"Evan, we need to pack first. Take it back upstairs." Sissy pointed up to the second floor.

Ignoring his aunt's instructions, Evan continued down the stairs. "I already packed."

"What do you mean you already packed?"

"I packed too. Should I go bring my suitcase downstairs?" Eddy asked. Like his brother, he was wearing his pajamas. He now stood next to his aunt, looking up to his little brother.

"Why would you boys do that? You're going to have to get your clothes out of the suitcase in the morning, and now they'll be all wrinkled."

"We have to unpack when we get home anyway," Evan said when he reached the first floor.

"You boys aren't going home tonight." Sissy reached down to take the suitcase from Evan.

"Yes, we are. You said Dad was going to be here pretty soon," Evan protested.

Setting the suitcase back down on the floor, she looked from Evan to Eddy. "Boys, there is no reason for you to go home tonight. You're already in your pajamas. I imagine your father is exhausted and just wants to get home and get some rest."

Eddy shook his head. "No, Dad said he was really excited to see us."

"Of course he is." Sissy reached out and ruffled Eddy's hair, to which he wrinkled his nose in a frown and took a step back away from her.

"I imagine your brother will want to take the boys with him," Bruce said from the archway separating the living room from the entry hall.

"Bruce, really, can't you be on my side for once?"

"I didn't know this was a matter of taking sides." He stepped into the entry. "But come on, Sissy, think about it. The boys have been worried sick about Ed; you really can't blame them for just wanting to go home."

"I-I-I suppose not," Sissy stammered.

Bruce reached out and took the suitcase from his wife. He looked at Eddy and said, "Go ahead and get your suitcase. But when you're upstairs, take another look around, and make sure you didn't forget anything. You too, Evan."

"Okay!" Eddy raced up the stairs. Evan followed him.

"Bruce, really…" Sissy let out a sigh and turned from the stairs, making her way back to the living room.

Bruce set Evan's suitcase near the front door and then joined his wife. "Come on, Sissy, you know I'm right."

"I know you are. And I'm so relieved my brother's okay. But I'm going to miss the boys, and I really did think Ed might enjoy a night of peace. He's been through so much."

"Does this mean you aren't going to be telling him what's gone on this week?"

"I have to tell him. But I hate doing it right when he gets home."

Bruce shrugged. "So don't."

"I'm sure Brian will tell him if I don't. And if he does, then my brother will probably be mad at me for not saying anything."

"True. I'm sure Brian will tell him about Evan breaking into Marlow House. So he's going to find out one way or another."

"Evan needs to apologize to Danielle Boatman," Sissy insisted. "So I suppose I should be the one to tell Ed."

"Is that necessary? I mean really, the poor kid was scared to death about his dad."

"I don't care, it was wrong. And Brian doesn't know about the other thing."

"You mean Evan lying about why he wanted to go to Heather Donovan's?"

"Hello, anyone home?" a voice called out from the hallway. It was Edward MacDonald, who had just walked in the front door.

Sissy immediately stood up, but before she reached the hallway, her nephews were already racing down the stairs. Moments after hitting the first-floor landing, Evan and Eddy flew to their father. Edward dropped to his knees and wrapped his arms around his boys, drawing them to him. From the archway Sissy and Bruce silently watched, while Sissy dabbed tears from the corners of her eyes with a tissue.

The boys were both talking at the same time, asking questions, yet not waiting for answers before asking another one. Sissy ushered the group into the living room and then left to fetch her brother a beer, which he gladly accepted.

"I thought Carol Ann might be with you," Sissy said as the commotion calmed down. Edward sat on the sofa, a beer in hand and a son on either side of him.

"I dropped her off at her house before I came here."

"Did they hurt you, Dad?" Eddy blurted out.

Ed smiled at his oldest son and ruffled his hair. "No, Eddy. They didn't hurt any of us. We were pretty lucky."

"What about Chris?" Evan blurted.

Turning abruptly to Evan, Ed cocked his head slightly and narrowed his eyes. "What about Chris?"

"Umm…I mean…wasn't he hurt?"

"Evan, your father said they didn't hurt any of them. Thank god," Sissy said.

"Well, actually"—Ed glanced from Evan to his sister and back to Evan—"Chris took a bad fall when we first landed in Arizona. He stayed back in Havasu in the hospital. Danielle's with him."

"Is he going to be okay?" Bruce asked.

"He's still unconscious—he has been since he fell. But they ran a battery of tests yesterday, and so far, the results have been encouraging. Danielle's working to get him back to Oregon."

"Dad, have you talked to Danielle much?" Evan asked.

"What kind of question is that?" Sissy asked with a laugh. "Your father has been with Danielle and the rest of them all week. I'm sure they talked a lot."

"Actually, we didn't. They held us in a large building. At first I thought it was a small warehouse, but I guess it was more of a storage building on private property. The kidnappers basically isolated us, so none of us did much talking. At least, not until we were rescued and they took us to the hospital."

"Dad?" Evan asked timidly.

"Yes?"

"After you were rescued, did you and Danielle ever get to talk in private?"

Narrowing his eyes again, he studied his youngest son. "Private? Umm…no, not really."

"Oh, I know what this is about. Evan, your father and Danielle don't know yet. I was hoping not to have to tell him until he had some time to rest."

Ed looked at his sister. "Tell me what?"

"Your son—I know he was upset about you being missing—but he ran away, and he broke into Marlow House."

Widening his eyes in surprise, Ed looked down at Evan.

"He was gone overnight," Sissy told him. "I was worried sick."

Reaching out to Evan, Ed tucked one finger under his son's chin and tilted it upward so that he could look him in the eyes.

"I had to, Dad," Evan whispered. "I knew you were alive."

Leaning briefly to the coffee table, Ed set his beer can down and then wrapped his arms around Evan, giving him a hug. In reply, Evan wrapped his arms around his dad and squeezed tightly.

"I do think he needs to apologize to Danielle Boatman for breaking into her house," Sissy added.

"I'm sure Danielle will understand," Ed said as he kissed the top of Evan's head. "But we'll discuss this with her, won't we, Ev?"

Pulling back from the embrace, Evan looked up into his dad's face and grinned. "Sure, Dad."

Evan settled back on the sofa and Ed reached for his beer and picked it up again.

"While we're clearing the air, there was another incident involving Evan."

"Really?" Ed took a sip of the beer. He didn't sound too concerned.

"We were down at the pier getting ice cream," Sissy began. "Evan asked to go to Heather Donovan's house, alone. He said he was selling her magazines for some fundraiser at school."

Ed cocked his brow. "Fundraiser?"

Sissy nodded. "There was no fundraiser. I spoke to his teacher the next day. I mentioned the fundraiser, and she didn't know what I was talking about. Evan lied. I have no idea why he wanted to go over there. And he refuses to tell me. I called Heather Donovan and asked her why Evan had really gone to her house—that I knew there was no fundraiser, and do you know what she told me?"

Ed shook his head. "I have no idea, what?"

"She said, 'Really? Evan told me he was selling magazines. If he isn't, then I guess that saves me some money. I can't afford them anyway.' And that was that. As if it was the most natural thing in the world for a first grader to try to sell her imaginary magazines."

"Hmm, Heather Donovan?" Ed eyed Evan curiously and took another sip of the beer.

"Edward," Sissy snapped, "you don't seem very upset."

"Well, Sissy, considering the week I've had—no. I'm not particularly upset with Evan."

LATER THAT NIGHT, while tucking Evan into bed, the chief sat on the side of the mattress and looked down at his son.

"Okay, Ev, it's just you and me now. So why don't you tell me what you couldn't tell your aunt."

Evan went on to tell his father about how he had run away and about the time he had spent with Walt, and how the two had plotted to get them home. He told his father about seeing Chris at the pier, and how he served as a go-between for Chris and Heather.

"Are you telling me the police found the plane and then found us because of you?"

"Not just me—Danielle, Heather, Chris, Walt—oh, and Percival."

"Who's Percival?"

"He's a ghost Danielle met. He helped her figure out where you were being kept."

"Danielle never told me that."

"That's why I asked if you've talked to her alone. I wasn't sure you knew. I didn't know all about it until last night."

"What happened last night?"

"Walt visited me in a dream hop to tell me all that had happened. I mean, I knew they found you, but I didn't know everything."

"So if you hadn't lied to your aunt and gone to Heather's and convinced her to go to Marlow House, then we might not have been found?" Ed asked.

"I don't know, Dad. I just know Heather was the one who called Officer Henderson and told him about the plane and then about you all being kept in Havasu."

"You know, Evan, I don't think Heather would have done that if it wasn't for you."

Evan shrugged.

"You're my hero, son. You saved our lives." Once again Edward wrapped his arms around his youngest son and drew him in for a hug. He held him there for a moment, silently counting his blessings.

"You know what, Dad?" Evan asked, still in his dad's embrace.

"What?"

"We can't tell anyone."

Edward smiled. Releasing hold of Evan, he kissed the boy's head and murmured, "Yes, you are definitely my hero."

THIRTY-THREE

"I really don't know why you just don't stay with me and Kelly," Ian said as Lily prepared to unlock the front door of Marlow House. "You're going to be here all alone."

"I told you. I just want to sleep in my own bed. Don't take it personally, but I'm just so happy to be home. And frankly, I was scared to death my parents would come up here anyway, even after I asked them not to. After what we've been through, the last thing I wanted to deal with was my mother hovering. I just need some—space."

"I suppose I understand. Kelly and I promised the folks we'd take a trip out to see them soon. By the way, sorry about not getting you that steak I promised. Tomorrow night?"

"Hey, that take-out burger tasted pretty good. At least it wasn't a freaking granola bar. Anyway, I just wanted to get home tonight. We'll take a rain check on that steak."

Just as Lily pushed open the front door, Sadie charged full speed in their direction, her tail wagging and body trembling. To Ian he saw a dog that was simply happy to see him because he had been gone over a week—what he failed to see was a dog who had been worried much of that time because she was aware of the danger her human was in.

"Wow, some greeting!" Ian laughed with delight as he dropped to the floor and allowed Sadie to trample his body and swipe his face with wet kisses.

"Someone's happy to see you." Lily closed the door. While Ian was distracted with Sadie's enthusiastic greeting, she glanced around the entry hall, wondering where Walt—and maybe Chris—might be standing. She spied Max, who stood by the doorway to the living room. The cat let out a loud meow and then sauntered panther-like to greet her.

Lily reached down and picked up the cat, who was already purring. "I'm glad someone's happy to see me." In the next moment Sadie shifted her attention from Ian to Lily. Lily found herself standing in the center of the entry hall, struggling to keep hold of Max while Sadie enthusiastically leapt up to give Lily equal time. Max nonchalantly batted the golden retriever's nose each time it bounced by his face.

A few minutes later Lily suspected Walt had given Sadie the command to simmer down, because the dog was no longer ricocheting around the room like someone had just spiked her kibble with uppers, but sat politely in front of Lily, her tail still wagging and her tongue hanging out the side of her mouth as if exhausted and trying to catch her breath.

Ian lingered for another twenty minutes or so, and when he did leave, he took Sadie with him. Lily stood by the window next to the front door, holding the curtain to one side, and watched as Ian and Sadie made their way down the walkway to the street. When they were out of sight, she dropped the curtain and turned to face the seemingly empty entry hall. Even Max was no longer in sight, as he had wandered off to the kitchen to nibble on his food.

"Walt? Chris? Are you guys in here?" Lily asked.

Her purse, which she had set on the small hall table, lifted into the air and then dropped to the floor, scattering its contents on the wood floor.

"Well, *that* was rude," Lily said with a chuckle. "I know you hate when we set things on your grandmother's table. But really, Walt?" She flashed the space where she imagined Walt stood a smile and then went to pick up her purse and scoop its contents back inside it. Instead of placing it back on the table, she hung it on the coat rack.

"Is Chris here? From what Dani tells me, he's like I was, and doesn't have any energy left to harness."

Motion from the corner of her eye caught her attention.

Turning to the doorway leading to the parlor, she spied a notepad floating in her direction. Just as she reached out for it, it started to fall, as if it had suddenly been released. Lily managed to grab it before it fell all the way to the floor. She looked at the pad. Writing was scribbled over the top sheet.

Call Heather. We need to talk.

Still clutching the notepad, Lily looked up and asked with a frown, "Heather? Seriously? I have to do that?"

In response her purse began to swing back and forth on the coat rack.

Lily let out a sigh. "I suppose I will take that as a yes."

LILY THOUGHT Heather looked like a Dr. Seuss character when she walked through the front door fifteen minutes later. It wasn't just her blaringly bright colored pajamas in dramatic shades of hot pink, lime green, and purple, but the way she had fashioned her high-placed pigtails into makeshift buns. Spikes of black hair randomly stuck out of each bun. She'd thrown on an overcoat for her walk over, yet removed it the moment she walked inside, and hung it with Lily's purse on the coat rack. She hadn't bothered to put on regular shoes, but instead wore fuzzy slippers.

What Lily hadn't expected was Heather's exuberant hug. One minute, Heather was marching into Marlow House in a no-nonsense manner, hanging up her coat, and the next she was suffocating Lily in a vibrant viselike bear hug while shaking the kidnap survivor from side to side, muttering, "I'm so glad you're safe!"

It was in that moment Lily felt like a total jerk. Heather might very well have saved all of their lives. At the very least, she had shortened their time in that gawd-awful wannabee warehouse. With a sigh, Lily returned the hug.

"ENOUGH ALREADY," Walt said impatiently as he stood a few feet from the embracing neighbors. "We want to know what's going on. And please tell Lily I'm glad she's home."

Heather released Lily and said with a snort, "I guess Walt is getting impatient." She turned to Walt. "Hello to you too. Is Chris here?"

"Yes. He's standing over there." Walt pointed down the hall.

Heather turned in that direction. "Hello, Chris, wherever you are."

"You can't see Chris? Just Walt?" Lily asked.

Heather shrugged. "I've seen flashes of him, even heard his voice a couple times. But nothing tangible where I can communicate with him. But Walt here," Heather said as she pointed in Walt's direction. "I can see and hear him as clearly as I see you. By the way, he wanted me to tell you he's glad you're home."

"And I'm glad to be here! Let's go in the living room. We can talk there," Lily suggested.

When they were seated in the living room a few minutes later, Heather said, "If Joanne asks if Dani gave me a house key and told me I could borrow the Wi-Fi here, please tell her yes."

"Dani told me about that," Lily said with a chuckle. "No problem."

"How did Danielle know?" Heather asked, glancing from Lily to Walt.

"Lines of communication have been open—so to speak—via dream hops with Walt. But I understand theirs was cut short last night. Hospitals are not the best place to get an uninterrupted night's rest, which is why I imagine Walt is impatient to hear what's going on."

Chris then asked a question, which Walt conveyed to Heather, which Heather repeated to Lily. "Chris wants to know about his body..." Heather paused a moment and shivered. "That sounds so...so...*creepy*."

"From what I understand, they gave him a crap load of tests last night, and so far, they haven't found anything significantly wrong with him. Fact is, they aren't really sure why he hasn't woken up," Lily explained.

"I can tell you why he hasn't woken up yet," Walt scoffed.

Heather glanced at Walt. "Why is that?"

Lily withheld her question and looked from Heather to where she imagined Walt sat.

"Isn't it obvious? He's here," Walt explained. "You can't have one's spirit just wander off from his body and expect him to suddenly wake up. Look at Lily." At Walt's suggestion, both Chris and Heather turned to Lily and stared. "If she'd stayed with her body instead of coming back here, maybe she would have woken up sooner."

Frowning at the way Heather was now staring at her, Lily asked, "What?"

"Basically, Walt thinks one reason Chris is still in a coma is because he's here—hundreds of miles from his body. He mentioned your out-of-body experience—"

"How did you know about that? I don't recall discussing it with you," Lily asked.

Heather smiled. "I've learned lots of things since you've been gone. But forget about all that..." Heather waved her hand dismissively and turned to where she believed Chris stood. "Maybe you should try going to Havasu."

"Chris is over there," Walt interrupted, pointing to the opposite side of the room.

Heather abruptly turned in Chris's direction. "It would be nice if you'd stay put!"

"I thought she just said I need to go to Arizona?" Chris asked lazily.

Walt chuckled.

"I think Dani wants to get Chris back to Oregon, to do just that—get his spirit back in his body. But maybe if Chris went there, it would speed things up," Lily suggested.

"No." Walt shook his head. "Not unless Chris isn't concerned about getting lost along the way. I suspect if he was never in Havasu when he was alive—and with his body—it'll be difficult to find his way. He could end up wandering indefinitely until his body gives out."

"Walt, you actually sound as if you care about me." Chris grinned.

"What I care about is Danielle spending endless time at your bedside while your spirit rambles aimlessly around the countryside."

"Oh..." Heather shrugged and turned again to Lily. "I guess Chris going to Havasu isn't a good idea. Something about him possibly getting lost and wandering around aimlessly. Walt seems to think the reason for your out-of-body experience was the fact your spirit wandered off when unconscious. He thinks it might not have lasted so long if you had stuck around your body."

"Actually, I've thought about that myself," Lily told her. "My theory, the reason I wandered off is that my spirit—or soul—whatever you want to call it—stepped out of my body after the attack, and I was afraid, so I fled to what my subconscious considered a safe place. I ended up here."

"Why did Chris wander off?" Heather asked.

"I suspect he was going for help in the only way he knew how," Lily said.

Chris looked at Walt and groaned. "Is she implying I felt compelled to come to you for help?"

Walt smiled. "Looks like it."

Lily spent the next forty minutes telling Heather about their ordeal and filling in the blanks for Walt and Chris. After she was finished, the subject shifted to the kidnappers—and where they might be now.

"Do the police have any idea who's behind this?" Heather asked.

Lily shook her head. "If they do, they haven't said anything to us. Danielle does know the first name of one of the kidnappers. Percival told her. But she didn't say anything to the police when they picked us up—it would be too hard to explain how she knew to Ian, Joe, Kelly, and Carol Ann. After all, we were together the entire time. But she'll be telling the chief when they can talk privately."

THIRTY-FOUR

Andy answered the phone; it was Sky. "Did you get back to Washington okay?" she asked.

"Finally. Next time remind me how much I hate public transit."

"At least we were able to sell the car in California."

"We?" Sky laughed. "Yeah, and for half of what we paid for the damn thing. But at least there's no way they're going to trace it back to us. It's probably in Mexico already, in parts."

"At least that's something."

"Stop trying to look on the bright side, Andy. Do you know how much this *adventure* cost us?"

"I told you it was risky."

"It wouldn't have been so risky if Clay had done his damn job."

"I never felt right about this anyway," she confessed.

"It's not over, kid."

"What do you mean?"

"Have you heard anything on Glandon? Has he come to, now that he's at the hospital?"

"It was on the news this morning. He and Danielle are still in Havasu. He's still in a coma. But from what I heard, the doctors really don't understand why."

"As soon as he wakes up, we'll try again."

"Exactly how do you expect to do that?" Andy asked. "Sky, this thing just blew up in our faces. We're lucky we're not sitting in jail right now, and if he happens to die, then we're really screwed if they figure out our identities."

"Then let's hope he's not going to die. Anyway, we need him so we can get that money."

"Do you expect him to charter another plane in the near future? Or do you plan to take him again when he flies home from Havasu?" Andy snapped.

"Our plan was too elaborate. I know that now. We should have just taken him in Frederickport."

"And exactly how would that work?" she asked.

"Nothing more than a home invasion, really. Use his own Internet to make the transfer. Like I said, our other plan was too elaborate before."

"No, Sky. Please. You can't do this."

"Listen, I didn't spend over a year working on this program for nothing. I know it's going to work, but I also know that after I use it, the banks are going to swoop in and fill in the hole. This is a onetime shot, and you know it."

"So how do we convince him to go along with us?"

"Remember how accommodating he and the rest were when we threatened to smack around that sweet innocent girlfriend of the police chief's?"

"What are you suggesting?"

"Take Glandon, along with the people closest to him, and then see how he feels about us mishandling one of them. I imagine just threatening will do the trick."

"And if it doesn't?"

"Then he isn't such a good friend after all, is he?"

"How do you intend to get away? That's one thing I especially liked about the first plan. No one had any idea where we were—and by the time the cops showed up the hostages would be safe and sound, with no sign of the kidnappers."

"Let me work out the getaway plan. You just pay attention to any news on Glandon. I'm not walking away from this ten thousand in the hole."

"WAS THAT ANDY?" Clay asked when he walked into the room and saw Sky hanging up the phone.

"Yeah. I just told her what we were talking about this morning."

"And? Is she going to fight us on this?"

Sky shrugged. "She isn't thrilled, but she'll do what I want. She always has."

Clay plopped down on the worn recliner and looked over at Sky, who now lounged on the couch, a beer in hand.

"Isn't it a little early for beer?" Clay chuckled.

"It's noon somewhere." Sky chugged the beer.

"You didn't tell her about our getaway plan, did you?"

"Why do you say that?" Sky smirked and drank more beer.

"Because I don't think she'd go along with it. I don't see Andy sitting back while you pump bullets into Glandon and Boatman."

Sky shrugged. "What's she gunna do about it? It'll be over before she can stop me."

WHEN THE CHIEF went into the station on Thursday morning, he was immediately besieged by his staff, who were thrilled to have him back. The happiest of the crew was Brian Henderson, who gratefully returned the mantle of power to his boss.

"You look like hell, Brian," the chief said with a laugh as he patted him on the back and followed Brian into his office. He found the office neat and tidy, with no stacks of paper littering his desk. What he didn't know, Brian had spent the previous evening getting the office back in shape.

"I haven't had a day off since you left. The next time you decide to take a vacation—don't. Or at least, don't take Joe with you." Brian sat down on a chair and watched as his boss slipped off his coat and hung it on a rack before taking the seat behind the desk.

"I imagine Joe would agree with you. I don't think either of us want to go anywhere for a very long time."

"I spoke to Joe a few minutes ago; he said he was going to be in a little late coming in this morning," Brian added.

"Yeah, I told him yesterday not to rush back today. It was a hellish week." The chief then went on to tell Brian more about their ordeal, beginning with the unexpected change of pilots.

"I wonder what would have happened had Glandon not hit his head," Brian asked.

"No idea. Not sure how the kidnappers thought they were going to get ahold of fifty million dollars while hiding out in Lake Havasu. But they must have had some plan."

"You might be glad you decided to come in today and not rest up at home." Brian leaned forward in the chair. "I got a call this morning; they finally tracked down the original pilot's girlfriend—or at least the woman he dated for a time and bragged to about Glandon hiring him." When talking to the chief on the phone after the rescue, he had told him about the woman they were trying to find.

"Where is she?"

"She's back in Frederickport. I sent someone over to bring her in."

"And Thomas and Wilson?" the chief asked.

"I just spoke to them. They're already in town and will be here in about five minutes."

ANDREA BANNER SHIFTED NERVOUSLY in the chair. She glanced around the small room and noticed the mirror on the wall across from her. Near it was a clock. It was almost noon. The door opened and in walked a man wearing a suit. He carried a manila folder.

"Miss Banner," the man greeted her. He closed the door behind him and approached the table where she sat. "I'm Special Agent Wilson from the FBI. Thank you for coming in today."

"FBI?" She sat up straight in the chair and watched as he took a seat across from her. "Why am I here?"

"We have a few questions for you." Wilson opened the file and glanced through it. He then looked up and smiled. "Do you know Mason Murdock?"

Andrea frowned. "Mason? Sure. We used to date."

"Used to? You aren't seeing him anymore?"

"The last time we went out was over a month ago," she explained. "It was never a serious thing. We only went out a few times."

"Have you seen him within the last month?" he asked.

She shrugged. "Yeah. I ran into him in the grocery store. What's this about? Has something happened to Mason?"

"Mason is fine—now. So tell me, do you remember him telling you about a new client? Chris Glandon?"

"Sure." She shrugged again. "I think he was trying to impress me. So what's this about?"

"Are you saying you don't know about Murdock's plane being hijacked?"

"Hijacked? Is he alright?"

"Yes, he is, fortunately. Are you telling me you had no idea about the hijacking and kidnapping? The story has been all over the news."

"I don't really watch the news."

"You don't listen to the radio in your car?" he asked.

"I listen to music. I don't like listening to the news; it's depressing."

"Where have you been this past week?"

"With a friend."

"That's who you were with—I asked where you were."

"You don't seriously think I had something to do with Mason getting hijacked, do you? I mean seriously, what would be the motive?"

"Fifty million."

Andrea's eyes widened, and she grew still. Licking her lips nervously, she asked, "Did Mason say I had something to do with it? I mean, I know he was kind of annoyed that I didn't want to go out with him again."

"No. According to Mason, he didn't think you had anything to do with the hijacking."

Andrea released the breath she had unwittingly been holding. "Then why am I here?"

"Just because Mason thinks you're innocent doesn't mean I do."

Expressionless, she asked, "What do you want?"

"You can begin by telling me where you were this last week."

"I went to Vegas with a friend."

"Who was this friend?"

"Just a guy I know."

"How did you get there? Your car's been in your driveway all week."

"He picked me up."

"But you came back on a bus; why is that?"

Andrea pulled her brow into a frown. "How do you know that?"

Wilson smiled. "We just do. So tell me where you were staying in Vegas."

Andrea shrugged. "Some apartment. The guy I went with has a friend in Vegas who let us use his apartment."

"Where was this apartment? Who can verify you were there?"

"I don't know," she snapped. "I don't even know where the apartment is."

"How is it you stayed in Vegas but don't know where?"

She slumped down in the chair. "I never pay attention when I'm not driving. I don't know my way around in Vegas. My friend picked me up, and when we got to Vegas, we went to his friend's place. I don't know where it was."

"How long did it take to drive to Vegas? It's pretty far from here. Kind of a long drive. So tell me, how many hours was the trip?"

Andrea frowned. "I don't know, I fell asleep after a couple hours, and when I woke up, we were there."

"What's the name of this friend of yours so we can talk to him."

"His name is Bob, but he doesn't live in Frederickport, and I don't know how to contact him. We sort of had a fight in Vegas, which is why I took the bus home."

"His last name?"

Andrea refused to answer immediately; instead she stubbornly crossed her arms over her chest and stared blankly ahead.

"His last name?" he asked again.

"I don't know. He told me it was Collins, but I found out that was a lie when we were in Vegas. He was married. Okay, are you happy now?" she snapped angrily.

"Okay, let's forget Bob for a moment. Do you know Herman Shafer?"

Andrea swallowed nervously. "Herman?"

"Yes, Herman Shafer. Do you know him?"

"Well, yeah…I guess…"

"You guess?"

"Herman is my uncle."

THIRTY-FIVE

Brian greeted Joe with a bear hug when he arrived at work later that day. "It's about time you showed up to work, you slacker!" After a few additional backslaps, Joe and Brian each took a chair facing the chief, who sat behind his desk. The conversation quickly shifted to the recent interview with Andrea Banner, which both Brian and the chief had observed from behind the mirror, along with Special Agent Thomas.

"We know she arrived back in Frederickport this morning. She drove in from Barstow," Brian told Joe.

"I thought she said she came in from Vegas?" Joe asked.

Brian leaned back in the chair. "She claims she got in a fight with this Bob character and got on the first bus she could find and ended up in Barstow. She had the ticket stubs to prove she came from Barstow, but she claimed she threw away her ticket stubs from Vegas. She paid cash for the tickets."

"I suppose they can check with the bus station in Vegas and see what they have," Joe suggested.

"I imagine they will. But getting home via Barstow is not exactly a straight shot. She headed south before going north," the chief said. "And if she was one of our kidnappers, it's possible she got to Barstow from Havasu in time to catch that bus."

"Banner admitted knowing about her uncle's properties. She

didn't hide the fact she'd visited the Havasu property a couple times when her cousin was alive," Brian told Joe.

"If her uncle knew that she'd visited the property, then denying it wouldn't be very smart at this point," the chief said. "I know Shafer, and if his niece is involved, I don't believe he was."

"The FBI isn't holding Banner?" Joe asked.

"No. They let her go, but I think they're still looking at her," Brian said. "Do you know if one of the kidnappers was a woman?"

"We only saw two of them; both were men," Joe said. "But Carol Ann said there were at least four of them."

"The chief mentioned they always wore masks when you saw them," Brian noted.

"Yes. Except in the beginning. We saw the pilot, but he was basically in disguise, hiding behind a beard, glasses and dyed hair."

"You said the two you saw were men, what about the other two Carol Ann saw?" Brian asked.

"According to Carol Ann, she didn't get a good look at them. They were wearing masks, and she said she couldn't really tell if they were men or women," the chief explained.

Brian's cellphone began to ring. He stood up and pulled it from his pocket. When he ended the call a few minutes later, he looked at the chief and said, "That was Agent Thomas. Something has come up, and he wants me to meet them at Lucy's Diner."

"Do you know what?" the chief asked.

Brian shook his head and put the cellphone back in his pocket. "He didn't say."

WHEN BRIAN WALKED into Lucy's Diner fifteen minutes later, he found Agents Thomas and Wilson sitting in a booth.

"Thanks for coming over," Thomas said as he scooted over on the bench seat to make room for Brian.

"What's going on?" Brian sat down.

"We found out where that call came from giving you the tip about where to find the hostages," Wilson explained.

"And?"

"Marlow House," Thomas said.

"Marlow House?" Brian frowned.

"Yes. According to the phone records, the landline at Marlow

House placed two phone calls during the time Danielle Boatman was being held hostage. The first was when Chief MacDonald's son called his aunt, and the second was the call to you, telling you they were being held somewhere in Havasu," Thomas explained.

"I don't get it. Who could have called?" Brian asked.

"That's why we wanted to talk to you first. What do you know about Joanne Johnson?"

"Joanne? She's Danielle's housekeeper. I've known her for years. She used to work for Danielle's aunt."

"I didn't think Danielle's aunt ever lived there," Thomas noted.

"No, she didn't. But she paid Joanne to clean the house once a week, and when Danielle inherited it, she hired Joanne to stay on," Brian told him.

"We need to talk to Joanne, and we'd like you to go over there with us."

AN HOUR later Brian Henderson sat in Joanne Johnson's living room with the two FBI agents.

"I was so relieved when I heard they'd been found," Joanne told the men as she took a seat on the sofa. "I understand the kidnappers are still on the loose. I assume that's why you're here to see if I know anything that might help."

"Were you over at Marlow House on Tuesday?" Agent Thomas asked.

"Tuesday? Why yes. I went over to Marlow House every day since Danielle and Lily have been gone. Twice a day at least." Joanne sat primly on the sofa, looking curiously from Agent Thomas to Wilson.

"Did you use the phone at Marlow House on Tuesday?" Thomas asked.

Joanne frowned. "Do you mean the landline?"

"Yes."

She shook her head. "No, I had no reason to. I have my own cellphone. But I don't remember using even that when I was over there on Tuesday." She looked directly at Agent Thomas. "What is this about?"

"Someone used the phone at Marlow House on Tuesday,"

Agent Wilson said. He then went on to tell her the exact time the call had been placed.

Joanne arched her brows. "That is interesting. I wasn't there at that time. I was sitting in my dentist's chair, getting a root canal. You can ask him if you want."

"Do you know who might have access to Marlow House?" Wilson asked.

"Danielle routinely changes the lock on the front door—because guests get a door key, and even if they return their key, there's no guarantee they haven't made a copy. I know she changed the locks after our last guests, and Marlow House has been closed for weeks because Danielle had a new heating and air-conditioning unit put in."

"So you can't think of anyone else who might have a key to the house?" Thomas asked.

"I assume you mean someone who wasn't with Danielle. Because of course Lily has a key, as do Ian and Chris. But aside from them, I believe Marie Nichols might have a key. But I'm not sure. I don't think Danielle gave one to Adam."

"No one else?" Thomas asked again.

Joanne started to say something and then paused. Tapping her index finger against her chin, she stared into blank space for a moment and then looked at Thomas. "I almost forgot. Heather Donovan has a key." Joanne shook her head. "To be honest, I was quite surprised Danielle gave her one. I questioned Lily about it when I talked to her on the phone earlier, and she confirmed what Heather had told me."

"Which was what?" Wilson asked.

"Apparently Danielle gave Heather a house key before she left, and told her she could use her Internet if she needed to—something about Heather's router not working correctly. I went over there the other day to feed the animals and was quite surprised to find Heather sitting in the library."

"What was she doing?" Wilson asked.

"Using her computer." Joanne shrugged. "She was using the Internet, just like she said Danielle told her she could."

"Why were you surprised Danielle would give her a key?" Wilson asked.

"I don't think they're all that close. Although, Heather did stay at Marlow House for a time when she was having some work done at her house. She just lives down the street. But now that I think about it, Danielle gave her a deal, because she was having some money issues, so I suppose it makes sense she offered Heather the use of the Internet while she was gone. I was just surprised Danielle forgot to tell me."

"Money problems?" Wilson asked. "What kind of money problems?"

Brian spoke up. "Heather inherited Presley House—it was located a couple blocks away from Marlow House. It burned down this past Halloween. Afterwards, Heather discovered she didn't actually own it anymore."

"How is that?" Thomas asked.

"Apparently her mother failed to pay the property tax," Brian said.

"Oh, that's right!" Joanne said. "Earthbound Spirits got their hands on it. She was kind of bitter about it. And then there was that thing with the emerald..."

HEATHER SAT in the Frederickport Police Department's interrogation room, staring across the table at Special Agent Wilson.

"No. I did not use the phone at Marlow House. Why would I? I have a cellphone. Anyway, I didn't go over there on Tuesday."

"According to Joanne Johnson, you have a key to Marlow House, and she found you there when she went to feed the animals."

Heather shrugged. "Yeah, so? Danielle said I could use her Internet. Ask her. And I'm sure Joanne will tell you that's what I was doing when she saw me there—using the Internet. But I didn't go there on Tuesday, and I certainly didn't use the phone."

Narrowing his eyes, Wilson glared at Heather. "Ms. Donovan, someone called the Frederickport Police Station from Marlow House and told Officer Henderson where they would find Danielle Boatman and the others."

Heather arched her brows and smiled. "Really?"

"Whoever made that call knows something that can help us find the people responsible for hijacking that plane and kidnapping your friends. While the caller did the right thing by coming forward with the information, they can't keep protecting the kidnappers. These are very dangerous people."

"And you think I made that call?" Heather asked innocently.

"I understand you've been having money issues."

"So? A lot of people have money issues."

"Perhaps, but you've had rather a bad string of luck lately, haven't you? You lived at Marlow House when Chris Johnson did, you probably figured out who he really was, maybe started resenting the fact he had far more money than he needed, and here you were, trying over and over again to do the right thing, but getting deeper in debt. Somehow you hooked up with the wrong people, got involved with the hijacking scheme, but when Chris got hurt, you realized you couldn't go through with it, so you made those phone calls. Come clean, Heather, and help us put these guys away, and I'll see what I can do to go easier on you."

"Interesting scenario, but total fantasy. I had zip to do with the kidnapping."

"No one else has a key to the house but you and the housekeeper, and she has an alibi for the time the call was placed."

Heather let out a sigh and leaned back in the chair, her gaze meeting Wilson's. "I didn't make the call. But…strange things happen at Marlow House."

"Strange?" Wilson frowned.

Heather leaned forward, her expression serious, and she said in a whisper, "Some say Marlow House is haunted."

"Haunted?"

"I think it's the ghost of Walt Marlow. He was murdered in that very house—they found his body hanging in the attic." Heather dramatically shivered and then added, "So gruesome."

"Are you trying to tell me a ghost called the police station?" Wilson asked indignantly.

Heather shrugged. "I have no idea who made that call. But I'm just telling you what I've heard about that house."

THE CHIEF SAT SILENTLY behind his desk and listened to Special Agent Wilson vent about his recent interview with Heather Donovan. Also in his office were Agent Thomas and Officer Henderson.

"Fact of the matter, anyone could have made that call," Brian said. "If that golden retriever can get through the doggy door, who's to say a small adult can't? We know a child can."

"I can't see just anyone going through that doggy door," Wilson said with a snort. "That's a good-size dog on the other side. I'd say whoever made the call was familiar with the golden retriever."

The chief chuckled. "Goldens aren't known for their killer instincts, and I imagine whoever made that call could have easily won her over while in the backyard by giving her a few dog treats."

"Perhaps. But I didn't appreciate all that nonsense about ghosts," Wilson snapped.

"In all fairness to Heather," the chief added, "she doesn't think it's nonsense. Heather does believe in ghosts."

WILSON CLIMBED into the driver's seat of the dark sedan and angrily slammed the door shut. "Someone made that damn call."

"You know what I kept thinking when I was listening to her?" Thomas asked as he leaned back in the passenger seat. He had been with the chief in the office next to the interrogation room, listening to the interview.

Wilson slipped the key into the ignition, yet he didn't turn the car on. "What?"

Thomas turned in his seat and looked at his partner. "I kept thinking of the times we've been to Marlow House."

Wilson stared at Thomas. After a moment of silence, he said, "Yeah, that's what I was thinking too. But I absolutely refuse to believe in ghosts."

"Something happened in that house when we were there, and you know it. We never talk about it, but we both felt it."

THIRTY-SIX

"We need to send him to Vegas," the doctor told Danielle that evening. He stood with her near the doorway to Chris's hospital room.

"No. I told you I want to take him with me back to Oregon," she insisted.

The doctor glanced over to the bed where Chris lay unconscious, showing minimal signs of life. "And I told you, Ms. Boatman, your hospital there is not equipped to handle Mr. Glandon. I know you have Mr. Glandon's power of attorney, but I'm willing to fight you on this. I sincerely don't believe moving him to Oregon at this time is in his best interests."

Danielle looked over to Chris and then back to the doctor. "What if he was conscious?"

"That, Ms. Boatman, is the problem. He's not conscious."

"But if he was, would he be able to return to Oregon?"

"Obviously, if that's what he wanted. But I don't really see your point," he said impatiently.

Looking back to Chris, she studied him a moment. Finally, she turned to the doctor and asked, "When are you planning to move him?"

"If you cooperate and I don't have to fight you on this, I was hoping to have him moved tomorrow afternoon."

"HOW'S CHRIS DOING?" Lily asked when she answered Danielle's phone call thirty minutes later.

"The doctor wants to send Chris to Vegas," Danielle said. "And honestly, I don't know how I can argue with him about this. They're better equipped to handle him in Vegas than our little hospital in Frederickport, and I understand why the doctor believes I'm being utterly irresponsible insisting I send Chris to a small Oregon hospital."

Lily responded with a loud snort.

"What was that about?" Danielle asked.

"I was remembering how Stoddard insisted they send me to Oregon when I was in a coma."

"We all know Stoddard didn't care what was best for you. But I do want to make the right decision for Chris."

"So how does he get back to his body if he's here and the rest of him is in Vegas?" Lily asked.

"Tell him to try!" Danielle said impatiently. "He certainly is not going to do it if he's hanging around there."

"I don't think it's that easy. We talked about it last night. Walt doesn't think Chris can just will himself to Havasu since he has never been there when he was alive. He might be wrong, but if Chris tries and Walt is right, that means Chris's spirit could end up wandering aimlessly until his body dies."

"That's *chilling*. Did Walt tell you that in a dream hop?"

"No. Remember, Heather came over and played interpreter." Lily had talked to Danielle briefly when she had arrived back in Marlow House, but their conversation was cut short when Danielle was interrupted by a nurse coming into Chris's hospital room.

"Then you bring him here," Danielle suggested. "And if he's not able to connect while he's still in Havasu, then he can follow his body to Vegas. That way he has a much better chance of getting back to normal."

"What do you mean bring him there?"

"Get the next flight back to Vegas. When I was checking flights, the best one is under five hours from Portland. In Vegas, you can rent a car and drive to Havasu; there's no direct flights from Vegas to Havasu and no bus service. Depending on the flight, you should be able to make it in about twelve hours. I know that's pushing it, but even if it still took a couple extra hours, you'd get here before Chris has to leave for Vegas."

"You want me to *escort* his spirit there?"

Danielle, who held the phone to her ear, nodded. "Yes."

"You do understand that I can't see or hear Chris, don't you? I'm no more sensitive to his type of spirit than I am Walt. In fact, Heather can't see him—only glimpses. So maybe you can't either."

"I'll be able to see him," Danielle insisted. "I saw you."

"You do know it'll be like I'm traveling with my imaginary friend," Lily told her.

"I know. But you can do this."

Lily let out a sigh. "Okay. I'll need to come up with a good story for Ian. After all, I haven't even been back twenty-four hours."

"Thanks, Lily."

LILY STOOD at the kitchen table, where she had just placed a pad of paper and pen. At the top of her voice she said, "Walt, are you in this room?"

The pen floated up from the table and then dropped back down. After it hit the table, it rolled off and onto the floor. Lily leaned down and picked up the pen, setting it back on the table.

"I will take that as a yes. Is Chris with you?"

Again the pen floated up, but instead of suddenly dropping down to the table, it wrote *yes* across the paper before settling gently back down on the tabletop.

"Good," Lily said matter-of-factly, taking a seat at the table. "Here's the thing…" She went on to recount her phone conversation with Danielle. When she was done, she said, "Okay, Chris, are you ready for a little trip?"

The paper with the "yes" written across it lifted up into the air and then floated back down onto the table.

Lily stood up. "Good. Now I need to check flights, make my reservation, and then come up with a good story to tell Ian."

"SHE'S GOING BACK to Havasu? But we just got back from there," Kelly said when Ian got off the phone with Lily.

"Danielle needs her. I guess the doctor doesn't want to send Chris back here, which doesn't surprise me. At least, not in his current state. Lily doesn't want Danielle to be alone."

Kelly shrugged. "I guess I understand, but why didn't Lily just stay in Havasu?"

"I don't know, Kelly. All of us were just so anxious to get home, we didn't think about how it was going to be for Danielle there all alone."

"Are you going with her?"

Ian stood up and glanced at his watch. "No. she wants me to stay here, since I have Sadie. Plus, she wants me to keep an eye on Marlow House and Chris's place."

"Does she need a ride to the Portland airport?" Kelly asked. "I was going to head home anyway. I could drop her off."

LILY FELT as if she were traveling with the Invisible Man. Although, from what she recalled of the Invisible Man, he was able to do Walt-like tricks, such as move objects, while Chris seemed unable to make his presence known. She just hoped he was still with her. It would be very embarrassing to learn she had misplaced him along the way, and the times in which she whispered to him—such as when she was about to go into the ladies' room and asked him to wait by the door—that she had actually been talking to herself. But then she remembered being embarrassed was the least of her worries if Chris wandered off and got lost en route to Havasu.

Getting to her ultimate destination took longer than Danielle's estimate. Lily rolled into the parking lot of Lake Havasu City's hospital a few minutes before 9:00 a.m. She was exhausted, having been up all night, and to keep awake she talked nonstop from the time she picked up the rental car in Vegas to when she parked her car in front of the hospital. It was a one-way conversation—or at least that was what she assumed. Lily never heard the times Chris shouted, "Please stop talking, or I am going to jump out of the car right now! I can do it, you know!"

DANIELLE SAT in the chair by Chris's bedside, looking at the inexpensive flip phone she had purchased at K-Mart. According to the instructions, she could send text messages. She was tempted to give it a try and send Lily a question, asking when she would be arriving. But then, she remembered that would not be such a terrific idea. The last thing they needed right now was for Lily to look at a text message and get in a car accident.

She was just setting her phone on the nightstand when Chris walked into the room, followed by Lily.

Jumping up from the chair, she cried, "Chris, you're here!"

Lily smiled. "I guess that means he made the trip."

"I almost didn't," Chris said with a grin.

"I'd love to give you a hug, Chris, but I'll hug Lily instead," Danielle said with a laugh as she threw her arms around Lily and gave her a quick welcome hug.

"Why do I feel like second choice?" Lily chuckled, accepting the hug. "Oh, I know why, because I am."

Danielle flashed Lily a giddy grin. She looked at Chris. "I've been so worried about you."

"*Oh, and thank you, Lily, for coming all the way back to Havasu. I bet you didn't get any sleep, you poor dear*," Lily muttered under her breath as she wandered over to an empty chair and sat down. She yawned.

Danielle turned to her roommate. "Lily, you have to know how grateful I am you brought him!"

Lily waved her hand dismissively and yawned. "I know. I was only pulling your chain." Lily yawned again.

Danielle turned back to Chris. "The doctor says they'll be transporting you to some hospital in Las Vegas." She glanced at her watch. "He said it would probably be right after lunch. But if you can get back in your body and wake up, then you can tell them you just want to go back to Oregon. According to the doctor, there's nothing wrong with your body. You had a concussion, but according to all the tests, there's nothing physically wrong with you."

Chris walked over to his body and looked down at it.

"We know why he hasn't gone into his body," Lily called out from the chair. "The same reason I stayed out of mine. Hard to reconnect when you're not in the same room." She yawned again.

"If there's nothing physically wrong with me, why do I have a bandage on my head?"

"You took a nasty fall," Danielle reminded him. "I guess you gashed your head open pretty bad. Carol Ann had to stitch it up. It'll probably leave a scar."

"No big deal," Lily said from her chair. "Chris was too pretty anyway."

Danielle couldn't help it, she chuckled.

"Good, you're here," a nurse said when she entered the hospital room. "She glanced over to Lily. "Oh, you have company?"

"This is my friend Lily. She came to be with me while Chris is transported to Las Vegas," Danielle explained.

"That's what I'm here for. They're going to arrive a little early to take him."

"How early?" Danielle asked.

"I'm here to get him ready," the nurse explained.

"Noooooo," came a groan from the hospital bed. A monitor blared.

Rushing to the bedside, the nurse began checking Chris's vitals while asking him questions. The monitor still blaring, Chris grabbed hold of the nurse's forearm and held it tightly, forcing her to look him in the eyes.

"I am not going to Las Vegas," Chris said in a raspy voice. "I am going home, to Frederickport."

THIRTY-SEVEN

"I guess he's not going to Vegas," the doctor said after he finished examining Chris. Danielle stood by his side while Lily remained in the chair, trying desperately to keep her eyes open.

Chris, who was sitting up, leaning against the elevated end of the hospital bed, asked, "When can I go back to Oregon, Doc?"

"I don't see any reason why we can't release you in the morning."

"Not today?" Chris asked.

The doctor laughed. "I'm glad to see you're anxious to get moving. But let's take this one step at a time. And when you get back home, I expect you to see your own doctor immediately."

"I promise." Chris grinned.

After the doctor left the room, Lily asked with a yawn, "What now?"

"I'll call the same charter service we used to get you guys home the other day. That way we can avoid the drive back to Vegas, and we don't have to fly into Portland. Plus, it will be easier for Chris."

"What about the rental car?" Lily asked.

"I'm sure they have a franchise here we can leave it at. We'll probably have to pay a little extra. But that's okay."

"Yeah, yeah, spending more of my money. Typical woman," Chris teased.

Danielle met Chris's comment with a grin.

"I'm exhausted," Lily groaned.

"I tell you what, why don't I drop you off at the motel room, and you can take a nap," Danielle suggested.

"If you want to stay here to visit with Chris, I can drive myself and come back later and pick you up," Lily suggested.

Danielle shook her head. "No. There's somewhere I want to go before we leave tomorrow."

"Where?" Chris asked.

"I want to go down to the London Bridge, see if I can find Percival. He left pretty suddenly when we were rescued, and I never was able to ask him all the questions I wanted to."

DANIELLE STOOD in front of the formal entrance to the English Village—a lacy wrought-iron fence with an arched gateway, its doors propped open and welcoming. Just inside the entrance was the fountain, water spilling down from its centerpiece. Beyond the fountain was the historic London Bridge, which arched over the manmade channel separating the mainland from what was now an island, yet had once been a peninsula known as Pittsburgh Point.

After leaving Chris alone at the hospital and dropping Lily off at the motel, Danielle had come down to the bridge site and parked the rental car in the lot just outside the English Village. After entering the gateway, she passed by the fountain and made her way toward the bridge. To her right she noticed a tourist information center housed in what appeared to be some old pub of sorts. But she was not interested in learning more about the local attractions, nor was she interested in visiting any of the gift shops or restaurants up ahead. Danielle had just one thing on her mind, find Percival if possible.

Just minutes after arriving at the English Village, Danielle stood on the concrete walkway under one arch of the London Bridge. To her right, the arches continued over the channel and to the island side. To her left, she spied a narrow granite staircase tucked along the right side of the bridge, leading to the roadway above.

There were a few people milling around, but it wasn't overly crowded. Along the concrete edge bordering the channel, pigeons foraged for food left behind by careless tourists. Instead of walking toward the water, Danielle made her way to the narrow granite staircase. If fog should suddenly appear—an unlikely possibility in the Arizona Desert—she could imagine herself transported back in time to London of the 1800s.

"I didn't think I'd be seeing you again," said a voice in a heavy English accent just as Danielle reached the foot of the staircase.

She twirled around and came face-to-face with Percival. "I came looking for you."

He smiled. "I assume you and all your friends are now safe?"

Danielle took her flip phone out of her pocket and opened it up. She placed it by her ear. "I hope you don't mind. But I find people don't seem to pay much attention to me when I have this while I'm talking to a ghost."

He frowned. "What is that, by the way? I'm always seeing people walking around with one of those things by their ears. Does it help one hear better?"

"Umm…not exactly." Danielle sat down on one of the steps. She scooted over to make room for Percival.

He accepted her silent invitation and sat down. "Your friend who was unconscious, has he come to?"

"Yes, this morning. We're going home tomorrow. Back to Oregon."

"And have they captured the scoundrels?"

Danielle shook her head. "No."

"I'm sorry they got away, but I'm delighted you and your friends are safe. It is so inconvenient to be snuffed out prematurely. *I know.* I wish I would run into someone else like you—someone who lives here—so I could have a person to talk to."

Danielle glanced up to the bridge on her right and then looked back to Percival. "I would expect there might be other ghosts—spirits—attached to the London Bridge. Especially considering its history. Someone else you might talk to."

"Oh, there are! And frankly, I'm a bit surprised they aren't crowding around, trying to get your attention."

"Then you aren't really alone. I mean you have other people to communicate with."

"You mean dead people?" He smirked.

"Well, yeah. But you're dead too."

"Yes, but have you any idea how tedious it can be talking to the same ghosts for almost two hundred years? It's not like they have anything new to say, and most of them are obsessed with the fact they're dead. As if they can't get used to the notion. But for heaven's sake, some of the blokes have been dead for far longer than I have. It's time they faced that fact and moved on."

"You know, you could always just move on to the next level," she suggested.

He frowned. "Next level?"

"This isn't all there is. There's more after we leave here."

"Such as?" he asked.

"I'm not sure, but I know there is. However, before you go, I want to ask you some questions."

"Ask away. But you needn't worry about me taking off just now. While I'm not able to communicate with any of the very alive young women who frequent this area, it doesn't mean I can't look." He chuckled.

"Look?"

He chuckled again. "It's quite astounding, really. Pretty young women wearing practically nothing at all, prancing about as if it is the most natural thing in the world. And it must be, considering the fact it seems I am the only one who ever really notices."

Now it was Danielle's turn to chuckle. "I get it now. You're talking about girls wearing bikinis—even skimpy thongs."

"Amazing," he muttered and then asked with a bright smile, "So, what was it you wanted to ask me?"

"The last time we talked, you left before I could ask you any questions. Most of our questions before were about where we were—but now—now I need to know what you know about our kidnappers."

"Ahh…why certainly. What would you like to know?"

"How many kidnappers did you see?"

"Three," he told her.

"Hmmm, according to Carol Ann, she's pretty sure there were four."

"Who is Carol Ann?" he asked.

"One of my friends who was kidnapped along with me."

"I only saw three of them. But I wasn't there the entire time. It's possible one of the kidnappers wasn't there when I visited."

"Did you ever hear their names?" she asked. "Aside from the one you mentioned before, Clay."

"Yes. I got the impression the leader was this fellow who went by Sky."

"Sky?" Danielle frowned. "Sky what?"

"Just Sky. Then, of course, there was Clay. But you already know about him."

"Any last name?"

He shook his head. "I only heard him called Clay. And then there was the woman. The men called her Andy."

"Andy?"

"Just Andy. I thought she might have been captured when the bobbies showed up."

"Why did you think that?"

"She wasn't in the car."

"What car?" Danielle asked.

"The car that ran over me when I arrived that day. Maybe I didn't see it coming, but I saw it when it went over me, and the only people in the buggy were Sky and Clay."

"So she must have left before they did? But where did she go?"

"I have no idea. Not long after they chose to run me over, the bobbies started showing up, and that's when I went to find you. Sorry, I didn't really stick around after that."

"Can you tell me what they look like?"

Percival described Clay and Sky. Danielle had no doubt the pilot that had flown them to Seligman was the one who went by Sky. She didn't believe she had ever met either man prior to the kidnapping. As for Andy, Percival basically described her as a woman about Danielle's age, who was of average height and build, with blond hair. She knew dozens of women—probably more—who fit that description.

"Can you remember any of the conversations you might have overheard?"

Percival considered the question a moment. "I know they were anxious for your friend to wake up. They wanted something from him. Sky was quite annoyed at Clay because it was his fault your friend fell. At one point, Clay wanted to get money from you instead of your friend. But Sky didn't want to do that because it wasn't enough."

"I'm surprised they didn't take what they could get and just left us."

"They said something about this being a onetime deal. And once they did it, they couldn't do it again."

"It's true Chris has much deeper pockets. Considering what they expected to get from him, I guess I'm not surprised the one called Sky wasn't willing to settle for what they could get from me."

"Andy, she just wanted to call it quits."

"She did?"

"Yes. She was quite upset about your friend. She wanted to get him to a hospital, but they wouldn't listen to her."

"What do you think the relationship between the three was?" Danielle asked.

"Relationship?"

"Do you think this Andy was married to one of them? Maybe a girlfriend? Related someway?"

"I got the impression they were all just friends. Maybe not friends exactly…"

"Partners in crime?" Danielle suggested.

"Something like that. But I don't believe Andy was in a relationship with either of them. There was never anything…"

"Intimate?"

Percival nodded. "Exactly."

"Did they ever mention where any of them lived?"

Percival shook his head. "No."

"Did they talk about how they chose Chris as their target? Did they mention if any of them had any kind of relationship with any of us?"

"What kind of relationship?"

"I'm just wondering how they found out about Chris. He's very rich."

Percival chuckled. "I already gathered that. They mentioned the amount they were attempting to extort from him."

"But the thing is, Chris never uses his real name. Only a small group of people back home know his true identity—and what he's really worth. Since he moved to Frederickport this past December—that's where I live—most people thought he was this guy who was between jobs. Everyone thinks he just recently landed a new job—working for a foundation that he actually founded. So I'm trying to figure out who knew he has access to that much money."

"Obviously someone did. If I were you, I'd take a closer look at your little group of friends. One of them might be a kidnapper."

THIRTY-EIGHT

Adam Nichols was just about to take a second bite from the cinnamon roll when he heard a soft knock at his office doorway. Looking up from where he sat hunched over his desk, he found his assistant leaning into the room.

"Beverly Klein is here. She wants to know if you have a minute to see her," she asked.

Grabbing one of the two napkins lying on his desk, he used it to wrap the partially eaten roll and hastily shoved it into a top desk drawer. He picked up the remaining napkin and wiped off his mouth. "Sure, show her in."

By the time Beverly walked into the office a moment later, Adam had already crumpled and tossed the used napkin into the trash can and had removed all evidence of the cinnamon roll he had been eating—all but the white chunk of glaze still on the corner of this mouth, which he had missed with the napkin.

"Beverly, what a nice surprise," Adam said as he stood up from his desk.

Beverly, crisply dressed in a designer pantsuit, with her strawberry blond hair perfectly coifed, strolled confidently into the office and flashed Adam a smile. Adam, who had just stepped out from behind the desk, offered her a hand, which she accepted in greeting.

"I hope I wasn't interrupting anything," Beverly said as her green eyes flashed from Adam's face to the trash can by the desk's side. She took a step back and sat down in a chair Adam pointed to.

"I was just organizing my day." Adam smiled and sat back down behind his desk.

"Old Salts?" Beverly asked with a grin, dropping the purse she had been carrying to the floor by her feet.

Adam frowned. "Old Salts?"

Beverly pointed to the trash can. It contained a crumpled sack from the local bakery. She then pointed to her own mouth. "And you have a little…umm…on the corner of your mouth."

By reflex Adam's tongue swiped at the frosting residue. He then touched the area with a finger to make sure it was all gone. With a shrug he said, "They have the best cinnamon rolls."

Beverly smiled. "They do."

Confident he was no longer wearing bits of his morning snack, Adam settled back in his chair. "So what is it I can help you with?"

"I would appreciate it if you keep this between you and me," Beverly began.

"Certainly."

"I have been considering moving from Frederickport. But I don't really want to sell the house. I was thinking one option might be to put it into your vacation rental program."

"It would certainly appeal to my high-end renters. From what I remember, you have a beautiful home."

"I figured that way I could leave without worrying about moving furniture and packing everything. I understand vacation properties need to be completely furnished."

"So you don't intend to take any of your furniture with you?"

Beverly shifted in the chair to get more comfortable. "No. I'm considering doing some traveling. I don't know where I'll land. Maybe even back here. But in the meantime, I could rent out the house, and if it's in a vacation rental program, if I do want to come back for a visit—or my kids want to come—we'll have someplace to stay. Of course, I understand we'd have to coordinate that with you—if you handled the property."

"Certainly. Most of my owners of the properties block out times for their personal use."

"So what's involved?" Beverly asked.

Adam went on to explain his vacation rental program, including the cost to the owners and the services he provided. When he was finished outlining the program, Beverly asked, "Then could you come over to my house and let me know what I'd need to do to bring it to optimum rental potential?"

"Of course. I could stop over this afternoon if that would work for you."

"Wonderful." Beverly started to stand up, but then paused and sat back down. "Have you heard anything about how Danielle Boatman and Chris Johnson are doing? I understand they stayed in Arizona. Do you know if he's still in a coma?"

Adam grinned. "I am happy to report Chris came out of the coma yesterday. They're flying back this afternoon."

Settling back in the chair, Beverly crossed her legs. "I'm glad to hear that. Although, I'm surprised they're releasing him from the hospital so soon."

"I was too. But according to Danielle, the doctors say there doesn't seem to be anything physically wrong with him, and they can't really force him to stay. Chris is pretty insistent about leaving and coming home."

"Is that a good idea, him going home alone after just coming out of a coma?"

"I spoke to Danielle last night. She promised the doctor Chris would stay with her at Marlow House for about a week and follow up with his doctor. If his doctor agrees there's no reason for Chris not to go back to normal, he'll move back home."

"So they should all be settling into Marlow House by this evening?" Beverly asked.

"It looks that way."

MASON MURDOCK HAD JUST GOTTEN off the phone when Andrea Banner walked into his office.

Mason stood abruptly. "Andrea…"

"Hello, Mason. Do you have a minute?" she asked hesitantly.

Mason's gaze swept over Andrea, noticing the jeans hugging her trim hips and how her snugly fitting cotton T-shirt wasn't quite long enough to cover her flat midsection or hide the glittering belly-button ring nor the elaborate tattoo peeking out from the shirt's hem. "It's good to see you."

"I hope I'm not interrupting anything."

Mason shook his head, insisting she wasn't, and offered her a chair, which she accepted.

"I heard about the hijacking. I'm so glad you're alright," she said after sitting down.

"Thank you. I wish I could say the same about my plane. I've been on the phone all morning with my insurance company."

"Your plane? I thought they found it."

"They did. But those maniacs landed it on an old dirt airstrip—one that wasn't even maintained. They did some damage." He then waved his hand dismissively. "But forget about that. I'll work it out. I'm just glad all my passengers are alright."

"I heard one of them was in a coma," Andrea said.

"My client. But I got a call this morning; he's out of the coma and coming home today." Mason smiled.

"Really? So he's okay?"

"He's out of the hospital, at least. But he's not going home right away. He'll be staying at Marlow House; that way he won't be alone while he recuperates. So tell me why are you here?"

"I don't know if they told you. But the FBI questioned me. They seem to think I was in some way involved. But I want you to know I had nothing to do with this. I wouldn't even know how to pull something like this off!"

"I don't believe you had anything to do with the hijacking, and I told the authorities that," Mason insisted.

"But did the authorities tell you about my uncle?" she asked hesitantly.

"Your uncle?" He frowned.

"That primitive dirt airstrip—the one where the kidnappers landed your plane—it was on the Seligman property my cousin Jimmy owned."

"The cousin you told me about? The one killed in that car accident?"

Andrea nodded. "Jimmy left that land—along with some property in Havasu—to his father, my uncle Herman."

"Havasu?" Mason frowned. "Isn't that where they found everyone?"

Andrea nodded again. "Everyone but the hijackers. That Havasu property where they were being kept also belonged to my cousin Jimmy. And well, now it belongs to my uncle Herman."

Mason narrowed his eyes and studied Andrea. "What are you telling me?"

"I need you to know I had absolutely nothing to do with the hijacking. I would never do something like that."

"But you did know about Chris Glandon." Mason's expression was less friendly than it had been when Andrea had stepped into his office.

She stood up and reached for Mason's hand. Before she could grab it, he pulled it out of her reach.

"You have to believe me. I had nothing to do with this!" she insisted.

CAROL ANN SHOWED up at the Frederickport Police Station bearing gifts—freshly baked cinnamon rolls from Old Salts Bakery. She sat with Joe Morelli in the break room while the chief poured them all a cup of hot coffee.

When the chief sat down with them at the table, he told Carol Ann, "This was sweet of you."

She smiled at the chief and then picked up a sticky roll. "I figured we need to celebrate now that Chris has come out of the coma."

"That is something to celebrate," Edward said before taking a bite.

Carol Ann glanced toward the open doorway and then looked back to the chief. "Where's Brian? I thought he'd be here this morning."

"Brian's taking a few days off. He hasn't had a day off since we went on vacation," the chief explained.

Joe let out a snort and then said, "Some vacation."

"At least we all survived the ordeal, even Chris," Carol Ann reminded him.

"Always the optimist." Edward chuckled.

"I was so worried about Chris. I'm just relieved he's awake and coming home. Do you know when they arrive?" Carol Ann asked.

"Ian's picking them up at the airport this evening," Joe told her.

"In Portland?" Carol Ann asked.

"No," Edward said. "The airport we used. Danielle rented the same plane we flew back on."

"When I talked to you the last time, you told me they aren't checking him in to the hospital here?" Carol Ann asked.

Edward shook his head. "No. But he isn't going home. He intends to stay at Marlow House for a week or so until his own doctor says it's okay for him to be at home alone. I'm going to stop over there tonight. You want to come with me?"

"I'd like to. But my brother's coming in tonight," Carol told him.

"Aww, I knew it!" Edward smiled. "He needs to see for himself his little sister is okay."

Carol Ann smiled. "Something like that. Tell Danielle I'll call her later, after they're settled in. Let her know if she needs me for anything, just call."

"I'll tell her."

"How did she sound?" Carol Ann asked.

"I haven't talked to her since Chris came out of the coma. We've been playing a bit of phone tag," Edward told her.

"I talked to her," Joe said. "She sounded pretty good. Happy to get back. I think she was anxious to talk to the chief about the case, but I told her the FBI is handling the investigation."

Carol Ann delicately licked frosting residue from her fingers and then said, "I suppose I can understand that. It would probably be something of a conflict of interest, since both of you were hostages."

"Not to mention the cost to our department. We're not really equipped to cross state lines—not with two different crime scenes in Arizona," Edward added.

"I wonder if Chris will be hiring some sort of bodyguard now," Joe speculated.

Carol Ann frowned. "Bodyguard?"

"Considering what happened. I think most people in that position have one." Just before Joe popped the last bite of cinnamon roll into his mouth, he looked at Carol Ann and asked, "I bet you never expected Chris Johnson to be some Richie Rich named Glandon."

Carol Ann smiled. "No. I will admit that one caught me by surprise."

"I hope you understand why I never told you about Chris's real identity," Edward said.

Carol Ann reached over and patted his hand. "I understand."

"You probably thought the kidnappers had screwed up and

grabbed the wrong people when they told us they expected Chris Glandon to give them fifty million dollars," Joe said as he wiped his hands with a napkin.

"Something like that," Carol murmured.

THIRTY-NINE

Chief MacDonald promised his youngest son he could go with him to Marlow House and welcome home Danielle, Chris, and Lily, who were due to arrive home in a couple of hours. But first, he and his boys needed to have dinner. Since there was no food at his house—he hadn't had time to go grocery shopping—he took the boys over to Lucy's Diner. After dinner, he planned to drop Eddy off at a friend's house.

The waitress had just taken his order when Beverly Klein walked into the diner. The moment she saw him sitting at a booth, she headed in his direction.

"Chief!" she greeted him when she arrived at the table. She then flashed a smile to the two young boys and then looked back to MacDonald. "I was so relieved to hear your trip had a happy ending."

"Thanks, Beverly. I am too." He glanced around. "Are you meeting someone?"

She shook her head. "No. It's just me. I find it's a little lonely eating at home these days." She smiled.

"Would you like to join us?" the chief offered. He scooted over in the booth to make room.

"That would be nice, thank you." She sat down next to him and smiled across the table to Edward and Evan.

"Boys, this is Mrs. Klein. I think you've met her before,"

MacDonald introduced. Each boy said a brief hello, neither looking particularly thrilled with the added dinner companion.

"You boys are sure growing up to be handsome young men. And Evan, you look so much like your mother!"

"You knew my mother?" Evan asked.

She nodded. "Yes, I did. A wonderful woman." Beverly turned her attention to Eddy. "And you look just like your namesake. My, a spitting image of your father!"

Eddy grinned.

Beverly turned her attention to the chief. "And how are you doing? I heard you had quite an ordeal."

"Glad to get home, that's for sure."

"I talked to Adam Nichols earlier today. I heard Chris Glandon came out of his coma."

Edward frowned. "I didn't know the papers listed Chris's real surname."

Beverly shrugged. "I have no idea. I didn't notice."

"Did Adam tell you who he really is?" Edward asked, his expression serious.

Before she could answer the question, a server showed up at the table and took Beverly's order. When the server left the table, Edward repeated the question.

"So I assume it's still a secret?" Beverly asked.

"How did you know who he was?" Edward pressed.

Beverly picked up the water glass the server had just filled. "I sort of figured it out. Didn't Carol Ann tell you?" She took a sip.

"Carol Ann?" Edward frowned.

"I ran into her a few weeks ago. She was shopping for cowboy boots for the trip. She mentioned where you were all going and how Chris was supposedly working for the Glandon Foundation. I'm naturally curious, so I did a little searching on my cellphone and came across a photograph of Chris Glandon. Even with the beard, it was pretty obvious who it was."

"Did you happen to mention this to anyone?" Edward asked.

Beverly took another sip of water and considered the question for a moment. Finally, she shook her head and set her glass back down on the table. "No. Only Carol Ann. I think she was surprised her host was a billionaire."

"NO. I don't want to go lie down," Chris told Danielle for the third time. They had arrived back at Marlow House thirty minutes earlier and were now in the living room. Lily and Ian had already gone across the street to Ian's house. Ian assumed Lily just wanted some alone time—and he was more than happy to oblige—yet the truth was, Lily knew the chief was on his way over to talk to Danielle, and it would be easier to do if Ian was not around, considering Danielle needed to pass on information obtained from a ghost.

"Stop hovering, Danielle," Walt chided. "He looks fine to me. Although I'm not sure why he's staying here. He has a perfectly nice house down the street."

"Walt, sometimes you don't make me feel very wanted," Chris teased.

"Sometimes you are rather perceptive," Walt retorted. He leaned against the fireplace mantel, smoking a thin cigar.

"I thought Chris would be a little safer here," Danielle told Walt as she took a seat on the sofa next to Chris.

"Safer?"

"Walt is going to love this," Chris mumbled under his breath.

"The kidnappers haven't been caught yet, and with Chris now conscious, he could be a target again. I just figured he would be safer here."

Walt stood up straighter, no longer leaning against the fireplace, and glanced from Danielle to Chris and back to Danielle again. "Safer, how?"

"Isn't it obvious?" Chris asked with faux innocence. "You're here."

"You expect me to protect you?" Walt began to chuckle. He took a puff off the cigar and shook his head at the idea.

"The truth is," Chris said, the teasing tone replaced by seriousness, "it's more about protecting Danielle and Lily."

The cigar vanished and Walt took a step toward the pair. "What do you mean?"

"The kidnappers intended to hold us while they forced Chris to transfer money to their account. I don't really know how they expected him to move that much money, but Chris and I just figured if he was here and we were here, it would be a little difficult for them to use our well-being as leverage," Danielle explained. "Not with you here."

Walt considered the situation for a moment. Finally, he said, "Very well, but you can't live your life out holed up in this house."

"You are," Chris quipped with a grin.

"That's different. I'm dead."

"True." Chris let out a sigh. "This is just until we figure things out. I'm still not one hundred percent, and maybe I do need to look into hiring some sort of security."

"You mean aside from a ghost?" Walt asked.

Danielle chuckled. "Walt, you just called yourself a ghost."

Walt shrugged. "It just seemed appropriate in this instance."

The doorbell rang. Danielle stood up. "I bet that's the chief and Evan."

A few minutes later Evan and the chief walked into the living room with Danielle. The first thing Chris did when they entered the room was thank Evan for all his help in bringing them home.

"He's my hero," the chief said as he ruffled Evan's hair.

"Why don't you let Evan stay in here and visit with Walt and Chris. I have a few things to tell you," Danielle said.

"YOU SAW PERCIVAL AGAIN?" the chief asked after Danielle told him about seeing Percival the day before. She sat alone with the chief in the parlor.

"I asked him about our kidnappers. He insists he only saw three of them."

"Carol Ann said there were four," the chief noted.

"I know. But it's possible the forth kidnapper wasn't there when Percival was. He didn't stay there the entire time we were there. The ones he saw were two men and one woman," Danielle told him.

"Carol Ann said they always had masks on, and she couldn't tell for sure if they were all men."

"Percival heard their names. Unfortunately, only their first names. Although, I suspect one was a nickname, considering they called him Sky. I don't think I've ever heard anyone named Sky—even as a surname."

"Sky?" The chief frowned.

Danielle nodded. "I'm pretty sure he was our pilot. The way

Percival described the man, sounded just like him. Fake beard and all."

"And the others?"

"The other man was Clay. Which you already knew about. The woman went by Andy."

The chief stood up. "What did you say?"

"Andy. I imagine that might be a nickname, too."

"What did she look like? Did he describe her?"

"Yes, but it's not much help. About my age, blond, average height and build. That describes a lot of women I know."

Edward dropped down into the chair, his hand now on his forehead as if he expected it to fall off at any moment and he needed to keep it attached. Whatever color had been in his face disappeared, giving him a ghostly appearance. Compared to him, Walt looked alive.

Alarmed, Danielle leaned forward. "Are you alright, Chief?"

Slowly shaking his head, he muttered, "No. I think I'm going to be ill."

Danielle jumped up from the chair. "What can I get you?"

Waving for Danielle to sit back down, he shook his head and said, "There is nothing you can get me for this. Sit down."

Startled, Danielle obediently sat on the sofa and stared at the chief. He looked up at her; their eyes met.

"What is it, Chief?" she whispered.

"I ran into Beverly Klein tonight."

"And?"

Edward licked his lips; they felt suddenly parched. "She knows about Chris. Who he really is. She figured it out when she ran into Carol Ann when Carol Ann was buying her cowboy boots."

"Are you saying Beverly had something to do with the hijacking?"

"No. But I know now, Carol Ann knew who Chris really was days before we left on the trip."

"I don't understand what you're getting at?"

"Remember I told you about Carol Ann's brother, the one who was in the military? The one who raised her?"

"Yes. Didn't you tell me he was really into computers?"

"He also flies planes. In fact, he can fly just about anything, which is why his friends call him Sky."

"Sky?" Danielle frowned. "No, you're not suggesting Carol

Ann's brother was our pilot—our kidnapper. No. It's just a coincidence."

"Carol Ann also has a nickname. Her brother gave it to her, because she was a bit of a tomboy when she was a kid. She doesn't use it now, but I remember her telling me her brother still calls her that, as well as some of her old friends she grew up with."

"What are you saying?"

"Danielle, Carol Ann's nickname is Andy."

FORTY

Carol Ann's porchlight was on, and there was a truck in her driveway. She didn't drive a truck. MacDonald turned off his ignition and sat in his car a moment, studying her house. They had been dating for less than a year, but until tonight, it had felt longer than that. Now he wondered if he really ever knew who she was.

After getting out of the vehicle, he made his way to the front door. Once there, he stood on the porch for a moment before ringing the bell. Several minutes went by and no one came to the door. Ed could hear voices from inside and footsteps. He rang the bell again. Finally, a moment later, the door eased open several inches.

"Ed?" Carol Ann said with surprise, peeking out the door. "I thought you were going over to Danielle's tonight." She eased the door open a few more inches.

"I was on my way home. Thought I'd see if you were still up, and I noticed the lights on and the truck in the drive. Is that your brother's truck?"

"Umm…yes, yes, it is." She smiled—a smile not reflected in her eyes.

Edward grinned amicably. "I thought it was about time we met."

Carol Ann glanced nervously over her shoulder and then looked at Ed. She smiled again and stepped back from the door, opening it so he could enter the house. "Well, of course. Come on in." By the way she initially had been hiding behind the door, one might assume she was wearing her nightclothes. As it turned out, she was wearing jeans and a pullover sweater.

Edward stepped into the house and glanced around. There was no sign of her brother, yet there was a light coming from the kitchen down the hall.

"Sky and I were just going to have some ice cream. Would you like some?" Carol Ann motioned to the kitchen and then started in that direction, expecting Ed to follow her. Instead, he paused a moment—hearing her use the name Sky felt like a punch to his stomach. While it was the name she always used when referring to her sibling, hearing it now after what Danielle had told him made him ill. He prayed that once he came face-to-face with her elusive brother, he'd discover he was short and fat—or exceptionally tall and skinny—anything but the body type of the man who had hijacked the plane. Taking a deep breath, Ed started to move, heading down the hall.

"Sky, I'd like you to meet Ed," Carol Ann said cheerfully as she entered the kitchen.

Her brother, who had been sitting at the kitchen table, stood up and smiled at Ed, extending a hand in greeting. "Well, we meet at last. Andy's told me a lot of good things about you."

Ed felt ill. While the man standing before him had a different hair color than the pilot and was clean shaven, Ed didn't doubt for a moment he was his kidnapper. It wasn't just that Sky had a facial rash—as if it had been irritated by a fake beard—the man had the same body type and height as the pilot. However, he had to admit, had he not been aware of the nicknames when dropping by Carol Ann's tonight, it never would have occurred to him that her brother was the pilot, even with the facial rash. *We often fail to see what is right before us,* he thought.

"Nice to meet you, Sky," Edward said with a forced smile as he shook the man's hand.

"Where are your boys? You mentioned you were taking Evan to Danielle's with you," Carol Ann asked.

"They're at a friend's house."

"Carol Ann was just telling me all about your harrowing experience. How is your friend who got hurt?" Sky asked as he sat back down at the table.

"Would you like some ice cream with us?" Carol Ann asked before Ed could answer her brother's question. She opened her freezer and pulled out a gallon of ice cream.

"No, thank you, I'm not hungry." Ed took a seat at the kitchen table.

"So how is your friend?" Sky asked again.

"He seems to be doing well." Ed forced a smile.

"Carol Ann was telling me he plans to stay at Marlow House for a while."

"That's the plan." Edward watched Carol Ann walk to the table, carrying two bowls of ice cream.

"Are you sure you don't want one?" she asked as she set a bowl in front of her brother.

"No, thanks."

Carol Ann sat down with her ice cream.

"Marlow House is a bed and breakfast, isn't it?" Sky asked.

"Yes," Carol answered the question.

"Do they have any guests staying there?" Sky asked.

Edward frowned. "Guests? Why do you ask?"

Sky shrugged. "After all they went through, I was wondering if they're open for business."

"They haven't been open for a while," Carol Ann said between bites of ice cream. "Danielle had some work done on the property; that's why we went on the trip—before the B and B reopened for business."

"Yes, I remember you saying that. But I was just wondering, now that she's back, is she taking guests?"

"They had some reservations, but they were all cancelled when our plane was believed to have gone down," Ed explained.

"So…the only people at Marlow House are your friend who got hurt and the woman who owns the place…what's her name? Danielle?"

"Yes, Danielle," Carol Ann told her brother. "But Lily also lives at Marlow House. Lily was one of the people who was with us, and her boyfriend. He lives across the street from Marlow House."

Sky smiled at his sister and then focused his attention on his bowl of ice cream. Edward sat silently and watched the two eat while wondering what he might say to the FBI agents to turn their attention to Sky—and to Carol Ann. Again, Ed felt ill.

When Sky finished his ice cream, he dropped the spoon in the bowl; it made a clinking sound. He looked up at Edward, his smile wide. "You know, my little sister here was really worried about her friend. She told me how she tried to help him, how she just wanted to get him to a doctor. I told her she did the best she could, and look—he made it. I don't think he'd be where he is now without her."

Edward's gaze fixed on Sky. "You're right. Chris has a lot to thank Carol Ann for."

"She has been talking about him all night. Andy told me how you were going over to see him tonight, and how she wished she could have gone with you."

Edward glanced over at Carol Ann. He knew her well enough to realize she hadn't a clue where her brother was going with this. But the moment she noticed Edward looking her way, she broke into an awkward smile.

"You know, my little sister means a lot to me," Sky said.

"Yes…she told me how close you are."

"One thing I learned in the military, when you go through battle with someone—and what you all went through is like battle—it forges a special bond. Carol Ann is very dear to me, and I'd like to meet these other people who were with my sister when you all went through that ordeal. It doesn't seem right that I don't know them. Hell, it doesn't seem right I just met you for the first time tonight, since you've been dating for months."

"But you have to go home tonight. Maybe next—" Carol Ann began, only to be cut off by her brother.

Sky grabbed hold of her hand and squeezed it, looking her in the eyes. "It's still pretty early. I think we should go over there now so I can meet your friends before I head back home, and then you can see your friend Chris—see for yourself he's alright. I know you'll sleep better tonight if you did."

"You want to go to Marlow House…tonight?" Carol Ann fairly squeaked.

"I think that would be nice." Edward spoke up. "But I need to call Danielle first and make sure they're still up. It's possible they've already gone to bed. They had a long day."

"You do that." Sky smiled.

Edward stood up. "I'll go out into the hallway and make the call. I also need to check on my boys and tell them I'll be a while."

After Edward stepped out of the kitchen, Carol Ann jerked her hand from Sky. "What are you doing?" she hissed.

"I just want to check out Marlow House. Get a feel for the place."

"You're not going to do anything tonight, are you?"

Sky smiled at his sister. "Of course not."

WHEN EDWARD, Carol Ann, and Sky arrived at Marlow House, Danielle greeted them at the front door and took them to the parlor, where Chris was sitting on the sofa. What they didn't see was Walt, who was leaning against the fireplace, keeping an eye on the new arrivals.

"Am I going to meet Lily?" Sky asked after he was introduced to Chris.

"Lily won't be back tonight," Danielle told him. "She's staying over at Ian's."

Sky glanced around the room. He spied the laptop sitting on the desk. "So it's just you two in this big old house?"

"Pretty much," Danielle said with a smile, her eyes fixed on Carol Ann's brother.

"I know Sky would love a tour of your house," Carol Ann told her. "If it isn't too much trouble. I've told him all about it. He loves old houses."

"Yes, I do." Sky strolled leisurely around the room, absently running his fingertips over the woodwork while looking around. He paused at the desk and looked down at the computer. "Oh, I see you have a MacBook. Do you like it?"

"Yes, I do. I haven't had it long. My other laptop died," Danielle explained.

Sky looked from the computer to Danielle. "Do you offer your guests Wi-Fi?"

"Why yes…we do." Danielle continued to study Sky.

"Do you get very good Internet here? It's pretty iffy where I live."

"Actually, ours is very good," Danielle told him.

"I'm really glad to hear that," Sky said just before he pulled a gun out of his coat pocket.

Carol Ann gasped. "What are you doing?"

"I want the two of you to sit on the couch with your friend, now!" Sky told Danielle and Edward as he waved the pistol in the direction of the sofa. The two did as they were told.

"Sky, what are you doing?" Carol Ann frantically asked.

"Shut up, Andy. Clay screwed this up the first time, and now I'm going to screw him. It'll be more for us."

"You're the pilot, aren't you?" MacDonald asked. "The one who hijacked the plane."

"You've a smart boyfriend, Andy. He catches on quick. But not quick enough. I told you he wouldn't recognize me when he saw me, and he didn't."

"My god, Sky, but they know who we are now! What have you done?"

"I'm getting us fifty million bucks. That's what I've done. If Chris here cooperates…" Sky waved the gun at Chris. "Then we tie them up and you and I will be out of the country and with our money."

Carol Ann began to cry. She looked helplessly from her brother to Edward.

"Don't lie to your sister," Edward said calmly. "You don't intend to tie us up after you get what you want. You plan to kill us."

"No." Carol Ann shook her head in denial. "Do what Sky says and he's not going to hurt you. He promised me. And Sky never breaks his promises."

Edward's eyes searched Carol Ann for answers. "Why? Why did you do this?"

No longer crying, Carol Ann shrugged. "I like you, Ed, I like you a lot. But I'm tired of sick people and dealing with bedpans. And you'll always be just a cop, and I don't really like kids that much. And fifty million dollars is so much money. Chris won't even miss it. No one's going to get hurt; you just have to do what he says. This is our chance."

"Your brother plans to kill us, he'll have to," Edward said with a sigh.

"No. He has a plan. We'll be far away before anyone finds you and lets you go."

"You think so? My boys are with friends—I already mentioned that—and they expect me to pick them up soon. When I don't show up, one of my officers will show up here. No way will you be able to get away that fast, and your brother knows it."

"Shut up!" Pointing the pistol at Edward, Sky's hand trembled.

He then pointed it at Chris. "You do exactly as I say or I'll kill you and your friends."

"Okay, I will. But can I ask you one question?" Chris asked.

Sky smiled. "Go ahead."

"How exactly am I supposed to get you the money?"

Sky began to laugh. "Carol Ann, go out to my truck and get me my laptop out of the cab." Still holding the gun on his hostages, he used his free hand to dig his truck keys out of his pocket. He tossed them to his sister. She caught the keys, yet instead of rushing outside, she seemed frozen to the spot.

"I'm assuming you expect me to log into my bank account and then give you my password."

Sky grinned. "Something like that."

"But even if I do that, even I can't transfer the kind of money you're talking about."

"Oh, I wouldn't be so sure of that." He looked over at his sister and snapped, "Andy, what are you waiting for? Get my laptop, now!"

Chris stood up and said, "Okay, Walt, now."

In the next instant the gun was out of Sky's hand—it twirled in midair, making Sky look like a cowboy spinning his gun—yet in this case the gun was spinning on its own. When it stopped, the barrel was pointing at Sky, and in the next moment it flew backwards, the handle landing firmly in the chief's hand.

FORTY-ONE

Officially, the gathering was a celebration of Marie Nichols's birthday. The native Frederickport resident had reached the impressive age of ninety-one. Like royalty attending court, Marie sat in a rocker on Marlow House's side porch and watched as Lily turned the crank of the old-fashioned ice cream maker. Other guests fluttered around the birthday girl, giving her special attention.

A chapter had closed, and the beginning of something new was on the horizon. What that actually meant for those attending the barbecue differed according to whom one asked. To Marie, it meant the passing of another year. For Marlow House, it meant the bed and breakfast was once again open for business. All its guest rooms had been occupied for two straight weekends.

For Joanne Johnson, it meant rain wouldn't necessarily prevent barbecuing in the side yard at Marlow House. On impulse Danielle had decided to end the debate over the pros and cons of an outdoor kitchen when she had one installed the previous week. It included an awning, which kept out the rain. However, on this sunny day, there were no rain clouds overhead.

For Evan and Eddy MacDonald, it meant the end of the school year and the beginning of summer vacation and a promise of a visit to Disneyland.

For Chris Johnson, aka Chris Glandon, it meant introducing his new puppy to his friends, a pit bull named Hunny, whom he had adopted from the local shelter the day before. While Chris understood that even with his kidnappers locked up, he needed to take steps to protect himself in the future, he couldn't bring himself to hire a bodyguard. His compromise was to install a security system at his house and adopt a dog. By the way Hunny aggressively attacked the MacDonald boys, pouncing on the pair as they rolled around on the side lawn at Marlow House as she energetically swiped their faces with wet puppy kisses, Chris suspected the pit bull he had adopted might not live up to the ferociousness of the breed.

For Danielle it meant being a millionaire again. Not only had her cousin's estate finished going through probate, she was now the official owner of the gold coins that had been found in Ian's house. She wasn't sure what she intended to do with them, so like the Missing Thorndike, they now resided in a safe deposit box at the local bank.

For Edward MacDonald, who sat alone on a bench at the far end of the yard, watching the activity, it was a time of reflection.

"Beer?" Danielle asked, holding out a cold bottle of beer to the chief. She held a second bottle in her other hand.

Ed looked up and smiled, accepting the offer. He hadn't noticed her approach. "Thanks."

"What are you doing sitting over here all alone?" Danielle asked as she sat on the bench next to him.

"Just watching everyone." He took a sip of the beer. Dressed casually in jeans and a long-sleeved cotton T-shirt, Ed had let his hair grow out longer than he normally wore it. Danielle wondered if it was a conscious choice, or if he simply hadn't mustered the energy to go to the barber.

"Are you okay, Chief? I'm worried about you." She sipped her beer.

"Oh, I'm okay." He leaned back on the bench.

"Have you met Carmen?" Lifting the hand holding her bottle of beer, she pointed it toward a dark-haired woman standing next to Lily at the ice cream maker. "She's staying for two weeks. You should meet her. She's a teacher in Portland. I think you'd like her."

MacDonald chuckled and took a sip of his beer. "Playing matchmaker, Danielle?"

She shrugged. "I just hate to see you like this."

"It's only been a month. I'm not ready to jump back into dating. I need to think about the boys."

They sat in silence for a few minutes. Finally, Danielle asked, "Have you heard anything about Carol Ann?"

"I talked to Agent Wilson this morning. Looks like she's cutting some deal with the prosecutor for a lesser sentence."

"Have you talked to her?" Danielle asked.

MacDonald shook his head. "No. And I don't intend to. I'm just grateful the feds are handling this."

"There is still the trial. I'm not looking forward to that," Danielle said with a sigh.

"Me either." MacDonald took a swig of the beer. "You want to hear something funny Wilson told me this morning?"

"Sure, what? Funny is always good."

"You know that program Sky wrote—that brilliant piece of software that would allow him to hack into the bank and steal money?"

"Yeah? What about it?"

"Turns out, it wouldn't have worked anyway." The chief let out a harsh laugh and took another swig of beer.

"Are you serious?"

"Yep." He chuckled.

"Didn't they test it out first?"

MacDonald shook his head and chuckled again. "According to what Carol Ann told them, once they used the program, the bank could identify whatever vulnerability Sky intended to exploit and then fix it. Which is why they didn't want to use it to extort money from you or the others. They were after the big money, since they believed they only had one chance to use it."

"So it never worked anyway?"

"It might have, had they tried six months ago. But apparently that particular hole had already been filled. I guess Sky has been working on this for about a year, that's when he first developed the program. But over the last six months he spent more time looking for the ideal mark and failed to realize his brilliant hacking scheme was already obsolete."

"I can't help but feel sorry for Carol Ann. I don't think she wanted to hurt anyone, but her brother had such control over her. He was all the family she has. I know what if feels like to be without family."

"Don't feel sorry for Carol Ann," he said gruffly, taking another sip of beer. "The minute she realized who Chris was, she went to her brother. This wasn't just Sky's great plan. It was Carol Ann's idea to land the plane in Seligman and take us to Havasu. She had been Mrs. Shafer's nurse and knew all about the Arizona properties."

"Wow," Danielle said in awe. Leaning back on the bench, she shook her head. "And all this time, I've been thinking she was another victim in all this."

"Hardly."

FROM A WINDOW on the second floor, Walt Marlow looked down at the side yard. The only time he had seen more people there—since his death—was eleven months earlier, at Danielle's July 4th Open House.

He had watched Danielle approach the chief, who sat off from the group. Walt could imagine what MacDonald might be thinking. He understood being betrayed by the woman you loved. Walt suspected the chief would eventually come to understand he had never been in love with Carol Ann, as he never really knew who she was. Just as Walt came to realize he never really knew his own wife. In some ways, that would help to soften the hurt—yet not immediately.

Walt turned his attention to Chris, who was now sitting on the lawn with the chief's boys, playing with the puppy. As it had turned out, Chris had only stayed at Marlow House two nights before he moved back to his own house. One reason, reservations were beginning to pour in for Marlow House, and with the kidnappers captured, Chris felt it was time to go home. Chris also had foundation work that needed to be attended to, which meant he had little time to hang around Marlow House and be an annoyance.

The previous evening, Chris had introduced him to Hunny. Walt found her to be a sweet little girl, yet if Chris seriously expected to turn her into a watchdog, she would need to get over some of her fears. Walt failed to mention said fears to Chris, as Hunny asked Walt not to share them with her human, as she wanted to give a good impression. The last thing the pup wanted was to be returned to the pound. Things that terrified her included water, loud noises, other dogs—and cats. Her initial meeting with Max and Sadie had gone without incident—yet that was only because Walt played referee. Only Walt understood how truly terrified Hunny was of the pair—especially of Max.

Walt's gaze shifted to Lily, who energetically cranked the old ice cream machine. He smiled. The previous week he had located it, where it had been stored in the basement, and brought it upstairs. Joanne had found it sitting on the kitchen table when she came to work the next day and assumed Danielle or Lily had placed it there.

With a sigh, Walt turned from the window and made his way to the attic, a bit resentful of the new outdoor kitchen, which drew everyone outside—a place he could no longer be.

DANIELLE OPENED her eyes and found herself again sitting on the bench in the side yard. Overhead the sky was clear and the sun shining. The guests from Marie's party were nowhere in sight, yet everything was set up as it had been in the midst of the party, with steaks sizzling on the grill and the ice cream maker filled with freshly churned ice cream.

"Hello," Walt said when he suddenly appeared, sitting on the bench next to her.

"Hi." Danielle smiled softly. "I thought for a minute you were going to leave me here all alone."

"It looks like Marie's party went well."

"I wish you could have been there."

Walt shrugged. "I watched."

"I'm glad you found the old ice cream maker. It was really a hit. Evan and Eddy especially liked it."

Walt smiled. He leaned back on the bench. "I'm glad they enjoyed it."

Danielle turned to Walt, studying him a minute as he stared ahead, seemingly looking across the yard at where the activity had been the previous day. "Do you know what Evan told me?"

Walt turned to Danielle. "What?"

"He said he felt bad because you could never have ice cream again."

Walt's solemn gaze settled on Danielle.

"You know, Walt, that's not necessarily true. You and I both know that when you pass over to the next level, it might be entirely possible to enjoy ice cream again. In fact, I'd be surprised if you couldn't."

"I know."

"Do you ever think about it—about going. About enjoying things like ice cream again?"

Walt smiled. "Someday, Danielle. But for now, there are some things I enjoy far more than ice cream." He leaned to her and brushed a light kiss over her lips.

THE GHOST AND THE LEPRECHAUN

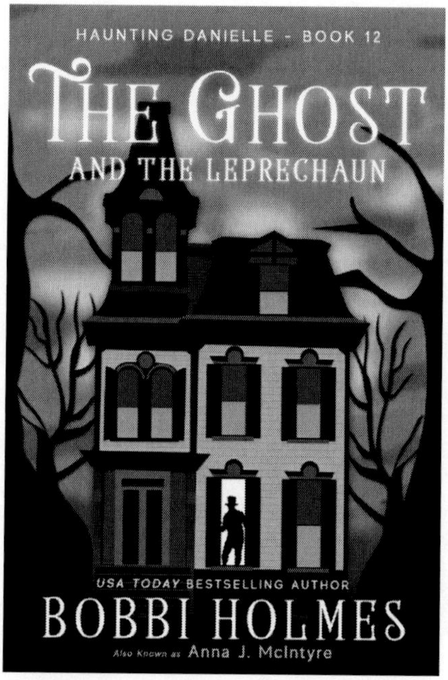

Return to Marlow House in

The Ghost and the Leprechaun

Haunting Danielle, Book 12

Everyone knows leprechauns are just make believe.

But wait, isn't that what they say about ghosts?

NON-FICTION BY

BOBBI ANN JOHNSON HOLMES

Havasu Palms, A Hostile Takeover

Where the Road Ends, Recipes & Remembrances

Motherhood, a book of poetry

The Story of the Christmas Village

BOOKS BY ANNA J. MCINTYRE

COULSON FAMILY SAGA

Coulson's Wife

Coulson's Crucible

Coulson's Lessons

Coulson's Secret

Coulson's Reckoning

UNLOCKED HEARTS

Sundered Hearts

After Sundown

While Snowbound

Sugar Rush